Nefarious

TEANNA DORSEY

NYX PUBLISHING

Printed in the United States of America

First Printing, 2015

ISBN 978-0-9949545-0-3

Nyx Publishing

www.nyxpublishing.ca

The Black Poison

Darkness. It lingers in unsuspecting places, waiting for something to latch on to. Something that it can poison and slowly contaminate to the point where it will never be the same again. Darkness is an infectious disease that remains contagious well after it has gone only to be caught by another as if it were the plague. No one is safe from its evil tendrils as they wrap around you and consume you. Once you have been touched, the darkness owns you. The only cure is light itself in its purest form and to find that is to look deep into one's self and find it amid the darkness. This is truly life's greatest challenge.

Molly St. Claire

Molly St. Claire stared out the school bus window becoming hypnotized with the passing landscapes. She was alone—the final stop on the long bus route. Molly sat in her usual seat at the back of the bus, discouraging any possible conversation from the bus driver, Merle. It was an exhausting day and she wanted to be left alone to her thoughts. Most days were ending this way lately. Molly noticed Merle watching her periodically through the rearview mirror. She hated the concerned look in his eyes, and it was almost like he knew her secret. The familiar houses passed one-by-one and it meant she was one step closer to home as each one disappeared from view. Molly's anxiety grew in an unsettled knot in her stomach as her destination grew nearer. Home wasn't a pleasant place these days and she longed for the haven of school each morning.

Since her mother left the month before, nothing was the same. Her home once joyful and happy was left empty and ominous. Laughter once ever-present receded into nothing but endless silence. The times it wasn't quiet, the silence was replaced with loud screams of bitter anger. Her father drank frequently and heavily and spiraled out of control into a vicious cycle of drunkenness. When he drank he became violent and soon Molly learned to fear him. The bus passed her neighbors' house and she began fiddling with a stray lock of her hair, twisting it around her fingers. It was a nervous habit not unnoticed by the bus driver. Merle knew exactly what happened. Most of the town knew, but only Merle suspected it was more than just the abandonment of her mother causing Molly to be so distant and forlorn. He pitied the girl and wanted to ask how everything was going. She seemed like a sweet girl and was intelligent beyond her years. He hated to see her ostracize herself and wanted desperately to reach out and make things better but Molly wasn't looking for help. She always was strong and willing to face her problems head on, without the help of others. Despite her pain she still tried to shield them from her burdens.

Molly stood and grabbed her bag as the bus began to slow. She could see her house standing alone on the big country property. Molly walked slowly down the steps and turned to watch the bus drive away, leaving her alone with her thoughts once more. The house stood daunting at the end of the driveway, as if daring her to enter. It seemed to have a menacing personality of its own creation. She took two deep breaths, calming her nerves before walking toward the door. It was becoming a ritual. She noticed her father wasn't home. A bonus she hadn't counted on, but it meant he was likely at the bar in town. He would be drunk by the time he arrived and the peace his absence brought was almost not worth the chaos it would later bring. Molly went to her bedroom and locked the door behind her. This was beginning to become an unsettling habit. Locking her bedroom door was the only thing that could make her feel safe. Her room became her sanctuary but the dark thoughts would still persist.

Molly checked herself in the mirror, and it was clear how her mother's absence impacted her. The girl who stared back was a mere shell of who she used to be. Molly was sixteen but her face was no longer young. Her green eyes, which once sparkled with happiness now held wisdom well beyond their years having no business on the face of a child. She was pale and under her eyes were swollen purple bags from nights of insomnia. The nightmares never ceased and were doomed to repeat the same day over again in an endless loop. Her dark brown hair used to be pretty and well kept but she might as well chop it all off now. She hated herself and tried to hide her thinness behind baggy sweatshirts. The loss of her mother took a toll on her body as well as her soul. Molly ignored her friends and soon they stopped talking to her at school and inviting her out with them and she was glad they moved on. It seemed everyone was talking about her and ridiculing her family. Wherever she went people stared, and her teachers pitied her. None of this mattered very much to Molly, because all she wanted was to be left alone. She didn't want to drag anyone into this mess and she was never one to mind what people thought. They could keep their opinions. So Molly went on shouldering the burden of her drunken father and flighty mother.

School was the only stable thing left in the world to rely on. It was always there and never failed her, providing a safe environment for six hours a day. Her marks gained importance and drove her to get the top grades for an education, which could save her from the mess her life became. University could change everything and she could leave and make something of herself. Molly wanted nothing more than to escape and she wouldn't look back. *Only two more years,* she thought. Her sophomore year was almost over and she decided to work during the summer at any job she could find, possibly even two but work would be difficult in town. She would do anything to leave the small town forever. Molly settled in to do homework at her desk when the front door slammed open, hitting the opposite wall with a loud bang. She heard her father muttering curse words under his breath and listened as he turned the television up full volume. She cringed at the sound, it was clear her father was drunk and it would only be a matter of time before he came looking for her. She heard him banging around in the kitchen in search for a snack and more beer. Maybe she would be safe for a little while longer if he kept his buzz but it was a long shot. Molly remained silent, even scared to breathe in case it drew unwanted attention to her presence.

Eventually Molly finished her homework and her stomach growled signally it was dinnertime. Molly desperately needed to eat some real food. She managed to stay unnoticed by her father and was reluctant to sacrifice her peace but eventually decided to make a trip to the kitchen. This would require her to venture out of her locked sanctuary and cross paths with her father. After formulating a plan, Molly unwillingly unlocked the bedroom door and tip toed quietly down the stairs. She peered into the living room and noticed her father passed out on the couch surrounded by spilled beer and an empty bag of chips balled up on the floor. She cleaned up as much of the garbage as she could before going to the kitchen. She scavenged yesterday's left over pizza and sat down at the table to eat it quickly. Molly wasn't allowed to eat in her room and found it hard to break rules that were in place her entire life, even if they were her mother's. As she ate, Molly surveyed the remnants of the house. The disaster zone, as she liked to think about it.

In its day, the home was immaculate and kept spotless. Her mother made sure nothing was ever out of place. Now dirty dishes overflowed the sink and spread throughout the counter tops. A layer of dust occupied everything and was thick enough to write in. Garbage and food wrappers littered the floor and Molly found she couldn't keep up with the amount of mess. The fridge and freezer were nearly empty excluding the large quantity of beer and left over pizza. Molly didn't know where her next good meal was coming from, but pushed the unpleasant thought from her mind. The living room was in just as bad of condition. The carpet seemed to be one big stain, and stunk of beer, sweat and vomit. The floor and couches were covered in crumbs and broken chip pieces and screamed 'vacuum me!' Molly sighed at the sight of the pigsty and knew something needed to be done but the task seemed a daunting one. It took everything she had to keep enough food in the house to keep them sustained.

"Molly, is that you?" Her father's voice said groggily from the next room. The sound of the tap water gave her away. Molly jumped and dropped the dish she was washing. It shattered on the floor into a million pieces. "Molly?" His voice was louder now and more awake.

"Yes, it's just me Dad. Who else would it be?" Molly said, her voice sounded stronger than she felt. She heard her father get off the couch with a struggle and step towards the kitchen.

"What was that noise, it sounded like something broke?"

"It's nothing Dad. Really! Go back to sleep, you don't have to bother coming in." There was desperation in her voice and she held her breath during the silence as her father deliberated whether it was worth the time to investigate. Molly was just about to start cleaning as her father came in to see it for himself. She had no time to react and braced herself in a corner for the verbal lashing to come. She stepped on a shard of glass in her haste and it wedged itself deep into the flesh of her foot. Molly shrieked in pain and felt the blood sticking to the floor as she tried to move away from the danger zone.

"What the fuck is all this!" Her father roared. His eyes fell instantly to the floor and then back to Molly. They bore into her angrily, and contained a deadly gleam that terrified Molly to her core. They were not the eyes of the father she had known as a girl. This man was a stranger to her. Molly was witnessing the person only her mother had known and hidden.

"I-I dropped a dish." Molly stammered shakily and cast her eyes to the ground. "I was about to clean it up." She added her eyes still on the floor. Molly spoke in a monotone, choosing her words carefully, assessing her chances of reprimand. Her father moved swiftly across the kitchen, somehow in his drunkenness managing to miss all the broken glass. He lifted her chin harshly, forcing her to look up into his face and into his eyes.

"Look at me, damn it!" He screamed, and Molly saw his menacing black stare before he slapped her hard across the face. Her nose, which had shouldered the brunt of the force, began spewing blood and she feared that it was broken. Her hands flew to her face and she let herself sink to the ground and curl into a ball. Molly desperately tried to hold herself together but it took everything she had not to cry and show her pitying weakness. She needed to remain strong, Molly didn't know why but she just had to. Her father crossed the room and was watching her from the doorway in vindictive amusement. His piercing glare was as cold as ice.

"Get up, you stupid bitch! Make yourself useful and clean up this mess." Molly, still in shock just nodded and started to pick up the bigger chunks of glass. Her nose was still bleeding and already forgot the glass in her foot. The shock numbed her pain, as she mindlessly followed his orders. All she could think about was the way his eyes watched her every move. There was hate in them in its purest form. Every move she made was being processed and analyzed. When the mess was cleaned her father went back to his hockey game with the volume turned up way too loud. Molly took her escape out the back sliding door, past the porch and into the late spring evening. The sun was just starting to set beyond the trees in the distance. As soon as she was down the last of the steps she ran as fast as she could go, not caring where her legs took her as long as it was farther away from this house which had long ago ceased to be her home.

Finally Molly stopped running and took note of her surroundings. She found herself at the far edge of the property where a large pond was dug in the back yard. It wasn't much of a surprise to her that her legs took her here. The place was one of her favorites as a child. She sat down at the base of a giant Elm tree, buried her head on her knees and cried without holding back. Her sobs scared away the family of ducklings on the pond and caused a deer to look up from where it was hidden deeper in the trees. The still evening air was refreshing and a little bit chilly as the sun set further. After some time Molly looked up and took in her surroundings. The sky was a beautiful orange glow that brought some courage to Molly as she regained her composure and strength. It wasn't the first time her father hit her, but there was something in his face that changed and led her to believe something snapped in him. It was like he didn't have a conscious and no longer cared about anything and least of all her. He could have been death itself. It was like staring into the face of evil.

In no time at all the sky grew dark and eerie. Molly heard an owl hoot and it seemed to be a bad omen. She didn't care to stay outside any longer and began the long walk back to the house. When she got halfway she noticed that only one light was left on in her father's bedroom. Her pulse beat faster and she forced herself to keep going onward. There wasn't going to be an escape, not yet. She was relieved the back door to the house wasn't locked like she feared as she quickly snuck back inside, sinking onto her bed in exhaustion. Molly was getting undressed when the doorknob wiggled and her father was banging for her to unlock it. The peace was over.

"Let me in!" He yelled and continued trying to push his way through.

"No, I can't!" Molly screamed back as she quickly threw on her old nightgown.

"Let me in right now! Where have you been all night?" When Molly didn't answer the banging continued more franticly for a few minutes and then silence. Molly listened and heard footsteps retreating but she knew her father well enough to know it was not yet the end. He would never give up this easily. Never. When he still didn't return ten minutes later Molly turned out her light and hid herself under the covers still trembling. There was nowhere else for her to go. The silence was the worst; she would have preferred the yelling and banging. At least she would know where the danger was. Now it could be anywhere.

When Merle arrived at Molly's bus stop the next morning he could see that it stood empty. He honked the horn and waited, her absence was rare. There was movement in the curtains in the bay window. Merle could make out the figure of Molly's father waving him onward and the simple action gave him an uneasy feeling. The next week was much the same, Molly remained absent and no one heard from her or caught sight of her since her last day of school. The house seemed to be deserted completely and even Molly's father was never home. The rusty old car, which usually could be seen either in the driveway, or in front of the bar in town called 'Morgan's' disappeared. Mr. Peterman began complaining to whoever cared to ask that Mr. St. Claire hadn't shown up to work in well over a week and rarely appeared at all before he left. Soon police became involved and both Richard St. Claire and Molly St. Claire were reported missing. The case ran cold and the old farmhouse was foreclosed, it had long since been abandoned anyway. No one knew what became of the St. Claire's and no one cared, except for bus driver Merle. He developed a theory about what happened and was certain there was more to the story than the father and daughter fleeing during the night. He often thought there was some horrible truth but he kept his silence.

Part One

Dream Home

1

Karen Williams was bursting with pride as she drove up her new driveway. It was her first time at the place since the papers were signed and the keys in her possession. Her husband Chase was still in the car, laughing at her giddiness. Karen fled from the vehicle the moment it stopped moving and darted towards her new home. She just couldn't believe this house was finally hers and she was at last a homeowner. It was beautiful, but not too extravagant in itself. It was the property she loved mostly. It was a ten-acre plot of land and the front yard had a nice white picket fence—the kind people dream about. The house was a three-bedroom farmhouse and perfect for starting a family. A typical country home that needed some repairs, but it was home and it was perfect. Chase joined her in the front yard and seemed just as happy about having a place of his own. It was great to finally be rid of their old apartment with the terrible plumbing and grouchy landlord.

"Are you ready?" said Karen happily, holding out the new house keys to 312 Bentwood Road.

"I was born ready," said Chase and he laughed heartedly. Karen put the key in the lock and heard the bolt let go in a moment of anticipation. She opened the door and they took the first steps into their new home. The first house either of them ever owned. It certainly needed work but had a homely feeling that Karen liked. It was an older home of thirty years, first built in 1982. From what Karen and Chase were told, it was built by the original owners, which were also the only real owners of the house. The Williams's were told the bank foreclosed on it in 1998 after it was deserted for years. The previous owners failed to keep up the payments. It was miraculous the place wasn't sold earlier, there wasn't anything bad about the house except for the dusty smell of stale air, which was to be expected of a house that had stood empty for so long.

"Well this is home," said Karen and Chase nodded in agreement as he went to open a window. He struggled to budge the old frame but it eventually slid up with an awful groaning noise.

"I think the moving truck just pulled in," said Chase, noticing the sound of squealing brakes. Sure enough when Karen went outside the movers had already lowered their ramp at the back of the truck. They were planning on how to empty the cargo with the least amount of damage. The rest of the afternoon was spent directing the movers on the positions of the heavy furniture and Karen's old piano.

Most of the living room furniture was placed in one of the spare bedrooms for the meantime. Karen decided her first order of business as the new homeowner was going to be replacing the disgusting old carpet in the living room with tasteful hardwoods. It was stained to the extreme and had a putrid smell even the open window couldn't help.

By dinnertime the movers were gone with an empty truck and Karen and Chase were left with the maze of piled up boxes. Neither one of them knew moving into a house would be so difficult and be so time consuming. There were so many things crammed into the small one-bedroom apartment and they just assumed compared to the three bedroom house unpacking would take no time at all. They couldn't have been more wrong. The only one enjoying the chaos was Timbit, their white Persian cat. He was sleeping on the top of one of the tallest piles looking like the happiest cat in the world.

Chase thought ahead for dinner luckily enough, and he produced a cooler filled with some beer, pop and two ham and cheese sandwiches made earlier as a surprise. To Karen, who was starving since missing lunch, it was a welcome meal. They sat at the kitchen table while they ate. Both of them were both too exhausted from the day's activities to say much. They stared out the window and watched as the snow fell. The snow seemed to be illuminated by the full moon and it gave the ground a sense that it was glowing. Karen wondered if the spring would be just as beautiful as the winter. She was dying to have a little garden of her own and to get her hands dirty. She was only able to fit a couple small potted plants on the balcony of their apartment.

"It seems so dark outside!" Chase remarked. The country was so different from the city at night. It was impossible to get away from all the streetlights and the bustle of activity at all hours of the night.

"I know, you can even see the stars!" said Karen happily before chewing another mouthful of sandwich.

"Everything seems so quiet too, it's peaceful." Neither Chase nor Karen had ever lived in the country before. Both of them were raised in the city and never lived in anything other than an apartment, even as children. Karen spent a year in a university dorm but that was no better. She was curious and eager to see what a house and the country were really all about. It was a great day when Chase signed the contract for his book deal. His publishing house gave him a large advance and wanted the book to be completed by the next year. They moved to the country with hopes that the secluded life style might provide him with the peace and quiet Chase needed to finish his novels. He always dreamed of being one of those authors typing away in some cabin in the middle of no where and Karen was more than willing to oblige, even if that secluded cabin turned into a country farmhouse on the outskirts of a very small town. She wasn't getting very many substituting jobs in the bigger city and hoped maybe she could apply for a full-time position at the local public school in town.

The first night they spent together in their new house was spent sleeping on the mattress on the floor of the small master bedroom. They were too worn out to bother looking for the tools and putting their queen-sized bed together. It took well over an hour to search out their blankets and pillows in the mess of boxes spread throughout the house. Luckily Karen remembered to pack each of them a suitcase filled with a couple days worth of clothes and their toiletries. The house only contained a single bathroom, which was on the smaller side. Chase and Karen fought for space, as it was difficult fitting two people over the sink as they attempted to both brush their teeth. The water pressure in the shower was good and Karen took a long warm bath before bed to help her aching muscles from the day's stresses. Even with the help of the movers she ended up doing quite a bit of heavy lifting of her own.

It was after two in the morning by the time they were able to retire to bed and both were struggling to stay awake. Even without any window coverings the room was in complete darkness. Karen was unable to see her hand in front of her face and she fumbled clumsily around in the dark as she made her way to the mattress. She almost fell over the sleeping Chase in the process. It was quite a change from the city where the world was never completely dark. Once in bed, Karen tried to sleep but found it wouldn't come. The house had new noises that kept her awake and startled her. She was never one to be comfortable sleeping in a new place. Sometime around four in the morning her bedroom door started swinging open and made a creaking sound that scared her and made her think an intruder was present. She was about to wake Chase when Timbit launched himself on her stomach and 'meowed' looking for attention. Relieved she stroked the cat's head before sending him on his way. She had no reason to be so paranoid.

The next thing she remembered was waking up in the fully lit room. It was morning and she must have finally gotten to sleep after all. She heard the calming sounds of birds outside her window. She felt the bed beside her and found it empty but the sounds of something frying on the stove were coming from the kitchen and she could smell the faint scent of cinnamon in the air. *Despite my restless night today is going to be a good day,* Karen thought and smiled to herself.

2

Chase didn't get much sleep himself, and he was tossing and turning all night. It simply was too quiet and too dark and the noises of the old house were still so unfamiliar. *It was just going to take some getting used to,* Chase told himself optimistically. When the morning sun began to rise in the window, Chase decided to give up on sleep and get a head start on unpacking. Karen was sound asleep and he didn't want to wake her now that she was finally getting some rest. It certainly was one long night for the both of them. Chase dressed quickly and as silently as possible, as not to wake his wife and went in search of some breakfast. There had to be some cooking tools somewhere and the groceries he brought. He sorted through the boxes in the kitchen and eventually found a frying pan, a bowl and the ingredients for French toast. The time on his watch read 8:30 a.m. Breakfast was almost complete by the time Karen walked sleepily into the kitchen and wrapped her arms around his waist.

"Good morning, honey," she said and kissed his neck.

"Morning." Chase replied and smiled at his wife. He couldn't help but notice she looked beautiful this morning. Karen wore nothing but an old t-shirt and her hair was messy from sleep but she could not have looked better if she had been wearing one of her fancy dresses and make-up. She had a way of looking attractive without trying. Karen smiled and there was a gleam in her eyes that never failed to make Chase smile back. They had been married for almost two years, since they were both fresh out of school. Their families were not happy they were married so young but they calmed down once they saw they could be successful. Chase had a couple mystery books published that were doing well and Karen was substitute teaching. It wasn't much but they got by.

"I'm so glad you made breakfast. After yesterday I'm starving," declared Karen as she set the table quickly and started the hunt for syrup.

"Me too, I think we should unpack the kitchen first. That way we'll at least be fed if nothing else."

"Sounds like a good plan." Karen agreed and started emptying the nearest box, putting things in the necessary drawers. Most of the groceries were already placed in the fridge but everything not needing to be kept cold was still packed away in the mess of unorganized boxes. The timer went off just as Karen finished with her first box and they sat down to eat. The warm French toast was just what they needed to start the day.

3

Shannon and Jim Ferrety were shocked at the sight of the moving truck in front of the old St. Claire place. No one wanted to have anything to do with the place for years. When the police first searched the house after Molly and Richard were declared missing they were disturbed of the state the place was in. There were stories the house smelt awful inside to the point where the cleaners who were hired needed to wear masks to go inside. Everyone in town old enough to remember the St. Claire's concocted their own version of the story with their own personal theory of what happened. The town's children were told campfire stories that the place is haunted. It soon became a rite of passage for young boys to bike up to the house and break in through a window. Once, a group of these adventure-seeking boys tried to spend a night in the house on a dare. Shannon wasn't sure if they managed to succeed or not. It didn't matter because she was sure the house was definitely not haunted. It was unlikely anything happened there at all but over the fourteen years since the incident the story became a legend, blown way out of proportion.

Shannon wanted to meet her new neighbors and see who braved the home's reputation. She was certain it wasn't anyone she knew from in town wanting to move further into the country. It must be someone from the outside. Either way, Shannon and Jim both were glad to have a neighbor again and they were curious as to the insides of the home. Shannon spent the good part of the afternoon baking a banana bread to bring over after the new people had time to settle in. She would show them what small town hospitality was all about while at the same time satisfying her need to see the so called 'haunted house' with her own eyes.

The new residents were not lost on the town. News spread quickly the St. Claire place was sold and the town was buzzing. It was a common topic of conversation and everyone wanted to catch a glimpse of the people brave enough to take on the house everyone believed should have been condemned. They wondered if the people would be as creepy as the place seemed to be. The town split into two groups on the matter. The first group consisted of the people who remembered the St. Claire's and were adults when they went missing. The second group consisted of the half of the town who were children when it happen or came after the St. Claire's disappearance.

The first half of the town was unhappy the place sold and believed firmly it should have been turned in to a pile of rubble years before. They knew Richard St. Claire was in a state before he left and was a known violent drunk. The disaster of the house was not a surprise to them one bit. To that half of the town the house was a symbol of hard times and a low class of people. They would have rather seen it gone. The second group believed the story was blown out of proportion and the house should have new owners. After all, there wasn't anything wrong with it besides a few broken windows already replaced before it sold. There could be a sort of charm to living in a farmhouse and the land it sat on was beautiful. That half of town believed a second chance was well deserved and was happy that it would be granted. All the house would need was fine people and a few renovations.

4

After a long week of unpacking, the house on 312 Bentwood Road was really beginning to feel like home. The boxes were put out in the recycling and almost everything found a place. Chase set up an office in one of the unused bedrooms and was back to work on his novel. Internet access was already up and running and so was the cable, not that they watched much television these days. A sense of normalcy was back and life was going on almost as if they hadn't moved at all. The late days of January were good ones. Karen sat down at her piano now placed on the new hardwoods in the living room, when there was a knock at the door. *I wonder who that could possibly be.* Karen thought as she went to find out.

"Hello, I'm Shannon and this is my husband Jim. We just live across the street and thought we would welcome you to the neighborhood," said Shannon cheerfully. Karen was ecstatic to have a real visitor for once. *This really is a small town,* she thought.

"Hello, come in," said Karen, as she moved so they could pass her and walk into the entryway of the house. They handed her a container with a loaf of banana bread and she thanked them, while being mildly amused that her views of small towns were in fact accurate. That never would have happened in the city. She waited for them to remove their shoes before motioning for them to sit on one of the two tan leather couches she bought for the room. They looked good on her new flooring. "Chase, come downstairs and meet our neighbors," she called to her husband. He was working away on his novel all afternoon and she hated to disturb him but also didn't want to be rude to her new potential friends.

"Hello, we're the Ferrety's from across the street." They greeted as Chase sat down beside Karen on one of their new couches.

"Hi, it's nice to meet you. We haven't really met anyone from town yet. I'm Chase and this is my wife Karen Williams" Chase greeted.

"We figured you might want to know who you neighbors are. After all this is such a small town. Believe me, give it a month and you'll know everybody by name."

"That's one of the reasons we moved to such a small town. It seems like a lovely way to live." Karen replied.

"It is nice but it definitely can get old pretty fast if you give it time. The town lives on gossip and you better get used to everybody knowing your business both good and bad," said Jim and he seemed to talk from experience. Karen picked up just a hint of regret in his voice.

"Where did you two live before?"

"Manhattan." Karen answered and was trying to remember if any of her neighbors in the apartment complex made a point of welcoming her when they moved in. Her mind drew up a blank but she didn't think so.

"That must have been nice." Shannon said, "Small town life might come as a change then."

"I certainly hope so. Living in the city can get so crazy some times. We're definitely looking for a change," said Chase. He was thinking about his novel and the peace of the country and the land.

"It's different having people live in this house again. We were beginning to think it would never be sold. It's been empty for fourteen years you know?" said Jim. Karen noticed he seemed to be hinting at something and she didn't quite like it.

"Did you know the original owners?" Karen asked inquisitively.

"I never knew Mr. and Mrs. St. Claire but I was in the same class as their daughter. She was an odd one, kept to herself mostly and never talked to anyone. Other than that she was a nice girl but her family left when I was in tenth grade so I couldn't tell you too much." Shannon answered cautiously.

"We were told that the owners just disappeared one night," said Chase.

"So they did tell you. The house has a reputation in town. Over the years people have made up stories about this place. I'm sure you'll hear them all," said Jim and he seemed a little relieved that the story of the house was relayed to the new owners after all.

"What story do you believe?" Chase asked, with some real interest. His novelist brain racking up the infinite possibilities, Karen was sure.

"I don't really think anything out of the ordinary happened, if that's what you mean? I think the St. Claire's knew they couldn't afford the house and just left it during the night to avoid being evicted, but who knows really. There's no reason to believe anything else happened here."

5

Timbit the cat was enjoying his newfound space. He was free to jump on the piles of boxes and even now that the boxes were gone, he had lots of new furniture in its place. The cat was enjoying exploring his new surroundings. The house was odd though, some of the rooms were much colder than others and the house was drafty. Timbit's favorite hangout had become the spare room. There was still no furniture in the room but Timbit was drawn there for some reason. It gave off a good vibe and he found it pleasant, a perfect spot to take an afternoon catnap on the floor. The carpet was soft and made a good bed but Karen still found it odd the cat preferred it to the new couches or her own room. In fact the cat seldom entered the master bedroom at all. Other than that Timbit seemed to adjust well to the new house and no one paid him much mind.

6

Chase was busy working on his novel and so far he was making real progress. It seemed the move did help his mind and sparked a round of creativity. Since he was back to work and now had his own office space he typed out fifty new pages that he was proud of writing. The third book was going to be completed sooner than he originally hoped and his publisher would be happy to hear the news. Now he had a solid foundation, so far entitled, 'Missing, Presumed Dead' Chase was eager to spend more time with his wife. Just the day before, they had gone on a walk through their back yard to check out the property. Karen found a large pond out back they didn't see before and now was pressuring him to buy some ice skates. The idea of skating brought back some memories of his hockey days as a child and his feud with his father, who had always been way too competitive for his own good. Chase had never been a great skater, but Karen on the other hand loved it and was a decent figure skater in her own right.

Chase was just happy they had more than enough land to buy a snowmobile and ride it. He always thought that it would be fun. It seemed a trip in to town would have to come soon. After the Ferrety's visit, it seemed all the neighbors on the street had the same idea and the living room often held guests. Many seemed to want a tour to see what they did with the place. Karen, with nothing else to do enjoyed being a hostess and gladly gave their nosy guests' tours. Most of their visitors came bearing some sort of dessert and they now had more than enough pies, brownies and different kinds of cakes. He couldn't complain about the near constant distractions, not while he was so well fed. He was sure he would recognize about half the people already when Karen and him did go on their shopping trip. It certainly would be interesting to see what the little shops and restaurants were like.

7

Karen was excited because her and Chase were finally going into town for the first time. They avoided going before because the dirt roads surrounding them were thoroughly covered in snow and ice. They hadn't been plowed all winter and the town was not easily assessable in their four-cylinder car; most of their neighbors owned a truck with four-wheel drive to navigate the hazardous ice and deep ditches. They agreed on the first day the weather improved, the drive to town would be attempted. It was a miracle the sun finally decided to make an appearance and melt a large chunk of snow that day. The lack of groceries in the house was becoming an increasing issue.

The drive into town was not as bad as they anticipated and only took them ten minutes. There was not much of a downtown, merely consisting of a grocery store and a few other family owned businesses and restaurants. Among those were a video store, hardware store, pizzeria, a pharmacy and a bar called 'Morgan's.' Further down Main Street was a city hall that doubled as a police station and community Centre. The town's second busiest road was called George Street, which intersected Main Street where the town's only sets of streetlights sat. On George Street there was a small white church and a public school that went from Kindergarten to eighth grade. After graduation students were required to go to the high school a town over which was a forty-minute bus ride away. Karen hoped to teach at the elementary school, if she was lucky but finding a job before the next year was going to be a challenge. The schoolyard was attached to the Towns Park, which held a baseball diamond, a soccer field, and basketball courts. Karen saw a couple tetherball polls and smiled, it was years since she saw one anywhere. The rest of the town consisted of a single subdivision with aged homes and a water tower that stood above everything else. The population sign she passed read 'Population 700'. She could not believe that it could possibly be accurate but by looking around she knew it was.

Chase pulled the little car up to the grocery store, the only building in town besides the school with any real parking lot. That was one thing the town seemed to have in common with the big city.

There were very few cars on the road and the parking lot was almost empty.

"Hello neighbors!" A man yelled over to them and waved to get their attention as he made his way over with two big brown paper bags filled with groceries—one in each arm. Karen didn't recognize him at first because of the amount of people who introduced themselves as her neighbors. She eventually placed him as the man who lived alone and ran a small dairy farm around the corner from her on Tatter Road.

"Hello Dan." Karen greeted as she smiled and waved. Chase still seemed confused as to who the man was and looked impressed.

"So you guys finally made it into town I see." Dan commented, stating the obvious. "How do you like it?"

"It's lovely," said Karen looking around admiring the quaint surroundings. The layer of snow did add to the beauty of the place.

"I can see staying here for a long time." Chase agreed and Dan seemed rather pleased.

"Most people do." After they waved goodbye and went in to the small grocery store. They saw a few other familiar faces as they walked the aisles and everyone wanted to have a conversation. Mr. Banner and his wife, who owned a small hobby farm beside them stopped to chat about how frigid the winter had been and how they were looking forward to the coming of spring. Karen didn't want to think about it too much, there was still a lot more winter left. She found out the Bennel's son wanted to learn piano and they hoped Karen was up to giving lessons. She was surprised they knew she even played but graciously declined saying she was too busy at the moment but maybe when they were more settled. She appreciated the offer. Maybe she could make some cash if teaching at the school turned into a dead end.

Chase and Karen came out of the store two hours later with a full cart of groceries. It had never taken so long before but then again no one ever wanted to talk to them back in Manhattan. It was a little inconvenient but they had time to kill and everyone was just so friendly. Navigating the grocery cart back to their car turned out to be a bit of a challenge. The snow turned mostly into slush on the warm tarmac of the parking lot and was a wet slippery mess. It took both Karen and Chase to steer the cart and they were having fun making a game of it. Only a couple slush balls were thrown at one another. By the time the small car was loaded to full capacity and groceries were stuck in every extra nook and cranny available, the whole afternoon somehow disappeared. The trip into town was dubbed a successful outing and Karen even managed to find a pair of figure skates in the hardware store she purchased. Chase was still looking to buy that snowmobile.

8

Mr. Peterman still worked and owned the hardware store. He was one of the first to notice the new neighbors made the first trip into town. He was an old man now at the ripe old age of sixty-four and he knew Richard St. Claire well. Then, Richard had been a dear family friend since boy hood. As Richard's friend he was one of the first to know something was wrong in the St. Claire household but he never mentioned it. In the last few months leading to their disappearance he watched from the sidelines as Richard drank himself into the ground on a regular basis. He always had a short fuse and often resorted to violence, a quality that was accentuated when he was drunk. Mr. Peterman had been too afraid to bring up any unpleasant topic to Richard for fear of a confrontation. He often looked back at those hard times and never forgave himself for his silence. Maybe something could have been done to help the poor man. He also wondered about Jennifer, Richard's wife. She was occasionally seen with bruises or a black eye. Secretly Mr. Peterman wondered how she came by those injuries and grew suspicious of the St. Claire's home life. He had no right to pry.

As an older man that knew the family well it didn't sit right with him that the St. Claire's house was sold. He was well planted firmly on the side of town that believed the house should have been condemned. It belonged in a part of the town's history that he believed was better off not remembered. Whether the house had seen a murder or some sort of violence did not matter to him or sway his opinion like the others. He stayed out of the theories and would only allow himself to believe the actual facts. In his mind 312 Bentwood Road would remain the St. Claire house and it would be nothing but a dark stain on the history of the town. The children were right when they used it as a haunted house but not because it was haunted but for the symbol it represented.

He watched the Williams' as they did their shopping and threw snowballs in the parking lot. They seemed young and a solid couple and he wondered how long they would remain that way. He was taught when something evil happened in a place it sometimes lingered well after the dark forces were gone. Living in close quarters with darkness had a way of affecting a person's soul.

9

"Come on, it will be fun!" said Karen as she twirled gracefully on the ice with her new figure skates. This was her favorite thing about winter and made the cold temperatures and the snow a little more tolerable.

"I'm not so sure about that," said Chase, as he stood clumsily in his own skates and held the base of a tree for support. Karen glided over and reached out to him and Chase unwillingly gave her his hand. She pulled and next thing he knew he was right up near Karen on the ice. She smiled and slowly started to skate around with him in tow. Karen thought Chase looked cute in his nervousness. It was years since they went skating together because Chase never liked it much. His father gave him a tough time as a hockey player in his childhood.

"That's not half-bad," said Karen, admiring her awkward husband as he attempted to skate backwards. He did seem to be enjoying himself.

"Ouch." Chase yelled as he hit a divot in the ice and fell backwards, arms flailing. Karen stifled a giggle, fearing if she laughed Chase might never come out here again.

"Nice one," said Karen, and skated over to Chase to help him up. He took hold of her hand and before she knew it she was lying on the ground beside him. They laughed for a while without bothering to get up.

"Look it's snowing!" said Chase and they both looked up at the sky. It was one of those snowfalls where the snowflakes were large and well defined. Karen stuck out her tongue and caught one and felt it melt.

"It's beautiful." She remarked and Chase seemed to agree with her in his mesmerized silence. The whole backyard was covered in a layer of white and sparkled as the sun kissed it and twinkled in the light, dancing. The trees were barren but were decorated in icicles and more snow, which seemed to hold the sunlight. The backyard property was covered in rolling hills of white and untouched land, even their footprints from earlier was almost covered up from the fresh falling snow.

"We should get up," said Chase, nudging her in the side.

"You're right." She replied as she suddenly became hyper aware that her backside was soaking through. They skated to the edge of the pond and Karen sat beneath the big elm tree and took off her skates. It felt good for her feet to be out of the tightly laced skates and into the much larger and warmer boots. Her fingers were freezing from the cold and wetness and she stuffed her hands into her pockets and waited for Chase. The snow soaked her hair and it was plastered to her head in a wet mess. She was looking forward to some hot chocolate with marshmallows and maybe a warm bath later. The walk back to the house was not a short one and it was made longer as they had to step through the extra foot of snow.

Job Opening

1

Karen awoke from a deep sleep to the sound of the phone ringing on the bedside table. It took a moment for her to realize what she was hearing and get her bearings. Chase grumbled and stirred in his sleep. Karen picked up the phone without first checking the caller id. *Who is calling this early in the morning?*

"Hello?" She said groggily.

"Hello Karen, this is Mrs. Elsing the principal of the public school." It took Karen a moment to comprehend this.

"Yes, might I ask why you are calling?" Karen asked with a bit of excitement.

"It seems we are in need of a teacher. Mrs. Meriwether had her baby yesterday and we need someone to fill in her maternity leave. From what I've been hearing though, I wouldn't be so sure she intends to come back at all. So this may turn out to be a full time position should you accept it," said Mrs. Elsing.

"Yes, of course I'll accept it. When will I start?" Karen asked.

"Next week is March break, so a week Monday."

"I'll be there, its good news about Mrs. Meriwether's baby. Is it a boy or a girl?"

2

"Are you nervous?" Chase asked his wife as they were sitting down for breakfast. She was dressed and ready for her first day as the new fifth grade teacher.

"It's been a while since I've done any teaching," said Karen truthfully. She was nervous and she never had to come up with her own teaching plan before. Karen couldn't have been more excited and more terrified. This was definitely what she wanted and now she would have a chance to make some real money to put towards the household. Karen could have something to be proud of like her husbands career. Chase watched her and seemed to understand.

They were living in their home for nearly two months and it was time Karen found some real work. Chase was making some progress with his novel and was a third of the way through the first draft. Karen watched him work diligently on his computer day in and day out and secretly wished she had something of her own to focus on. She didn't want to admit it but she was bored.

"I'm sure you'll do fine, honey," said Chase reassuringly and he meant it. Karen knew she would, but decided she would feel much better about it after a couple weeks when it was no longer so fresh.

"I'm sure your right." She answered as she finished up with breakfast, gave Chase a kiss goodbye and left out the front door. She parked her car in the mostly empty grocery store parking lot. She was one of the first teachers to arrive. Her nerves were beginning to take over as the reality of her job seemed to sink in. It was only eight O'clock when Karen opened the big front doors of the small elementary school. Finding the Principal's office wasn't a challenge as it had often been back in New York. This school had only a single hallway and the Principal's office was the first room on the right and was clearly marked. Karen entered the small office and walked up to the desk, a nameplate read Mrs. M. Elsing.

"Hello Karen," Mrs. Elsing greeted happily. The principal wasn't what she was expecting. She was an older woman of about her mid to late fifties, but she looked good and was professional. Her long hair was kept in a bun and was obviously dyed a natural looking golden color. Her hair didn't show any grey but Karen was suspicious. Mrs. Elsing quickly started a tour of the school as they talked about her new duties. She brought Karen to the staff room and showed her to her new classroom. It was the only fifth grade class in the school and there were only to be fifteen students in her care. This calmed Karen's nerves a little bit and for once she saw what her day would be like and felt a bit more confident. Mrs. Elsing gave her Mrs. Meriwether's notes and lesson plans to give her an idea where the class was and then she left her to get prepared.

"The warning bell rings at 8:50 a.m.," said Mrs. Elsing on her way out the door. *Only twenty more minutes*, Karen thought as she wrote 'Mrs. Williams' on the blackboard. She took a seat down at her new desk and took in the feel. It was awkward being left alone in the empty classroom and she felt out of place. She straightened her papers out on the desk and quickly looked over the notes left to her by Mrs. Meriwether. The class was a little behind in the curriculum, most likely because of their teachers progressing pregnancy. She was going to have her work cut out for her to get to everything on time. Luckily she had the advantage of having taught many fifth grade classes before. Karen mentally reviewed her plans for the morning in her head in careful detail.

The bell rang and the students gathered outside the school began to line up. The sounds of screaming and children outside her window began to quiet down. There was a period of silence before the sounds of the kids flooded down the hallway. Lockers slamming and mindless chatter came from just outside her door. Soon the first of her students walked in and took their seats. Karen wondered if there was a set-seating plan and shuffled through papers to look for it, before noticing it was taped on the clipboard that held the attendance sheet. The students were giddy and Karen heard parts of conversation mostly about March break adventures as she walked and took her place at the front of the class. The bell rang and the national anthem filled the room coming from the ancient intercom system in the corner. The morning announcements followed immediately and the sound of Mrs. Elsing's already familiar voice came on and was followed up by sounds of some of the students doing a really corny skit to advertise the school play try outs for next week. Then the intercom died and the attention was immediately on Karen. Fifteen sets of eyes looked at her as if they suddenly realized the absence of their usual teacher. One boy in the back raised his hand and Karen called on him.

"Where's Mrs. Meriwether?" He asked and everyone seemed to nod in agreement at the question. It was clear they were all thinking the same thing. She was the elephant in the room.

"She had her baby a week ago and I will be replacing her as your new teacher until the end of the school year. My name is Mrs. Williams." A few of the students seemed thrilled at the news of the new baby but most of the class seemed indifferent. Some chatter began to rise up again, and Karen cleared her throat to redirect the attention back to herself.

"We need to do attendance; I hope to learn all your names soon but in the mean time, say 'here' when I call out yours." Karen went through the list and everyone was present and she felt she might remember a few of the names already. That was a good sign; she hadn't expected to remember them so fast. Fifteen names should only take her a few days to get a handle on. "We are going to start today by doing what I know everyone is dying to do." Some of the students looked at her in blatant disbelief and most seemed bored already. "You are going to stand up one at a time and say what you did during March break for the class." A few of the bored students seemed a little more interested and Karen knew her tactics were working.

"Do we have to go up to the front of the class?" A girl in the front row asked. Karen looked at the seating plan quickly and saw her name was Sarah.

"Only if you want too, but other than that you can stand where you are." A few students, including Sarah seemed relieved. She forgot how shy most ten and eleven-year olds were when it came to presentations.

"We'll start at this end of the class and work our way across the rows until everyone has a chance to say what they want." She pointed to the boy in the front right corner of the classroom. She believed his name to be Braydon.

"During the break my dad and I went on an ice fishing trip together, just the two of us. I caught a big fish and we brought it home and had it for dinner one night." Braydon sat back down and Karen could tell he was proud of himself and his fish. They continued for the rest of the morning and the exercise seemed to be a good success. She had everyone talking and getting along and participating fully. That was never an easy feat, if only it would be so simple once the real work got started. The bell rang and the class was let out for a fifteen-minute recess. When they got back she was going to have long division worksheets on each of their desks. If only she could find the copier room.

3

"How was your first day?" Chase asked as he greeted her in the driveway. Karen was full of energy despite her long day and was quite pleased. She was glad to see Chase and ran up and surprised him by kissing him passionately.

"Was it really that good?" said Chase smiling; he seemed surprised at her outburst and was amused at her mood.

"I had a great day. I'm teaching a class of only fifteen and they are all really great kids. They seem very eager to learn and I think they like me!"

"Who wouldn't like you? Who wouldn't like the person who gave them homework and made them do math?" He mocked teasingly. Karen could tell he was proud of her and her new job. She wondered how she could have ever been nervous in the first place. It seemed stupid now.

"I got a call from my publisher today," said Chase with a bitter edge to his voice.

"And?" Karen waited, her good mood partially gone. Chase seemed worried.

"They said the first couple chapters are good but complained that they didn't get how the third and fourth chapters followed the story line. They want me to rewrite it."

"I read those chapters yesterday; they made perfect sense to me. They're just being nitpicky. When they have so much money tied in to something they want it to be perfect. I'm sure the chapters you wrote would have been fine."

"No, I think they're right on this one. I don't know why but when I sat down to write those chapters my hands wanted to type a different story and no matter how much I tried to get back to my original plans, the other ones kept coming back to me. I couldn't stay focused," said Chase. He was beating himself up over this and Karen wanted to help him but she didn't know what to say. She hated to see him so tortured, it was worse than when he struggled with writers block.

"What is it that you have in your head?" Karen asked putting her hand on Chase's shoulder sympathetically.

"It's dark and cold, I can't see anything except for the mist that surrounds me. I'm being followed by something but I don't know what. All I know for certain is I must seek shelter." Chase took on an ominous tone and seemed to be quoting something. It didn't sound like anything Chase had written before.

"What is it?"

"I don't know. Those are the lines I keep writing over and over again whenever I try to get back to my novel. I wish I knew, I don't even know where it came from and how it got in my head but it has. I think it's the beginning of a story that needs to be written but I can't write it now. Not when I promised a sequel to my last novel."

"What if you wrote out just a little bit more of the story? Just enough to see where it's going?" said Karen helpfully.

"If only I had more time, but I don't."

4

"Karen surprised me." Maggie Elsing admitted. She originally was dead set against hiring her as Mrs. Meriwether's replacement but the lack of qualified people made her the obvious choice.

"I told you she would be a good fit." Mathew, the fourth grade teacher replied. They were alone in the staffroom well after all the other teachers left for the night. Karen was on the job for a week and she heard nothing but praise for the twenty-six year old teacher. All the students liked her and she was teaching them at a quicker rate than Mrs. Meriwether managed. She was worried because Karen only ever taught as a supply teacher before and never took on a whole class of her own. She was still fresh out of school and inexperienced in Maggie's eyes. She also didn't care to admit that she didn't like her because she wasn't known. Not too many people knew her very well and Maggie never trusted people she didn't completely know. It was her cautious nature.

"I see I was wrong now. She is a good teacher and is fitting in with the class. Let's just hope she meshes in with the parents. People in this town don't always take to new comers." Mathew just chuckled.

"They do when those new comers are young beautiful women." He replied. Maggie stared him down with a sharp look and for a brief second Mathew feared she might slap him.

"She's happily married," said Maggie coldly from between gritted teeth. "And she's not that pretty."

"Not when you compare her to you of course," said Mathew, attempting to mend his mistake, "but marriage never stopped you." He said mockingly.

"Lets shut up about this and talk about something else." Maggie replied, effectively ending that conversation. She never liked the fact that she was married to be brought up when she was with Mathew. The two of them had been secretly sneaking around ever since the year before when Maggie's husband Michael started shutting her out. She was drawn to the much younger teacher's arms mostly because he offered her things her husband could not: respect and attention. Mathew liked her because she was older, experienced and intelligent and he thought the more of her for it. Michael feared her dominance and often put her down and belittled her in an attempt to feel superior. Mathew boosted her self-confidence and made her feel young and good about herself for once in her life. After all she did deserve it, right?

"We're alone," said Mathew, acknowledging the absence of the other teachers who had left long ago. The hall was silent of footsteps and the lights were out. The room was reduced to shades of grey.

"I think your right." Then the fifty-eight year old principal let herself feel thirty again.

5

"My mom told me you lived in a haunted house," said Tommy casually to Karen one day. She was on recess duty and was walking slowly around the big field. Some of her students flocked to her for conversation. Every once in a while she would have to look up to make sure the kids weren't beating on each other and were playing fairly. A nice game of freeze tag had broken out and everyone for the moment was getting along so Karen answered the boy's curiosity.

"My house isn't haunted. It's the same as everybody else's house." She replied, she hadn't heard anything on the topic before and would have found it funny if any of the parents had told her that the nice quiet farmhouse once was referred to as 'The Haunted House'. She hadn't learned boys were often terrified of it.

"So its not haunted. I don't know why everybody was scared of it then," said Tommy and it peaked Karen's interest.

"Who's scared of it?" She asked.

"Lots of the older boy's, they rode their bike over to it once on a dare. I think my parents are scared of it too."

"What makes you think that, that's silly?" said Karen. She couldn't believe two grown adults could be scared of a house.

"They talk about it lots. I don't think they like it for some reason." Karen wasn't sure what to make of that. Kids often said things they shouldn't and she definitely was not suppose to hear that the town disliked her house and talked about it. She couldn't even think of a logical reason for that kind of a reaction.

"I can assure you my house is fine. No ghosts there," said Karen and Tommy looked relieved. They talked about school for a little while longer before he ran off to join in on the game of tag. Karen heard a scream from the far end of the field and noticed little Sarah was crying and holding her knee. Karen sprinted over to her and all memory of the previous conversation vanished.

6

Chase was beyond frustrated at himself. He just couldn't focus. The words, which had flowed endlessly to him in the first month, now ceased to exist. It wasn't that he didn't know what to write and how to write it. He did, which was the part that stumped him. *If that was the case, how come I can't put my thought down on paper? It should be so simple. How come whenever the words come to me I mess it up by writing something else? Something completely different!* Chase slammed his fist onto his desk in frustration and pushed his computer chair away. This wasn't working and Chase had been an author long enough to know that if he had to force it, the words would never come.

Completely giving up, Chase sighed and walked down the stairs into the kitchen. He leaned against the counter and brewed himself a fresh pot of coffee. The house was silent and felt empty without Karen. He was used to her being home and now that she had a full time job he missed her when she was out of the house. It was only noon and the day had hardly gotten started. Karen wouldn't be home for hours. If only she was home he would feel better about being behind in his work. She always had a way to calm him down and see that everything would turn out all right. The coffee finished brewing and Chase poured himself a cup; he always drank it black when he was stressed. The walk back upstairs was slow and reluctant but he couldn't put it off any longer. A thought popped into Chase's mind, it was something Karen said once. 'Maybe you should write out a little bit of the story? Just to see where it is going?' It seemed like a time consuming idea at the time but maybe she was right. He really could use a writing exercise. At the moment he was willing to give everything a try. It had to be better than not writing anything at all.

Chase minimized the word document with his novel and opened up a blank page. It was a start and he could feel himself already getting excited. *Maybe this might just work!* Chase typed: It's dark and cold. I can't see anything except for the mist that surrounds me. I am being followed by something but I don't know what. All I know for certain is I must seek shelter. I must survive and to do that I must find the light, but all I see is darkness. This danger could be lurking anywhere. It could be right behind me, the sound of the wind effectively masks out the sound of footsteps. I'd have no warning before the danger got me, no warning before I died.

Chase read over the paragraph many times and knew he would never be able to make sense of it. He was completely clueless as to how and why this bit of literature was in his head. He didn't write horror novels and never wanted to. He wrote mysteries and people rarely ever died. Chase had the eerie feeling that those words he wrote were not his own, but yet he had written them. Still confused but slightly more focused, Chase deleted his writing exercise and went back to his main novel. He knew instantly that it was a success; the words he found himself writing were the right ones for once. His publisher would be happy and for the moment that was all he cared about. He would have to remember to thank Karen when she returned from work. Writing the story had mainly been her idea.

When Karen walked through the door three hours later Chase had written the two chapters he was required and was in the middle of sending them to his publisher. He was certain that this time they would not be returned. Everything was officially on track.

7

"Didn't anyone do the homework I assigned last night? Anyone at all?" Karen was saying to her class. Her day was exhausting and she was on her last nerve. Sarah sprained her ankle during recess and Karen was the one to call her mother. Sarah's mother wasn't impressed and said some rather sharp words to her even though the accident wasn't her fault at all. It was the fault of a raised root from one of the trees that Sarah tripped over. She wondered where Mrs. Elsing the principal went, as her office was empty when she went to drop Sarah off. Karen quickly used the office phone and was relieved when Mrs. Elsing stumbled in ten minutes later, still before Sarah's mother picked her up. Relieved to have missed seeing the brutal women, she went to take over her class from Miss. Lanley, the school's secretary who Karen recruited to watch her class while she played Principal.

"I did the homework," said Jessica, waving her hand up in the air. This did not surprise Karen. Jessica was the class smarty-pants and wanted it to be known.

"That's good Jessica. Did anyone else do the work I assigned yesterday?" No hands went up and she saw the class all look down at their desks. This was not her day. She planned the next period to be based on the assignment.

"Mrs. Meriwether never made us do homework." Dakota protested from the far corner of the room. He was a brave one, and loud spoken.

"I'm not Mrs. Meriwether and when I have you do homework you better do it. I'm the one who gives you your grades on your report card and the next one comes out next week!" She stretched the truth a little bit. She wasn't teaching the class long enough to grade anything that would change any of the students' marks. She was using the same grade Mrs. Meriwether already sent in for the reports. Her threat seemed to work, and the class was silent enough.

"I did my homework," Jessica chimed in again, breaking the silence. She was met with grumbles from the rest of the class. *Yes, today was definitely not my day.*

Karen spent the rest of class writing a note on the blackboard and explaining the lesson they were supposed to have already finished in the worksheet she assigned. She was originally planning a group exercise on the topic that would have been preferred by the class. At the end of the day she reassigned the science worksheet and added another one to be finished for the next day. As the final bell rang all her students seemed thoroughly bored and in about the same mood as she was. Karen wasted no time after her students left and she quickly crossed the parking lot to her car. For once she was the first teacher to leave instead of one of the last and her head was fuming with stress and frustration all the way home.

As if on cue the one stop light in town turned red just as she got there. *Of Course! Just when I'm close to being home that would happen,*

Karen thought bitterly. She was at the point where her day was beginning to seem like a comedy act, she found herself laughing neurotically by the time the light turned green. The whole time the light was red not a single pedestrian or vehicle crossed the intersection, a fact that Karen was not oblivious of. The rest of the ten-minute drive home was not as bad. March came in like a lion and was leaving like a lamb. The snow, which once was deep, was melting in the ditches. The ground was a mix of dead grass with little mini icebergs of snow that seemed to shrink by the day. Spring was so close it was almost touchable.

Karen pulled off the dirt back road and into her long driveway. It felt good to be home at last. She went in the front door and must have slammed it harder than usual because it instantly peaked the attention of Chase.

"What's up?" Chase asked with concern from his office upstairs. Karen heard him already getting up and coming to meet her. The squeaky computer chair gave him away. Karen sighed and threw her purse down on the table by the door and shook her boots off of her feet, not caring where they landed. Chase watched her from where he was standing at the last step from the bottom of the stairs. He looked deliberating whether or not it was going to be safe for him to approach.

"I've just had a day from hell. First one of my students sprained her ankle during recess on my supervision duty and when I took her to the principal's office Mrs. Elsing wasn't even there. I ended up having to deal with the student's mother who just about tore my head off even though I personally had no control of the fact that her daughter is clumsy. Then when I finally got back for my class I find that my students are testing me! Only one of them bothered to do their homework. I had my lesson planned on that worksheet and I put extra care to make sure it was a fun activity but I'm never going to get a chance to use it now. I even got a red light at the single stop light in town. How does that even happen?" said Karen. During her rant, Chase moved from his post on the stairs and helped Karen out of her winter coat and put it away.

"Well first the light was green and then yellow and then it turns red, I don't think it's that complicated," said Chase, attempting to be funny. Karen slapped him playfully and gave him a reproving look. "It does sound like you had a hard day and if it makes you feel better I'm sure tomorrow will be better. It can't get much worse can it?" He asked, he was leading her towards the living room couch and she allowed herself to be led and took her usual seat.

"I guess it can't." Karen muttered, starting to feel better after venting out her problems. She was home and it was over and that's all that mattered. Chase started massaging her shoulders and some more of her tension was letting go.

"I bet that you taught those kids a lesson today and they won't 'forget' to do their homework again." Chase laughed and she remembered what she had told the kids, she may have lost it a little bit. Karen joined in on the laughter.

"I did really lay into them," said Karen. Chase never failed to make her feel better. She was about to ask him how his day had gone but Chase began kissing her neck which effectively erased her train of thought. She turned herself around enough to kiss him and he pulled her closer holding her tight.

8

Something had changed in her world. She didn't know what it was and began to fear it at first, but the fear eventually gave way to indifference. She was only slightly aware she was becoming stronger. An awareness that only surfaced at all at the realization her world, which had once been small and dark, had expanded. Her thoughts were forming in more detail and she found she was almost able to regain some control. She had no idea the cause to this change in events but she adapted. It seemed she would always be adapting. Nothing ever really stayed the same for too long and if she learned nothing else in life was that nothing could be trusted. Even the most solid, stable people could fail—could betray. Places that once were places of great comfort could be made to be places of great pain. Tortured memories still lingered everywhere and she clung to them with everything she was.

She could not bring herself to let go. If she did something terrible would happen, she just knew it, and she felt it. She carried these memories as proudly as battle scars. The only thing that connected her with her past, a tangible thing that allowed her to see her past did exist and was not just a dream. If she gave up that, a whole part of her would just be gone, where everyone else had forgotten she wouldn't. Hope must not be lost; and it wouldn't be as long as one person remembered. Her life was worth something as long as one person knew.

9

"Maybe we shouldn't do this anymore." Maggie was saying to Mathew. "People are going to find out."

"What makes you think so?" said Mathew, a little hurt and taken by surprise.

"Karen was in my office yesterday when I got back. She was waiting for me and I could swear she knew something. She gave me a dirty look and it felt as if she could see right through me. My husband can't find out and the other teachers can't find out. I may lose my job over this. This is serious." Maggie was worried and anxious since her run in with Karen. She knew she shouldn't have left her office during school hours. This affair was affecting her job. Maggie and Mathew were together in a booth of a restaurant in the bigger city. It was Sunday afternoon and they were far enough from home that they were safe from being spotted. Maggie kept moving anxiously in her seat, she was paranoid she would be discovered.

"Karen knows nothing. I talked to her yesterday in the staffroom before school started and she didn't mention anything. All she wanted to know was what the plans were for the spring school trip. Where it was going to be and who was planning it." Mathew had always been overly confident everything would turn out fine. This was great at first but now she was beginning to see that maybe things hadn't been such a good idea. After all Mathew had nothing to lose if this ever got out. He was young with no other woman in his life and really just starting his career. Maggie on the other hand would never be able to get a reputable job again and she would have to move. It would be a shameful disgrace on the town and to her family. Her marriage, which was already crumbling would be ruined. A divorce would be imminent and she really did love her husband. Maggie would lose her whole life.

"Can I take your order please?" The waitress came back to their table a second time.

"I'll have a beer and an order of chicken wings," said Mathew as he smiled at her charmingly.

"Nothing for me." Maggie replied. "I was just leaving." Maggie got up, grabbed her purse and left the restaurant feeling slightly better about her future. She heard Mathew calling after her but she didn't look back. Maybe it was about time she called her husband. As Maggie pulled out of the parking lot she caught a glimpse of Mathew's face. It was one of pure hate. She wouldn't think about it as she drove down the road that would bring her back to town. She would deal with Mathew later.

10

"I'm proud of you," said Karen as they sat down to dinner. Chase was telling her he finished the chapters that had to be rewritten. She read them for herself before dinner and was impressed. Karen was worried Chase was struggling and she knew he doubted his work for once in his life. Doubting yourself was a dangerous thing.

"I used your advice." He was saying as he was putting food on the table. It caught her attention.

"What advice?" She question, since when had she given Chase any good advice recently?

"You told me that I should see where the other story went. So I tried to write a little more and I have to admit it was a little weird." He stopped what he was doing and looked at her seriously.

"Weird how?"

"First it didn't sound like anything I had written before; it was as if it wasn't even my words. If I saw it written anywhere else other than on my computer I would never have guessed it came from me. It wasn't even the same genre, I was writing about someone who feared death was imminent."

"It had to have come from somewhere, maybe in a dream." *That must be it,* Chase thought, but he hadn't had a dream he remembered in a while but maybe it was something in his subconscious.

Gossip

1

"Something is going on," said Catherine suspiciously, her eyes fixed on the empty doorway as if expecting someone to walk by at any minute. Catherine was the second grade teacher and the same age as Karen. The two women got along almost instantly after she started her job.

"I don't see it," said Karen. They were talking about Mrs. Elsing. It was brought to her attention Catherine suspected the principal of having an affair with Mathew the fourth grade teacher. Karen did not have a problem with Mathew before, and she found him quite friendly. It was Mrs. Elsing who was often missing when she should have been working and that did look a little suspicious. Most of the other teachers had grown leery, Mrs. Elsing and Mathew were staying alone together long after the others left and sometimes both went missing at the same time. Was this a coincidence?

"Didn't you say Mrs. Elsing was gone when you needed her that one recess?" Catherine said with a bitter undertone to her voice.

"Yes, but that doesn't mean anything." Karen liked to see the best in people.

"Just watch," said Catherine and the bell ringing effectively ended their conversation. Karen couldn't help but notice she seemed more than a little bitter. Why did it really matter if Mrs. Elsing was having an affair or not, it didn't affect her and wasn't really any of her business. None of the small town citizens seemed to agree with her. It seemed everyone made it a full time job to know the business and personal situations of every member of the town. Still Karen wondered if Catherine and Mathew had at one point been an item. She did notice a hint of jealousy in her actions and maybe the bitterness was justified.

Chase was right when he predicted Karen's class would not try to skip out on homework a second time in a row. She was grateful for the fact and her good spirits were renewed. Today was going much better than Friday. Her class worked diligently on textbook work in pairs. They were remarkably silent to the point where Karen wondered if maybe she had been too successful into scaring her class into respect. She felt a little guilty at losing some of her patience with them but it had to be done. Karen was no longer getting walked over by her students and they still liked her despite the extra workload.

With time on her hands, Karen sat at her desk at the back of the classroom. She was planning on using this time to grade some papers but her mind began to wander as she worked. She found herself thinking about the house and plans for a garden now that she had gotten her first real paycheck in a while. She wanted to plant some fruits and vegetables in the backyard and maybe some sunflowers. Soon she began thinking about town life in general and her neighbors, some of them seemed to act oddly distant when they talked to her and she wasn't sure if she was liked or just tolerated. She did have some new friends; Shannon and Catherine were the main ones and they even invited her out on a girl's night. The two of them and a few other girls from town went to the bar on Friday nights. Karen promised she would attend on the coming Friday to see what it was all about. She felt honored to be inducted into their close nit group when she still felt like such an outsider in a new world.

"Mrs. Williams?" A small voice asked from her desk and Karen realized she was completely zoned out. Zachery stood in front of her and was holding up his half-finished worksheet.

"What do you need help with?" She asked pleasantly. The boy looked confused and she noticed his partner Tyler kept glancing back at them. She knew they both needed the answer, whatever it happened to be.

"We can't find the definition of the word amphibian anywhere? Its not in the section you told us to read." Karen looked through her own textbook and realized the mistake.

"Try the glossary at the back of the book. That will give you a definition."

"Thanks." He said and walked quickly back to his desk. Karen decided she better announced to the whole class, who likely hadn't spotted the problem yet or had and didn't want to ask.

"Zachery brought up a good point. You may have noticed the word amphibian is not in the pages I asked you to read. You will have to go to the glossary to find the definition." Zachery looked proud of himself for the recognition and some of the confused faces seemed to change to understanding. Karen let the students continue and went back to her marking and pondering if she was ever going to fit into this tiny town.

2

The date was April 3, 1998. It was the first day Jennifer St. Claire failed to show up for work at the music store downtown. She was the piano teacher and when she was not giving lessons she could always be found behind the counter. She knew everything about any given instrument and was always helpful and friendly. It was an odd sight seeing her missing from behind her usual post and even more unusual that she failed to call in sick. Tom Bantting, the storeowner was shocked at her absence and immediately phoned her home to make sure everything was all right. After ten rings the phone picked up.

"Hello?" said a drunken voice on the other end, which Mr. Bantting decided must be Jennifer's husband.

"Is Mrs. St. Clair there?" He asked and there was a long pause.

"No, she's gone," was the only reply and the phone slammed down on the receiver before the line went dead. Mr. Bantting called back again every hour that day but there was never any answer at the St. Claire house. The weekend passed and neither one of the St. Claire's were spotted in town or heard from. Monday came around and Jennifer still hadn't called or come into work, and when there was yet no answer on the telephone Tom Bantting closed down his shop and drove the ten-minute drive to 312 Bentwood Road. He immediately saw Jennifer's beat up Camry was missing from the long driveway. Only Richard's Pickup truck was parked in its spot, for some reason this terrified Tom. He was secretly hoping to catch Richard out of the house. The man always sparked fear in him for no real reason. Facing his fear, Tom walked up to the door and rang the doorbell. He waited but there was only silence on the other end. He was slightly relived he didn't have to face Richard in person. Clearly Jennifer was out, maybe she had gone to work after all and he had simply missed her on his way. After a couple minutes Tom was backing down the front porch steps when the door slammed open, causing him to turn around in surprise.

Richard was stood in the doorway in a defeated stance. He looked worse than he had ever been and was clearly hung over badly. The bags under his eyes and looked like he had not slept in days and hadn't changed his clothes for just as long.

"What do you want?" Richard stammered grumpily. He seemed distant and less threatening than he usually came off. Tom took a couple wary steps closer.

"I was looking for Jennifer. She didn't come in to work again today. Do you know where she is?" There was no reaction from Richard; he just stood there looking pitiful.

"I told you yesterday she was gone. I don't know where she is. If you see her by any chance let me know but my advice for you is to start looking for someone to replace her. I doubt she intends to return any time soon." Richard started to close the door.

"Mr. St. Claire?"

"One more thing, don't bother coming back and bothering me again. Good bye!" Richard closed the door and Tom heard the deadbolt. The thought of Jennifer leaving in the middle of the night was unheard of. She loved her daughter and the town. She definitely would not have left without first telling her boss to hire someone else. This was so unlike her but it wouldn't be the first time people stumped him. They always seem like one thing when they really are another. Richard was never the perfect husband and Tom became aware he might even have been abusive in the past. Perhaps Jennifer was forced to take dramatic measures. If that had been the case he would forgive her.

<h1 style="text-align:center">3</h1>

Chase woke up to an empty bed on Monday morning. Karen must have slipped quietly out of bed to let him sleep in. He was so tired he never even heard the alarm. When he checked the time it was already nearly eleven and Karen would have been long gone. He was alone in the big house once again. He reluctantly scrambled out of bed and into the shower and then finally made it down to the kitchen to look for something to eat for lunch. Chase's stomach was growling in protest to his missed breakfast. It wasn't often that he let himself sleep in this late. He opened the fridge to scavenge for the supplies to make something but found it to be empty. He was disappointed with the results and when the cupboards turned out to be equally as empty he decided a trip to the grocery store was warranted.

The decision to purchase an old pickup truck came the month before, after Karen started work. They now had excess money and without the benefit of public transit a second vehicle was desperately needed. Chase was glad he had a truck of his own but was still getting used to the standard transition. He back out of the driveway awkwardly changing gears and the car lurched forward unnervingly as he put it back in drive. He was sure he was burning out the clutch but he had to admit he was improving. The parking lot at the grocery store was filled with cars. He knew most of them were only parking there while they were working in other buildings. The grocery store itself was mostly vacant besides the employees and the odd retiree that were there mainly for entertainment and social interaction.

Chase took one of the shopping carts and started loading it with supplies mindlessly. At first he wasn't aware of the two ladies chatting rather loudly on the other side of the aisle. That was until he clued in on Karen's name. Chase stopped where he was and listened silently hidden by the rows of canned goods.

"Did you hear Karen is teaching at the elementary school now? My granddaughter Melinda teaches there. She says that she is strict but she's really nice and all the students like her." The first lady was saying, she had a high-pitched nasally voice and was speaking louder than necessary.

"It's nice to see the new people getting involved. For big city folk they certainly are nice. I hear they are from New York City. It's a shame that out of all the houses in the neighborhood they had to purchase the St. Claire place. It looks nicer than it has in years, possibly better than it's ever looked but I still believe it should have been torn down years ago. That place has been nothing but bad news for the whole town."

"I agree with you completely. I would hate to see a repeat of what happened there before. Something about that house is just plain bad news. I don't like it one bit. I'm just glad there are no children living there." The loud high-pitched voice was saying.

"Amen to that, history won't be repeating itself for a while at least. The Williams seem to be good people though."

"People thought the St. Claire's were nice people." After that there was no words exchanged between the women for a few minutes and Chase stopped listening. He wasn't sure how to react to what he heard. It did manage to explain a few things. Chase went on with finding his shopping list and caught a glimpse of the gossipers when he reached the checkout line. The two of them were older women, probably in their early eighties. They were on to a new topic and Chase's presence didn't faze them. They either long forgot their previous conversation or didn't recognize him. Either way Chase was glad to be back in his beat up pickup truck. For the first time he was questioning the purchase of his new home. Was it possible the two women had a point?

4

"You would never guess what I overheard today!" Chase was saying over dinner. Karen was sat in her usual spot across the table and was enjoying some of Chase's homemade Chicken Noodle soup. "I was out getting groceries and people in the aisle over were talking about our house…and you." This caught Karen's attention.

"What about our house?" She questioned, eyeing Chase curiously.

"I couldn't see who was talking but they were saying that the St. Claire house was looking better than it ever did in years."

"Well that's good isn't it? What's wrong with that?"

"Hold on, they also said they didn't know why we chose to live here. There was more to the conversation but what I got from it, it sounds a lot like people were under the impression that the house should have been torn down. They don't seem to like us living here." Karen thought for a moment. The information didn't faze her as much as it should have.

"You don't seem surprised." Chase continued. He was still waiting for a reaction.

"It's just that I heard something like that before from one of my kids at school. They told me that his parents were scared of this house. It seems a little silly though."

"People do seem to act differently to us sometimes. Like how everyone seemed more than a little cautious to be inside our house and how they wanted to be shown around." Karen knew Chase well enough to see he was trying to over analyze the situation and put an imaginative, farfetched reason behind it. It was the curse of the writer.

"They just wanted a tour because the house was deserted and they were probably curious what was in it. It is an old house and it has a backstory."

"What if there is more to the story than we were told," said Chase and Karen didn't like what he implied.

5

Maggie sat alone at her desk. It was early and no one else was at school yet. The light in her office was the only one turned on in the entire building. She typed on her computer in an attempt to catch up on work. She'd gotten behind in the previous months. She felt free now that Mathew and her was no longer an item and she could give her husband the attention he needed. She was relieved she got out before anything bad could come from her mistake. Her job required a certain amount of respect and an affair would have ruined her. She was happy and saw her old dreary life in a new way. She just needed to get it out of her system and had in a big way. Other people in her position hadn't always been so lucky.

The footsteps startled her because it was still quite early for anyone to be at work. She ignored it and passed them off as some teacher getting a head start on the day and forgot about it. The copier machine began running and Maggie settled back into her work. She started humming a song in her elated mood as she was looking over her paper work. The school was getting good marks and the district was pleased. They were getting more results out of their students than any of the bigger surrounding schools in the area. She didn't notice that the copier machine stopped running but she was beginning to be aware of a presence in her office. Someone opened the door and was standing watching her. Maggie knew before she looked up that it was Mathew. He was seething and fidgeting; making it obvious he was uncomfortable. Maggie didn't speak and waited for Mathew to make his point. She didn't like this.

"I didn't like how you left me at the restaurant. Don't you think you could have maybe accomplished your goal with slightly less humiliation on my part?" He paused, but Maggie didn't answer. She wanted him to talk himself out. If she spoke an open argument was certain. At least now she had a slight chance to restore her peaceful morning. Hopefully none of the other teachers chose to come in at that moment. "Don't you think it was harsh? You were the one to seduce me in the first place!"

"I did no such thing." Maggie yelled suddenly. It came off louder than she intended. She then went on more quietly. "This started when *you* came on to *me*. I shouldn't have fallen into your boyish charms. It was a mistake."

"No, no. If you were dumb enough to perceive my friendliness as coming on to you, you would be mistaken. It was clear you wanted me and I would have been a fool to ignore that."

"Does any of it really matter anymore? It's over, why don't you just leave." Maggie said. It was clear there wouldn't be an easy end to this.

"I don't want to. I want you." She watched, as a sly smile spread across his face, his eyes were hard.

"I'm not going to take you back. I love my husband."

"I was afraid you might say that." He looked down at the papers in his hand. That's when Maggie began to get nervous. They both heard footsteps echoing down the halls. It sounded like whoever it was were wearing heels. On cue Mathew leaned over and closed the door. Maggie felt trapped in her own office and was beginning to feel claustrophobic. Mathew took one of the papers and placed it in front of Maggie on her desk. She looked at it quickly and looked away in disgust.

"Why?" She asked. She was terrified.

"If you don't take me back these might just find their way onto some teachers inboxes. I'm sure they will find it very interesting." Mathew left her office then and took the rest of his copies with him leaving her to stare at the remaining one. *Oh, what did I do to deserve this?*

Maggie answered the question for herself.

6

Derrick Munroe often frequented the music store. He wasn't a true music fan but he was a fan of Jennifer St. Claire. He came in everyday to say hello to Jennifer under the pretense of looking for new sheet music that arrived. Every Tuesday morning he would have a piano lesson and Jennifer was a good teacher, he found himself actually learning something. In 1998 they were the same age of forty-one. Jennifer looked young for her age and had a bubbly personality that never failed to pick him up when he was in a bad mood. There was never anything between them and there never would. Jennifer was married and had a teenage daughter. Derrick never made a move to woe her, but felt no harm in coming to see her every week. It was the first Tuesday of April when Derrick went to the music store for his weekly piano lesson. He was shocked to see Mr. Bantting behind the counter; he seemed to be in a foul mood.

"Where's Jennifer?" Derrick asked but he assumed she was in the back room with the piano already. Tom looked up at him, finally acknowledging his presence.

"She's not here. She's not coming back either." This comment startled Derrick; it was the most shocking thing he could have heard. "I tried to call you but you weren't home, but I'll have to postpone your lessons until I find a replacement. It could be a while."

"Did she quit?" Derrick thought it would have come up in conversation if she decided to leave. She never once let on of her intentions. A pained look came over Tom. He clearly wanted Derrick to go away and didn't want to be talking about Jennifer. It made Derrick even more concerned.

"No, she didn't quit. She just stopped coming to work. I talked to her husband and he doesn't think she'll be back. Said she left him and her daughter." Tom looked back down at his desk; Derrick could see he was working on a crossword puzzle.

"That can't be right?" Derrick mumbled and when he saw that Tom wasn't going to respond he slipped out of the store. Confused and unprepared for the events of the day he sat in his truck, mind whirling. Later that night at Morgan's, Derrick told a few of his buddies what had gone on. By the end of the night everyone who had been at the bar knew that Jennifer St. Claire the pianist left her husband and daughter and fled town. Neither one of them thought it was odd a motherly woman who loved her daughter would just disappear. She soon became nothing more than a name and an interesting piece of gossip that took the town by storm. Over the following week a steady stream of homemade lasagna and potato salad ended up on Richard St. Claire's door. The town went into over drive to comfort the newly single man and his daughter.

7

Everything was dark as night; she was in a world where the line between night and day ceased to exist. Memories of the way thing used to be filled her head and she spent most of her time working out what she could of the past. She put together the puzzle pieces and found that once she did, still nothing made sense. Something big had to be missing. Something big, but she didn't know what. She was confused the first time she heard the voices. They came and went and were not familiar to her at all. The voices did not yet have faces but she realized for the first time in years she was not alone. Whether the voices were friend or foe did not matter. They just complicated matters, but it did comfort her to know somewhere out there, others existed. She lived in an alternate reality, but as the nights marched on the boundaries were growing thin.

She knew she was dead. She had to be, as it was the only thing that made sense. Time had passed and lots of it since she died but it felt like only seconds. Wasn't death supposed to be the end? She was supposed to be at peace and enjoying another world where problems didn't exist. Somehow she did not reach her end, she still had something to accomplish. Instead of her world of bliss, she was in a world of darkness and only a vague sense of reality and time passing. How was this even possible? She had no body to confine her, only her energy still existed and it was a weird, lighter than air feeling. Was she a ghost, she wasn't sure but she didn't like it.

Her days had not always been like this after her death. Something has woken her from her slumber. She was feeding off the energy of something and it made her stronger. Things in the real world had begun changing. Now was going to be her chance to save herself and her memory. Whatever unfinished business she had now had a chance to be fixed. Maybe then the earth's hold might release her spirit to whatever happened next. She was hopeful as she waited out her turn.

8

I can't do this? Maggie thought as she paced back and forth in her office. The picture of her kissing Mathew still sat on her desk. She didn't want to touch it. It could have been worse but in a small town it was just as bad as porn. She was married! How could she have done this to her husband and to herself? Maybe she deserved what was sure to come to her. As Maggie saw it she had two options. Option one was to return to Mathew and continue on as she was. Option two would be to plead guilty and go public with their affair before Mathew released the pictures. If she took Mathew back now she would be miserable and she would probably just be caught later. It would delay her downfall but it would come and she would never be happy again. If she went public with the affair she would be forced to resign and possibly a divorce would follow. There was no good outcome to this.

There was a knock on her office door and Maggie became aware that during her mental turmoil the school became swarmed with children. So much for her productive morning, Mathew ruined it and he might ruin her. The warning bell rang, signaling the school day was starting. Maggie quickly swept the incriminating picture into her top right desk drawer and let in two of the students to do the announcements. The day had to go on as if nothing happened at all but she was no longer certain if it would end that way. By the end of the day a big change would be made. She was sure the next twenty-four hours would drastically change her future. The question was for better or for worse. It certainly wasn't looking great for her.

9

Karen was early to work which was typical of her. She witnessed Mathew leaving the principal's office with a stack of photocopies. Something about his demeanor tipped her off and set her women's intuition running wild. Mathew was anxious, nervous and walking faster than usual down the hallway in the direction of his classroom. Luckily for her, the fourth grade teacher's classroom was directly across from her own. She was able to follow him without drawing attention to herself. Mathew turned sharply and entered his classroom and the door slammed shut behind him. If Karen had been able to ignore his obvious tension before, the door was a sure sign something wasn't right. Her attention was drawn to something on the floor; it was one of the papers Mathew was so carelessly carrying in his flight. Curiosity got the better of her and she picked it up gingerly. Karen didn't know why she felt so guilty, like she was prying into something she shouldn't. It was probably just a worksheet for his class he was photocopying. There was nothing outright weird about the paper.

That was what Karen originally thought, but her intuitions were spot on. It was clear this was no worksheet. *Oh shit!* Karen thought, and immediately she wished she hadn't bothered to look. It turned out Catherine was correct in her suspicions after all. Karen was torn between what her next course of action should be. She could not forget what she saw or take back what she now found. She couldn't unlearn information. Karen wanted to put the photo where she found it and walk away and let someone else, anyone else, find it. That was the whole problem; if she did put it back someone else would find it. Karen decided she couldn't do that, it was morally wrong. She had to decide to hide the evidence or tell Mathew what she found and give it back to him. She had inadvertently involved herself in something completely unnecessary and wrong. Why did she feel the need to cover up an affair between her married new boss and a young teacher?

Karen tucked the photocopy under her arm and hid it as she walked into her classroom. She buried it immediately at the bottom of a stack of test sheets she had to mark which hid it from view. Then Karen started attendance as if nothing happened. It seemed all of her students were present. Today was already turning out to be quite the eventful one. If only she could have stayed out of other people's business. Maybe she was already becoming a part of the gossipy small town. But she was sure curiosity was just a part of human nature that would never be repressed.

After the attendance, the daily announcements and the national anthem had been completed, Karen through herself directly into a lesson about algebra. She was explaining how to balance the equations to solve for X. Meanwhile Karen was thinking about life and if she could just solve for X and have the answer to her dilemma. She was a variable in the equation and she could be anything. The equation wasn't solved yet and it was far from being simple. Later she gave her class some textbook work to practice on and let them work silently in groups. Soon, as always with fifth grade students, working silently gave way to mindless chatter that tested the volume of their 'indoor voices'. Karen spent the period answering questions and helping a few students that were falling behind. It seemed nearly everyone needed extra help in math except for Jessica, the class genius. That didn't stop her from attempting to gain Karen's attention every few minutes.

By lunch break Karen was mentally drained and could not wait for the bell to ring. Once it did and the students fled out of the classroom to grab their lunches, Karen sat down and rested her head in her hands. She had a killer of a headache and was very thankful that she had neither lunch or recess supervision that day. As the students started returning from their lockers Karen grabbed her keys and headed out. She nodded to Catherine as they passed in the hall;

she was the lucky one with lunch supervision. Karen attempted a half smile that made it obvious the stress she was under. Catherine gave her an understanding look in return and entered the war zone of her classroom. She bypassed the staffroom, wanting anything to avoid Mathew and Mrs. Elsing that day and headed to the parking lot. She unlocked the small car and sat in the driver's seat; glad she had made it out without running into anyone she was avoiding.

She was ruffling through her purse on a search for some Advil when someone began tapping on the driver's side window. Karen looked up and her heart dropped to her stomach as she saw Mathew staring in at her with a blank expression on his face. Karen couldn't read him but he didn't look angry, just amused.

"Are you going to roll down your window or just stare at me?" Mathew said, but it was muffled through the glass. Karen pushed the window button and it didn't do anything. In her nervousness she forgot the engine wasn't on. She gave up and opened the car door reluctantly, mildly embarrassed at herself.

"Sorry about that. I wasn't expecting anyone." Karen stammered in her awkwardness. "What did you want?"

"I was looking everywhere for you. Don't you usually eat in the staffroom?" said Mathew. Karen still wasn't sure if Mathew suspected that she knew anything or not. She got the feeling he was feeling her out and she wasn't going to cave in just yet. She was nervous, and she had a tendency to talk too much when she was nervous. A bad thing when you wanted to be sure you didn't say the wrong thing.

"Yes, no, not all the time. I was headed out to the coffee shop down the street. I didn't bring a lunch today." Karen looked around to make sure her bagged lunch wasn't in the car to give her away.

"Okay," said Mathew slowly, he looked as if he didn't quite believe her but didn't care. It was possible she was just overanalyzing every minute detail. He probably was talking normally.

"So? Why did you want me again?" Karen asked, hoping to be rid of the terrible awkwardness.

"I was looking for you because I knew you were inquiring about the spring school trip and I just found out what it is this year." Karen was relieved; clearly Mathew had a legitimate purpose for looking for her. It was a little weird that he would come all the way to the parking lot just to let her know about the spring trip but she ignored it for now.

"Where are you going?"

"It's actually where WE are going. It was agreed upon that you should come chaperone if you were willing since the trip is to New York City, Manhattan specifically. We would love for you to have a say in the trip since you did live there. What do you say?" Karen couldn't believe what she was hearing. She never dreamed she would be asked to partake in the school trip since she was so new of a teacher.

"Of course I would love to," she said with real excitement.

"Great, I will let the others know," said Mathew happily. The others must have really wanted her to join, and Mathew did seem pleased.

"Who else is coming?"

"It will be Melinda, you, myself and a few parent volunteers. Not many of the details are set in stone. There will be a meeting right after school regarding busing, and permission forms and such. I will expect you to be there."

"I will be," said Karen, just then the bell rang for lunch break to be over and recess to start.

"It seems I'm keeping you from lunch. I hope you don't have recess supervision duty," said Mathew and he started to back away.

"I don't but I better go now." Karen slammed her door closed and backed out of the parking lot. Her mind was still reeling from mixed emotions of the conversation. She went from nervous to excited, in a blink of an eye. Now more than ever she wished she hadn't picked up that damn paper. The coffee shop was busy and it took the whole recess break to get back to the school. She made it in the door as the bell was ringing for the students to line up and come back inside. The weather was getting nicer and the students were probably going to take their time. A door opened and Mrs. Elsing came out of her office carrying a box filled with new textbooks. Karen kept her eyes on the floor to discourage conversation and watched as Mrs. Elsing ducked into Kevin Hull's classroom near the end of the hall. He was the seventh grade teacher and Karen hadn't talked to him much as he kept to himself. She was saved from her awkward situation and hurried into her classroom before she was late. She just sat back down at her desk when she heard the flood of students come running down the hall and the shouts of children having fun.

10

"Hello?" Chase finally answered the phone just as she was about to hang up. That meant he was probably getting somewhere in his writing. She felt bad for having to disturb him at work. Karen was on her cell, it was three-forty pm and all of her fifteen students had left the building. She was alone in her empty classroom and her voice was causing an echo.

"Hi honey! I just wanted to let you know I'm going to be late today. I got invited to be a part of the teachers involved in the junior school trip. They are going to Manhattan for the day. There's a meeting I have to attend and I don't know when it will let out."

"That's awesome news Karen! I'm happy for you." Chase responded. Karen saw Mathew poke his head in the classroom quickly and motioned for her to hurry up.

"Listen, I have to go. You can get back to your writing."

"Okay, see you when you get home."

"Love you."

"I love you too," said Chase and then disconnected the phone. Karen pressed the end button on her cell and headed down the hallway toward the staff room. When she walked in the door she could see Mrs. Elsing, Mathew and Melinda and Mrs. Lanley already there. She did notice that Mrs. Elsing and Mathew were sitting on opposite ends of the table and they seemed to be avoiding eye contact. There was obvious tension in the room between them but Melinda seemed to be unaware of it. She was sitting between them and watched as Karen took the seat on the opposite side of the table. Karen felt all eyes on her and she wasn't sure what to do, she felt like the odd one out because she was the newcomer. With both Mrs. Elsing and Mathew sitting around her it just made everything more awkward as she remembered the picture she found and was currently hiding. She managed forget for most the afternoon but now she was confronted with it again.

"Okay, this is the second meeting regarding the Junior Spring trip to Manhattan. It was agreed upon last meeting that the trip should take place in early May 2012. We haven't actually got it down to any specific dates. Now that Karen has joined us and she got the experience of living there maybe we can all agree upon the best tourist attractions." Melinda looked over at her and smiled kindly, then glanced over at Mrs. Elsing to speak. Karen was beginning to wonder how much of a say she was going to have on the trip. It seems like they wanted her to make decisions. That was something she never really counted on and she grew a little nervous at the new expectations.

"That is correct Melinda, and I propose the trip be on a Friday. What day would that be?" Mrs. Elsing said looking around the room. Karen noticed how the principal's eyes seem to skip over Mathew. She wondered if Melinda noticed anything, but if she did she wasn't letting on.

"The first Friday of May is the fourth, and if that doesn't work the second one is the eleventh," said Mrs. Lanley after flipping through her calendar.

"Is everyone okay to have the trip on the fourth of May?" said Mrs. Elsing. Karen thought through her schedule. She wasn't busy either of the potential days. As it turned out everyone agreed the trip would fall on Friday, May 4, 2012. The meeting continued and the focus was now on Mathew.

"I think we should avoid having both the Top of the Rock and the Empire State Building in the itinerary, they are sort of one in the same."

"I agree," said Karen her first words of the meeting. "If I had to choose between them I would say there is more to do at the Rockefeller."

"The Rockefeller it I," said Mrs. Elsing.

"I told you this would work better with Karen," said happily. The way Melinda looked at him, made Karen instantly aware that Mathew must have been the one to push for her to join them.

"We definitely need to go to Central Park," said Melinda excitedly.

"Most definitely." Karen concurred and the ball was rolling on making plans. They all seemed to agree with everything she said and valued her opinion. The excitement of the trip they were planning was getting to everyone, especially Melinda. Soon everything was planned, Mrs. Lanley was doing up permission forms and looking into a travel company to do the booking. Mrs. Elsing didn't seem too impressed but the group seemed to ignore her sour mood. Karen was the most in tune to it, but even she forgot about it as she walked to her car with Melinda. They were both talking excitedly about the trip but the conversation ended when Melinda reached her car.

11

"So, how was your meeting?" Chase greeted her at the door.

"It was great! I can't believe they asked me to go, they could have gotten anyone else," said Karen as she quickly took off her shoes and coat. The weather was warming up and pretty soon she wouldn't need it anymore. Everything was getting pretty exciting. April was coming along.

"You're such a good teacher they had to ask you," said Chase as he led Karen into the kitchen where he prepared dinner. He made chicken with mashed potatoes and gravy. Everything looked and smelt wonderful. Chase even added a centerpiece to the kitchen table. It was a shame they didn't have a dining room.

"What made you do this? It's perfect," said Karen happily. She was expecting to order in for the night since it was so late.

"When you called and said you were going to be late I decided to have dinner ready since I knew you wouldn't want to make it," said Chase sweetly.

"Well, thank you honey," said Karen and kissed him before sitting down in her usual spot. Karen watched as Chase took his seat across from her. "So what did you do today, besides this fabulous dinner you made?"

"I was doing some editing and a little writing. Work has slowed down a bit again. I'm just over half way done now, so it can't be too much longer." Chase sighed, clearly not believing his own words.

"That's good news at least. You were originally expecting to have this book written by June, I think you can do it."

"I'm not so sure about that but I'm not as far behind as I thought. If only I could get another big section out of the way but I keep finding distractions," said Chase in a serious tone.

"What sort of distractions." Karen watched as Chase rose from his chair solemnly and walked first away from her and then back towards her again. At first Karen was worried she said something wrong but then her eyes fell on the twitch of a smile in the corner of Chase's mouth just in time to be surprised by Chase swinging in on her and grabbing her from her seat.

"You silly, you distract me by being so darn pretty." He whispered in her ear. Karen was still shocked by the explosion of events and let Chase hold her in his arms for a moment.

"May I ask what brought this on?" said Karen looking over at her still yet untouched food. Her stomach rumbled signaling for Chase to clue in and let her go.

"Sorry," he said as she sat back down. "I'm just in a great mood today. I got lots of writing done before you called me and I think you may find the scene rather interesting." Karen smiled knowingly in Chase's direction before finally shoving a bite of chicken into her mouth. She wasn't aware how long it had been since she had eaten until that moment.   After dinner she would read his new chapter in which one of the character's had been inspired by herself, it would be interesting, Karen gave it that.

The Note

1

Jennifer St. Claire had many reasons for wanting to abandon her life. More reasons than anyone could have possibly known. There was also one great reason to stay. Molly, her daughter could not be left alone with how things were. The trouble started with Richard, everything always revolved around Richard. Her husband was a great loving man, but he was also self-centered and incredibly controlling. These attributes seemed to only get accentuated with age. Richard always had a temper and even when Jennifer met him at only nineteen, Richard had a minor drinking problem.

He and Jennifer met in their first year of community college. Jennifer was taking a music degree and art classes on the side, and Richard was completing a construction apprenticeship program. He wanted to start his own company someday. Jennifer wanted to teach piano or maybe painting or even photography. She was always into everything creative, no matter the discipline. The red flags were there with Richard from the beginning but Jennifer was young and too blinded by love to care. It was possible it wasn't love yet at that point but Jennifer would not have known the difference in her youth. Richard was lazy and unmotivated to complete even the easiest of assignments. He was a bad influence and wanted to cut classes more often than Jennifer could afford to. She had high grades and potential but found she was drawn to Richard's bold bad boy image. He was kind, as long as he got his way and could be extremely fun and easy to talk too.

When Richard and Jennifer were twenty-two they got engaged. They were together for three years and were still going strong. Jennifer found a job relatively quickly in the music store in town. She was working behind the counter selling musical instruments and supplies but she had the chance at eventually moving up and teaching lessons. Mr. Bantting liked her attitude and kind nature and she grew to enjoy the job. It wasn't as high paying as she had hoped and still was only part time at first but she was happy and liked her boss. Richard got a full time job in construction. He was happy but wanted to save enough money to start his own company so he could be his own boss. They didn't have much money but it was as good of start as any and she was engaged to the man of her dreams. They were living together in town in the apartment above the bar called 'Morgan's'. Richard befriended the owner Jeff Morgan and he offered them cheap rent. The only arguments Jennifer had with her fiancée were about late nights spent drinking, but Richard only got drunk on weekends and she was able to live with that. Later she would wish she hadn't.

When they were engaged for two years, now twenty-four, Jennifer finally became Mrs. Richard St. Claire. There was a small June wedding and only close family and friends attended. It took place outdoors in the park and the weather could not have been more perfect. Richard had personally been building them a house from scratch since they got engaged and after the honeymoon in the Bahamas' the couple moved into the small farmhouse on 312 Bentwood Road. Jennifer thought it was beautiful and homely and she could see the influence she had on the place. Everything she asked for of the house was present. The land they chose was beautiful and even had a pond out back. She'd always wanted a pond and some fish. The trees were mature and mostly Elm and Birch trees. The house was new and in its glory days there was a charm to it and was the talk of the very small town that was somehow even smaller back then.

When Jenifer was twenty-five, a year into marriage she became pregnant with her daughter, Molly. Richard was pleased to now have a child and had a new reason to work. His laziness and the drinking subsided temporarily and Richard broke off and finally started that construction company he was talking about all those years. Jennifer thought maybe now the money would come. Her first years of marriage were not as great as she built them up to be in her head. In 1982 her daughter was born. She took maternity leave from her job at the store to care for Molly and tend to the house. As much as

Jennifer loved her child, she hated to be cooped up in her home all day doing housework between the cries of the newborn baby. She found she suited being a mother and had a great maternal instinct she never knew existed before but lack of sleep and being stuck in the house made her frustrated and irritable. Richard on the other hand loved the situation and began referring to Jennifer as his little housewife. A term she wouldn't shake for nearly three years, despite Richard was well aware of her hatred of it. The knowledge of that just drew him to use the name more often.

In 1987, by the time Molly was five and Jennifer was thirty-one, things slowly started to fall apart. The money Richard promised of his company simply wasn't appearing. Even with Jennifer back at work in the music store and with her teaching lessons on the piano for extra cash the little family was hurting. Richard was losing money left and right and keeping the house was becoming a real concern. Somehow Jennifer knew from the start this would happen but was afraid to say 'I told you so.' The company came to an end the day Richard accepted a job in Mr. Peterman's hardware store. The two were close before and Mr. Peterman wanted to help out a friend in need. The end of the business devastated Richard and the minor drinking problem seemed to step up a notch. Instead of only frequenting the bars on the weekends, Richard would go for a beer after work and occasionally would come home drunk. The issue wasn't as bad as it would become but the problem was getting more and more pronounced. Richard walked around the house grumpy and lashing out at her occasionally with a sharp word or reprimand. At least Jennifer managed to shield her daughter from her father's bitterness.

By 1992 the man had lost all hope of making anything of himself, and he began to completely give up trying to succeed. He frequently skipped work as he did school and Jennifer suspected he went into Morgan's on such days. Once she confronted Jeff about it but he didn't say anything to her but gave her a shameful look and she knew she was right. She left in a hurry after that discussion and cried, her worst fears coming true. When before she was only belittled and yelled at now the drinking was getting even worse. Richard struck her a couple of times and it bruised her, once she got a black eye that she managed to hide behind dark sunglasses. She loved the man but it was making life hard and Jennifer feared for her daughter. Richard had not sunk so low as to ever be harsh to Molly but Jennifer feared it was coming. If a man could strike his wife, he was just as likely to strike his daughter.

By now, early 1998 Jennifer put up with years of mental, physical and occasionally sexual abuse from her husband Richard. The reasons for leaving outweighed the reasons for staying. They were on the brink of losing their home, Richard almost never worked and he certainly was never sober. Molly needed a more stable life and she should have never allowed it to go on this long. She filed for divorce and was going to leave with Molly in tow. She would wait until the school year was over and leave in the middle of the night. Jennifer stayed up late at night planning their freedom. Chaos ensued long enough, and everyday was a nightmare. Jennifer feared for her safety and sometimes her life. In the dark of the late March night in

1998 she lay awake beside the snoring Richard. She thought about happier times, the earlier years of their marriage and wondered how she ever overlooked the red flags that were there. She wanted to talk to her younger self and warn her of the dangers of the future. How different her life would have been.

Jennifer wanted nothing else but to be free, she had stopped being blinded by love years before and possibly crossed the line over to hate. *Yes,* she thought, *I hate you, Richard St. Claire and you will never treat your daughter like you treat me. Not over my dead body!* Jennifer rolled over in bed and went to sleep to another night of nightmares. It would be over soon.

2

"I promise it will be fun!" said Catherine to Karen as she popped into her classroom. The students were gone for the day and Karen was sorting papers on her desk quickly. Catherine came to make sure that the girl's night was still a go. They were going to Morgan's.

"I never disagreed with you," said Karen as she finished with the papers, they were math tests she planned to bring home to mark over the weekend. Karen picked her purse up from under her desk, slung it over her arm and fumbled with the math papers.

"I'm glad I'm only a second grade teacher," said Catherine, eyeing the stack of papers still left on the desk. "A lot less things to mark."

"Another thing I agree with you on," said Karen as she started toward the door. They walked in silence until Karen reached her car, which was closer than Catherine's in the parking lot.

"It starts at eight-thirty. You promise you'll be there?"

"I promise. Who else is going?"

"You, me, Shannon Ferrety, Tammy Elsing and Suzie Martin." Catherine ran off the list. Karen knew the first couple, but the other names were foreign and one in particular caught her attention right away.

"You said Tammy Elsing?" She questioned.

"Oh, yes it is Mrs. Elsing's daughter. She's a year younger than us but fun to hang out with. Don't worry, she doesn't get along with her mother and nothing will get back to her." Catherine said, "I think she works out of town actually, as a hair dresser in a beauty salon. We went to public school together, but she was a grade younger. I think you'll like her."

"Alright. Who's Suzie Martin? I've never met her either."

"She works in the music store down town where I get my supplies for my class. She is pretty fun but doesn't get out much since she has a three-year-old at home. He's the cutest little man. I'm actually his god mother," said Catherine proudly and smiled, it was clear Catherine loved kids, something that Karen and Catherine had in common. Lately Karen was thinking about starting a family more than she was caring to admit. Chase hadn't said anything about it and Karen wasn't sure how to bring up the topic. It would be better to wait until they were more settled and when Karen knew for sure if she had a full time teaching job or not.

"Okay, I'll see you at the bar at eight thirty on the dot," said Karen as she got in the car. It was a long time since she went out for a night and she was actually looking forward to it. Maybe she would meet some new girls that she could get along with and join a new circle of friends. Karen hadn't really had many, even when they lived in New York City. Karen had numerous acquaintances and a few colleagues she kept in contact with for business purposes but no real friends. Now she had a chance at a new life and a chance to join a real social circle and be a part of something.

3

"How was your day?" Chase said as she came home, he greeted her at the door like usual.

"Not over yet, the fun part is going to be later tonight!" said Karen excitedly. Chase smiled at her enthusiasm.

"That's right you have a thing tonight. A girl's night out?" Chase knew his wife was excited because she rarely ever got a night out. Sure, the two of them went out on a date night once every couple of weeks but Karen never went out with friends. They didn't even have any married friends to double date with. Karen couldn't seem to stand still and her hair was moving on her shoulders like fire dancing in the wind. Her hair suited her personality perfectly, especially today.

"Yeah, it's a girl's night out. Morgan's has lots of discounts on Friday nights and I think it's about time I had some fun outside of the house."

"What's wrong with being inside the house, it's perfectly safe in here." Chase laughed teasingly as Karen gave him a reproachful look and ran up the stairs taking them two at a time. No doubt she was looking for an outfit to wear. Chase wished that he could accompany Karen and get out of the house for a change as well but he was glad she was getting a night with other female company. It wasn't good to not have friends to talk to once in a while and he would make sure she had that. A few minutes later Karen came down the stairs holding up a little black dress she just found.

"That looks perfect!" said Chase and Karen looked pleased. "I bet it will look even better on you."

"It's too early to get ready just yet, let's make something for dinner and then I'll get dressed."

A few hours later after a dinner of spaghetti and meatballs both of them helped to prepare, Karen came down the stairs wearing her stunning little black dress. She curled her hair and had half of it tied down with a sparkly barrette at the back of her head. *She could have easily been a model,* Chase thought as he watched the twenty-six year old descend the stairs.

"Well you look stunning!" said Chase and kissed her at the bottom of the stairs. "I wish I was going."

"You can come next time. Maybe I'll meet someone we can double with," said Karen as she grabbed the keys to the car. Chase put out his hand and took the keys from her.

"Let me drive you. That way you won't have to worry about how you're going to get home if you drink too much."

"That's a great idea." She said and climbed into the passenger side of her car. Chase backed out of the long driveway and turned onto the dirt road.

"Do you remember Shakoes?" He asked. It was the bar where they first met.

"Yes, I do very well. That was the best college hangout. We had so much fun back then, didn't we?" Karen was reminiscing just as much as he was.

"Yup, we did. A little too much."

"Those days weren't that long ago really, it's only been a few years. We've come so far since then."

"Well back then I never thought I'd marry that pretty red haired girl in the bar." Chase smiled.

"I definitely never thought I'd marry the mysterious writer either."

"I'm glad we did, this is definitely where we are destined to be right now."

"I agree, and things turned out exactly the way they should."

"Do you regret moving here? It's a small town and I know you moved here because it was my dream?" Chase had actually been wondering this for a while. He worried that Karen wouldn't fit into the small town being the Manhattan girl that she was.

"It is very different but it's a good different. Sure I liked New York where everything was nearby and where you could order in any type of food you could possibly want but that's not life. We had few people we truly knew well and we didn't know our neighbors. People were outright rude sometimes and life was busy. Here it's a little bit slower. I have a full time job where I actually had it long enough to remember the names of my students and that wasn't easy to come by in New York. There's something about life here that draws you in and makes you want to stay." Chase was relieved. So Karen really did like small town life. He believed every word she said.

"I'm glad; I just love it here too. It's weird how you said that something seems to be drawing you in because I feel the exact same way."

4

Karen watched as Chase drove away in the direction of home. It was sweet of him to offer to drive because she would have been worried about getting home later. She suspected that the ladies she was meeting might actually be bigger partiers than she was used to. Morgan's was fairly crowded and it seemed like most of the twenty-something's in town were gathered at the bar. A classic rock band was playing something on a small stage in the corner. It was a song that Karen didn't recognize right away. All over people were starting to dance and a few were seated at tables along the far wall or on barstools trying to order in the crowd. It was still early in the night and people were awkward having not gotten into the booze yet.

"Over here!" Catherine yelled from one of the larger tables and waved at her. She was alone and Karen took up the seat directly across from her. "I'm so glad you came, and you're the first one here!"

"Yeah, Chase drove me."

"That's good, my husband would have never thought of that."

"Hi, Karen, Catherine!" A familiar voice yelled above the crowd. Karen knew only Shannon could be that loud. Shannon took the seat beside Catherine and dropped her small clutch on the table. She turned to Catherine.

"I see that you saved our usual table!"

"Actually I don't have to anymore. People seemed to have figured out that this one is ours the first Friday every month."

"Yay, we officially stole it from those uptight bitches who work in the city!" Shannon seemed in a really good mood even for her usual upbeat self.

"You've been drinking already haven't you?" Karen asked.

"Hell yeah! Who wouldn't when the prices are as high as they are?" They all agreed with that but Karen actually thought prices seemed better than they ever were in the Manhattan bars. Soon Tammy and Suzie came together and sat down. Karen was surprised when she recognized Suzie from the girl she was talking to in line while waiting for her coffee.

"Hey, I know you, Karen right?" said Suzie as if on cue.

"You know each other?" said Shannon, and everyone seemed a little confused.

"Kind of, we met once in line for coffee," said Karen.

"It was one long line." Suzie added in. "Seems like everyone in town meets there." They all laughed. The lines really were long.

"Karen, this is Tammy, our wonderful boss's daughter." Catherine introduced, a little heavy on the sarcasm.

"Karen, nice to meet you!" said Tammy and extended her hand for Karen to shake. Tammy looked like Mrs. Elsing but was about thirty years younger. Even in the short time that Karen knew Tammy it was clear that she was indeed nothing like her mother. She had a diamond nose stud and a tattoo that was barely visible on her right shoulder blade. Her long chocolate brown hair covered most of it. Karen suspected the shade was also her mother's natural colour.

"Now that everyone is here, let's order some Jell-O shooters!" Shannon yelled. Karen wondered what was in store for the rest of the night. Shannon wasn't even drunk yet and she was loud and the rest seemed like they could be hard-core partiers. Karen wasn't really comfortable being mixed in with people she hardly knew, but another part of her was willing to embrace it. Hell, tonight was going to be a girl's night and she was going to have fun! The Jell-O shooters came and they each downed theirs and headed towards the dance floor. More people flooded to the bar as the night went on and the music was getting into some heavier rock.

Karen was awkward and totally uncoordinated on the dance floor at first but she ordered herself a rum and coke and by the time it was gone as well as a tequila shot Catherine forced her to take, Karen loosened up. The music went on and they danced up a pretty good sweat and Karen was finding herself feeling completely comfortable and close with her friends. The drinks were going to her head and she wished she ate more that night instead of just spaghetti. Catherine and Shannon still seemed completely sober but Suzie was visibly intoxicated. She was dancing with a strange guy and he was buying her drinks. Tammy was keeping a close eye on Suzie but was a little tipsy herself. The two girls were obviously close friends.

"Are you having fun?" Shannon yelled above the steady beat of the music. A new band came on and there had been a brief pause in the dancing. The new band was playing some songs Karen or the others never heard before and weren't particularly great at it. No one really noticed or cared.

"Yes, this is awesome!" Karen yelled back.

"I'm glad you're having fun, you should come with us every month!" said Catherine happily. Her words were a little slurred and betrayed her.

"Why every month? I say we make these nights every Friday!" said Shannon and Karen got the feeling Shannon did frequent the bar more often.

"I'm afraid I wouldn't be able to handle that. There's a reason we don't go out as much as we used to," said Tammy and as if to make her point Tammy's foot got caught under her and she tripped.

Catherine reached out in an attempt to grab her but it wasn't needed because Tammy stabilized herself again. She surveyed the group as if daring anyone to laugh. No one did.

"I agree with Tammy. I just can't handle nights out as much as I used to be able to," said Catherine.

"You are only twenty-six! That's still young so you are forbidden from using that excuse for at least another nine years!"

"I agree, me without sleep is a nightmare. If zombies existed, I could easily be mistaken for one if I get anything less than seven hours. As a teacher I have to work on the weekends with marking and shit," said Karen.

"See, work is an excuse but still not a very good one!" said Shannon pouting.

"I can use that too!" Catherine complained. "I'm a teacher, same as Karen."

"You're a second grade teacher, how much marking can you possibly have?" Shannon asked.

"Touché, but you don't work at all. So there!" Tammy laughed and it was clear this conversation better end before any real arguments broke out amongst them. No one was giving in to the weekly girl's night idea except Shannon the childless, house maker. Karen and Catherine both had some work on weekends and valued sleep over loud music and binge drinking. Tammy was a lightweight herself and only came to hang out with Suzie, and Suzie was a young single mother of a three-year-old son and had no free time at all. Everyone had busy lives except for Shannon Ferrety.

"Looks like Suzie made a few new friends!" said Catherine as she watched the girl flirt with a few older men and coerce free drinks from them. She was completely smashed. Suzie would probably, need help walking out of the bar and someone to put her to bed and pay the babysitter.

"I better go stop her. She's only hurting herself," said Tammy and started towards the bar. Catherine grabbed her wrist and stopped her in her tracks.

"Oh Tammy, let her have fun. She doesn't get out much and it's not like she is going home with anyone. Stopping her now isn't going to make her any less drunk. Let the bartender decide to stop serving her." Tammy grumbled something that sounded like 'hmm alright.' But if she pukes I'm making *you* clean it!'

"I'm getting tired of dancing. I think I'm going to go order another drink and sit down for a while." Karen said, she was lathered in sweat and her perfectly tidy hair was coming undone. Some rebellious strands of hair were free from their hold and were hanging in Karen's face.

"I'm going to join you. I'm getting tired," said tammy and yawned as if to make her point.

"I'm not through with dancing just yet." Shannon pouted.

"Me neither," said Catherine and shook her shoulders in time to the music. They both stayed behind as Tammy accompanied Karen to the bar. After a few minutes they ordered another rum and coke for Karen and a Cosmopolitan for Tammy. The tables were full of people listening to the band playing. They found one occupied by a couple of underage teenagers that had to be no more than only eighteen or nineteen.

"Get lost! Bars are for grownups!" Tammy stammered at them angrily.

"We're both twenty-one." The brunet girl said calmly. The blonde one across from her looked nervous and Karen saw their weakness.

"I don't care if that is what your fake driver's license says. Beat it," said Karen, trying to mimic Tammy. It wasn't usually in her to confront anyone but she found she enjoyed it.

"Maybe we should leave." The blonde pleaded with her stubborn friend.

"Who said anything about leave, I just want the table. Go underage drink elsewhere." Tammy sold the deal and the two girls grabbed their purses and headed to the bar, probably to buy some more drinks. Karen took the blonde's place and Tammy sat down across from her.

"That was kind of fun," said Karen and giggled. Not being responsible was great for a change. Tammy laughed too and it wasn't long before they were in hysterics.

"It's great that you came with us tonight. We really can be a fun group of people," said Tammy and they both looked at Shannon and Catherine grinding with some of the younger guys. Everyone was laughing and having a good time. Suzie rejoined the main group but wasn't exactly, dancing, just kind of swaying out of time to the music.

"I can see that. I was a little worried about going to the bar with the daughter of Mrs. Elsing, the big bad principal!" said Karen.

"I'm not really on speaking terms with my mother." Tammy swiped a stray hair from her face. "Not really on any terms with my mother."

"Catherine said something along those lines. May I ask why?"

"Um, I guess. My Mother was never much of a mother figure to me. I was more of my Fathers daughter. The two of us just never really got along. It's conflicting personality, and that whole deal. She never did anything with me as a child, never respected me as a teen and now as an adult she disapproves of all of my life choices. I also hate how she treats my father, she ignores him and I've often wondered if she's even been faithful." Karen's face betrayed her. "What?" Tammy was immediately suspicious.

"I'm not sure you really want to know."

"You got all weird on me when I mentioned my Mother's fidelity. Do you know something you're not saying?" said Tammy and Karen looked deep into Tammy's expression. She seemed hopeful and not at all angry so Karen decided it was probably safe to go on.

"I have reason to believe that Mrs. Elsing has been cheating with a young teacher at the school named Mathew."

"A young teacher?"

"He's about thirty, maybe thirty-one." Karen answered quickly.

"How do you know? Do you know for sure? I've been looking for years to find proof that my Mother wasn't loyal." She was really hopeful now and Karen was glad she had this conversation. She needed to get what she knew off of her back.

"Not concrete evidence but a picture. It shows the two of them kissing really passionately in what looks like her office. Maybe there's another completely reasonable explanation but I sure can't think of one."

"Where is it and how did you find it?" Tammy was completely unleashed now. She was fidgeting in her chair with excitement and a little bit of renewed hostility directed towards Mrs. Elsing. Karen was completely lost at what she should do. The calm conversation had taken an unexpected turn. At least it wasn't fury directed at her but somehow Karen felt herself getting pulled deeper and deeper into the mess.

"I found it when Mathew was walking down the hall with some papers and he dropped one. I went to pick it up and meant to give it back to him but it was the picture and there was no way I wanted him to know I found it. I hid it right away under a pile of papers on my desk and then I did something else with it but I don't remember where it is."

"We have to find it. We need to show everybody!" Tammy was getting a little crazy. She jumped up in her excitement and then stood forgetting for a second why she did that.

"Tammy, sit back down and calm down. There's nothing we can do right now. You should think about the meaning of what you just said and the effects it will have on your Mother's career before you do anything rash."

"Can't you find it tonight?" Tammy yelled, this time it was directed at her.

"Tammy, there's no way anything is getting done tonight. If and when I find the picture I'll forward it to you but I don't want to have any part in this."

"Fine!" She said sharply, and then she burst out crying. Karen didn't know what to do. Catherine, Shannon and Suzie whose attention had already been caught from all of Tammy's yelling were hurrying over to see what was going on.

"WA-what di-did you say to her!" Suzie slurred, she looked as if she might throw a punch. Karen backed away as far as she could from the angry drunk girl.

"Yeah, what happened?" Catherine asked, looking confused. Tammy looked up at her friends and waved them off.

"Le-leave Karen, aa-lone. It wasn't her fault. I'm drunk." Tammy sobbed and put her head back down on the table. Shannon put a hand on her back. Suzie gave Karen a dirty look but backed away to a safe distance and was back to being her non-threatening self.

"What happened, Karen?" said Shannon. As Karen looked around she noticed that most people in the bar were staring at them.

"Don't tell them!" Tammy yelled, louder than she needed to. She had stopped crying and looked at Karen long enough for her to see all of her mascara was smudged down her cheeks in two waterfalls. Karen shrugged at Shannon, who understood. They were both surprised at Tammy's outburst. Karen looked at her barely touched rum and coke and took a large sip of it. She wanted to be out of this awkward situation. The whole bar was watching and it made her uncomfortable.

"I'm alright now. I just need some bread and water and to go to the bathroom to clean myself up." Tammy started to stand up but fell immediately back in her chair.

"Gravity bad." She said annoyed and then started to laugh at herself.

"Gravity bad." Catherine parroted and started laughing. People started looking away and Karen finished her drink and felt it go directly to her head. She was worried about when she would have to stand up herself.

"Let me help you," said Catherine and took Tammy's arm and wrapped it around her shoulder. Catherine was probably the soberest. Suzie looked embarrassed that she couldn't offer her help. She was standing while swaying side to side and was clearly most likely going to end up on the floor at some point.

"Thanks." Tammy said and Catherine and Tammy walked off toward the bathroom.

"Final call!" One of the bartenders yelled and people headed toward the bar. Karen hadn't realized that it was two-thirty in the morning.

"I better go outside and call my ride," said Karen and prepared herself to stand up.

"That's probably a good idea. I think we've all had enough fun for one night." Shannon for once sided with the rest of the group. Karen stood up slowly and felt the alcohol go to her head like she expected. She felt lighter and warm which was pleasant and comforting.

"Let's all go outside." Shannon said, acknowledging her two friends were lightweights and shouldn't be left alone. Karen didn't argue. All three of them made it through the hoard of people who were still on the dance floor. The band was wrapping up and now with the supply of drinks cut off, everyone would soon hit the streets. They made it to the door and past the bouncer who stood watching them. Karen leaned against the building and fumbled around in her purse for her cell phone, it took her a few minutes but she eventually found it.

"Give it to me," said Shannon firmly and extended her hand. "I'm not going to let you drunk call anyone. You'll probably dial a wrong number." Karen stuck her tongue out at Shannon childishly but relinquished the phone willingly.

"I-I wouldn't h-have," said Karen but she knew better. It was lucky Chase didn't let her drive herself. She wondered if there were any cabs in town, Karen had never seen one before.

"Hello Mr. Williams?" There was a pause and Karen listened in and out of the one-way conversation. "Yes, outside of Morgan's…your welcome…thanks for the offer but I'll be fine…See you then." Shannon snapped the phone closed and handed it back to Karen who then slipped it in her purse.

"Suzie, are you okay?" Shannon asked and Karen noticed Suzie was looking a little green.

"I'm fine; I'm just starting to feel a little sick." Suzie leaned against the wall beside Karen and held her stomach.

"Oh, please don't puke!" Karen said, thinking mostly about her cute dress.

"Don't worry; I don't think I am going to," said Suzie softly but Karen couldn't quite believe her. She inched away just as a safety precaution.

"You two are so lightweights. You really should get out more." Shannon laughed. She was clearly slightly drunk herself and was easily amused but she had also drunk the most and was still light on her feet. Karen knew she was drunk but didn't feel she was as bad a Shannon made her out to be. Suzie and Tammy on the other hand were completely and pathetically intoxicated. The night sure would be memorable, or for them very forgettable.

"There you guys are." Catherine greeted as her and Tammy came out of the bar. People were starting to leave in groups and the five of them had to move away from the door a little farther. Tammy looked in a daze and didn't say anything.

"How are we getting home?" said Suzie and Catherine was the only one of them that was still safe to drive. She only had a couple shots at the beginning of the night.

"I can drive some people depending on where you're going." Catherine offered.

"Tammy, do you want to crash at my place tonight?" Suzie asked. Tammy only nodded her head yes. She looked as if she was close to passing out. It was either that or she was still angry about what happened.

"I was planning on walking home but I really don't want to have to do that." Catherine understood.

"How about anyone else? Shannon how are you getting home, I'm not letting you drive."

"I'm perfectly fine to drive!" She insisted sharply, just further proving she wasn't.

"No you're not."

"She can come with me; Chase is picking me up any minute now and it's on the way," said Karen.

"That's perfect," said Catherine and hit the door unlock button on her keys. The lights on a nearby SUV lit up and the three of them walked toward it slowly. They said their good-byes and Karen waved as they drove off toward Suzie's apartment. Karen saw Chase coming up in their small car.

"I don't need a ride. I see my friend Cammie over there and I'm sure she'll give me one," said Shannon quietly to Karen.

"Okay, but promise me you won't drive." She mustered up the sternest look she could.

"I promise." She walked off just as Karen got in the passenger side and sort of fell into the seat.

"Opps," said Karen and fumbled around for the seatbelt.

"I see you had a good night," said Chase sounding amused.

"What do you mean?" Karen played dumb.

"Oh, nothing." Chase pulled away and Karen assumed it was toward home.

"You weren't sleeping when Shannon called, were you? I know it's late?" She felt bad having Chase have to pick her up.

"No, I was writing. Actually getting lot's done. So, are you going to tell me what happened tonight or not?" Chase laughed.

"What makes you think it's so interesting?"

"Maybe, because you're drunk?" said Chase.

"I'm fine!" Karen defended but she was aware that she was unable to remain still and was swaying a little. When she tried to focus on Chase she was aware that he had a separate outline. Her vision was blurred and doubled. It was almost as if this was a dream but she knew it was reality. She had been drunk enough before to know that it always was. Chase gave her a blank knowing stare, so she went on.

"It was fun, everyone was nice. I met my boss's daughter and she is nothing like Mrs. Elsing at all. She's actually a hair stylist in the city. Anyway we were talking and I may have made her cry." Chase opened his mouth as if to say something, but Karen went on talking fast. "It wasn't my fault but apparently she gets emotional when she is drunk. We were dancing and having fun most the night. I think I'll go out again with them. Shannon is loud on a good day but she is so much worse when she's been drinking."

"Karen, we're home." She became aware that the car was stopped in their driveway.

"Oh." Chase got out and came around to her side to make sure she was okay. Karen didn't think she needed help but she took the opportunity to wrap her arms around Chase's waist and lean into him, he smelled nice.

5

Chase watched Karen as she kicked off her heels and put her purse down on the table. It was too close to the edge and it fell on the floor. He bent down to pick it up and noticed for some reason Karen was running up the stairs, she tripped on a couple of them but thankfully didn't fall. *Where does she think she's going?* Chase thought. He followed her lazily up the stairs bemused.

"What are you doing, honey?" Chase yelled at her. He heard her in their bedroom. He hadn't seen Karen this drunk in a long time. Clearly she was hanging out with a bunch of party girls. He never liked Karen getting drunk when he wasn't there, she had a way of getting herself into trouble and she was easily influenced. Chase finally found sitting on their bedroom floor quickly emptying papers from her laptop case. She appeared to be looking for something.

"What is it?" Chase asked and sat down beside her.

"I just remembered where I put something," said Karen and she pulled out a photocopy of a picture.

6

It was time to make the first move. Doing nothing was getting nowhere. She was tired of lurking around in the shadows and watching. One had come home drunk and it brought back even more memories. It frightened her, stirred up something buried deep inside, some feelings left untouched for years. Forgotten emotions she thought had died away but instead were buried deep inside. Death benefitted her in ways she hadn't expected. She gained knowledge and insight into important things. She knew now the real horrors of life, the truth was worse than she could have imagined. There was so much more her mind could never have comprehended, for knowledge of it would have destroyed the soul and drove her mind to insanity. Death was the refuge, she could hide behind it, but at the same time it hindered her and her new goal. The memory must go on and the truth finally out for all to see but what could she do. She was still so weak, newly awoken and she didn't exist.

7

Karen was in the middle of a restless sleep. It was approaching four in the morning by the time she passed out. In her dream she was hiding from a man with a knife, he was trying to murder her and she was running. It was one of those slow motion situations where she felt like her legs were in molasses and no matter what she could move fast enough to save herself. Then in the flash of a second she was hiding but the man was nearby and it sounded like he was getting dangerously close. The rhythmic sound of his footsteps as he paced brushed across the floor. As she listened in her terrified state, she noticed something wasn't right. The knowledge she was dreaming startled her to consciousness.

Karen was uncomfortable and drenched in sweat from her nightmare. Her head was pounding and felt like it had a pulse. Suddenly the rhythmic noise of something brushing against the hardwood floors continued and it was nearby. Karen started to fear it momentarily and looked over at Chase to see him peacefully snoring. Karen had the urge to throw the covers over her head and hide like a little child. The only thing stopping her was the headache that only got worse with quick movements. There was a meow that came from under the bed. Karen nearly jumped out of her skin.

"Timbit?" said Karen softly and then silence, followed by an answering meow. Karen unwillingly freed herself from the comforting bed sheets and looked under the bed, trying to give her eyes time to adjust. Sure enough Timbit stared back at her, eyes glowing yellow. "What do you think you're doing?" She snapped at the cat. He ignored her and went back to playing with something that kept scrapping against the floor. It was the source of the noise that somehow mingled with dreams giving her a nightmare.

"Come here stupid cat." Karen tried to fish the cat out from under the bed. She thought it was odd that he was even there. Timbit never entered their bedroom; he always slept in the spare room. The cat moved to avoid Karen's hands but she managed to get a hold of what Timbit was swatting at. A single piece of notepad paper was stuck between the hardwood floor and the baseboard. She never noticed it before but Timbit must have pried it loose. Now with his source of entertainment gone Timbit gave Karen an evil stare before trotting out of the room with his tail up. Karen followed him out and took a couple Advil from the medicine cabinet and a long drink of water. Her hangover subsided a little. After that Karen took a look at what she found, on the yellowed piece of paper was a note. It read:

Thursday, April 2/1998

To my husband and daughter,

I am leaving, possibly forever. I can't live this way anymore. I've had enough and I'm going to make myself a new life. I'm terribly sorry for the pain this will cause you. I can't stress how sorry I am. I do love you both and I want you to remember that. I can't tell you where I'm going so I'll just tell you that I've gone. Please don't go looking for me. I promise you I'm fine.

–Jennifer

The note was sloppily written, probably someone in an emotional state of mind. It was old and belonged to the long gone owners of the house. She wondered how long it was lost under her bed. She fought the urge to run and show Chase her discovery. It was proof of the homes checkered past and it made her want to know more.

Part Two

Nightmares

1

Success at last, had never before been so bitter sweet. It bothered her the means she used to get here but she pushed the guilt to the back of her mind. It didn't take much to forget it completely. What did it matter anyway? She was pushed and pulled in all directions and very nearly tortured. She had a hard life and it hardened her in death. She was going to do what she could to end it all and soon, no matter the consequences to the living. The fact of their innocence meant very little to her as she decided their fate as pawns in the greater scheme of things. The future didn't matter, only the now.

2

It was dark, too dark to see anything and Karen wanted to see everything. She was lying in bed and it wasn't her own. She laid completely alone in the darkness and she wanted Chase. She kept calling out for him but he never came. When she finally gave up, there was someone banging on the door, 'let me in!' The angry male voice screamed. It was Chase's voice but there was malice in it and Karen wanted to let him in, but fear gripped at her and held her in the single bed, something wasn't right. Karen tried to call out but when she opened her mouth no sound came. The banging and yelling behind the door continued but the voice morphed into something else in Karen's ears. It was a foreign language, and it seemed evil and almost demonic. It spoke in low undertones and repeated like a chant.

Hysteria set in and Karen threw the covers over her head, holding them tight around her. She was aware if anything were to break the locks she would be discovered in an instant by the source of the demonic voice. The dreaded banging from behind the door suddenly gave way to an eerie silence. A silence she soon found to be worse than the noise itself. Trembling, Karen lifted the sheets off of her head just enough to peer out into the room around her. The endless darkness persisted and even the darkest shadows were made to be invisible.

If there were any danger here–and Karen was certain that there was–it would never be discovered before it killed her. Karen felt like a little child as she remained in her blanket sanctuary and cried.

3

Something awoke Chase from his deep sleep. He took a moment to get his bearings and wipe the sleep from his eyes. The sun was shinning brightly through their bedroom window. The weather seemed to be pleasant that day and it put Chase in good spirits. He noticed the bed shaking slightly on his wives side and she was crying silently in her sleep. His good mood dampened with concern and he tried to jiggle her awake.

"Karen, wake up. What's wrong?" He whispered soothingly into her ear. She never did this before and it concerned him. Karen slowly opened her eyes, and looked panicked. Then without saying anything she sat up quickly and raised her hand to cover her mouth. Before Chase could realize what was going on, Karen darted into the bathroom and was heaving over the toilet. Unwillingly Chase got out of bed and followed his hung-over wife to the bathroom where he stood just outside the door not wanting to look. Just hearing her heave was making his stomach do flips. "Are you okay or do you want me to come in there?" said Chase. The toilet flushed and he heard the tap turn on before Karen appeared in the bathroom doorway. She looked pale as if she'd had a long night.

"Sorry." She said, looking embarrassed.

"That's alright, but maybe you shouldn't drink so much next time. You look like you were hit by a train," said Chase as he ran a cloth under cold water and took two Advil's out of the cabinet.

"I really didn't mean to drink so much, and I definitely won't be again!" Karen took the Advil and the cold cloth from Chase and went to go lay back down in bed. Chase followed her and analyzing her every move.

"Why were you crying just now?" He asked once she was back in bed. Karen just gave him a confused stare.

"I was crying?"

"Yes, that's why I woke you." Karen paused and thought for a moment.

"It must have been a dream. I don't remember anything."

"Well at least you don't remember. It was probably just a nightmare. I'm going to make something greasy for you." Chase turned and was about to leave the room.

"Wait! There is something I remember from last night. I woke up earlier because Timbit woke me up. He found something underneath the bed. I put it on the dresser." Karen pointed across the room to the piece of old yellowed paper. Chase picked it up and saw that it was a note scrawled out on an ancient notepad. *What was that doing under our bed?*

4

Karen woke up on Monday, April 9th and dreaded going to work. The weekend crawled by and nothing she intended to do got accomplished. Saturday was spent in bed nursing her hangover and that night Karen had another nightmare. It was too bad she was never able to remember them. It was the same with Sunday night and now Karen felt like a walking zombie as she drove into work. Facing a classroom of kids was the last thing she wanted to do. She really longed to go crawl back into her warm bed and not have to face the day. The note and the picture of Mrs. Elsing were tucked away carefully in her bag. She wasn't sure if she should turn it to Tammy. She did have a mind to destroy the picture; it was the only way to keep the leak from spreading. If only Tammy didn't know, that conversation was a whopper of a mistake. It was hers, and she would have to deal with it whether she wanted to or not. Karen was surprised to find Catherine sitting on her desk waiting for her when she got in.

"How was your morning?" She asked and Karen knew she wanted to know about Saturday.

"Terrible." She answered and sat down at her desk and put her head in her hands.

"Suzie puked in my van that night and Tammy passed out before we got home. I'm so glad I didn't drink much."

"Fun," said Karen sarcastically. "The hangover wasn't the worst part of my weekend though." Catherine looked at her curiously, waiting for her to continue but she didn't. The warning bell rang and Catherine got up. *Saved by the bell.*

"I better go. We'll talk later." Karen followed her to the door and began writing a bell work assignment on the chalkboard. The first half of the day went by slowly and Karen wondered if it only seemed like that to her. At lunch she had supervision duty and she made her rounds throughout the school. She found Mathew in his classroom unexpectedly reading a newspaper.

"Shouldn't you be out to lunch?" She asked.

"No, I traded Kevin for supervision duty again." That explained why Karen saw Kevin walking into the staff room earlier with his lunch. She was about to leave and check on another room when Mathew stopped her.

"No, stay and talk a little. We haven't really spoken much yet and I'd like to get to know you."

"Well I'm not that interesting," said Karen, she decided she wanted to leave, something was off about Mathew but Karen couldn't pin point what it was.

"I'm sure you are. It was me that requested you join us on the spring trip. Just between us Ma-I mean Mrs. Elsing doesn't really like you." Karen was shocked at how blunt Mathew was being.

"I don't know what to say," said Karen calmly.

"Don't worry about it. She doesn't like you because you weren't born here. I don't know why that's such a big deal but it is to the old timers, you know how it is. If it helps, she did tell me she thinks you're doing a good job and I agree. I like you." Karen wondered if she heard that correctly. His voice was full of implications, and it made Karen uncomfortable.

"Okay?" said Karen wanting to bolt out of the room.

"So how do you like it here? Bored out of you mind yet?" Mathew seemed a little overly friendly but Karen wasn't sure if she was over reading things a bit.

"No, I love it here so far. The town is great. I-I really should be going. I need to check on the kids." Mathew looked at his class, and they were seated in groups and chatting away. A couple had started playing a card game. Karen heard some shouting from down the hall and took it as an excuse to leave. She practically ran out of the room. For once she was grateful for some fighting kids. *What the hell is he up to?* Karen thought as she quickly made her way to the loud classroom.

Once the commotion was over and everything was sorted out Karen went outside and walked down the hall. She avoided Mathew's classroom carefully and was trying to figure out what was going on. She was operating on little to no sleep and it was quite possible that Mathew was just being friendly and making normal conversation. After all she was probably just on edge about the affair. He couldn't possibly have been hitting on her. There was just something about that guy that made her uncomfortable. She didn't like being alone with him. Karen decided the problem was her own and she calmed herself down by the time she returned to her classroom. The class was finishing up their meals and everybody was getting along so Karen sat down and got ready to eat her own lunch.

BRING! The bell went off suddenly and startled Karen awake. She almost fell asleep at her desk and jumped at the noise. Her lunch was untouched and still in its bag. Her students slowly filed out of the classroom.

"Karen, can I come in?" It was Catherine, she had two coffees in her hand and Karen hoped one of them was for her.

"Please do." She answered; glad to have some company that didn't weird her out for once. She did want to talk to someone about what was going on, if she didn't she would burst. Catherine suddenly seemed like the most perfect person to vent to.

"Drink this, it has a double espresso shot, you look like you need it." She said, handing Karen the coffee.

"Thanks, I was worried about how I was going to stand another three hours of this." Karen took a sip from the coffee; and let the caffeine work its magic.

"So, you were about to tell me about your weekend earlier. What happened?" Catherine pulled herself up a chair from one of the student's desks and stat down. Karen wasn't sure where to start. Catherine waited for her to speak; she did seem to genuinely care.

"Well I've been having these weird night terrors every time I fall asleep. It's been happening ever since the Friday night. I don't even remember them, I just wake up terrified and I don't know why and what it is I'm so afraid of."

"That sucks; do you have anything on your mind lately that could be stressing you out?" Karen thought for a moment and smiled. She realized she was under a lot of stress and Catherine may have hit the root of the problem in one guess.

"Actually, you may be right! There is a lot going on in my life lately out of the normal and it's probably just getting to me."

"Tammy?"

"What about Tammy?" Karen was surprised at Catherine's suggestion.

"You had a fight with Tammy at Morgan's Friday. That was the night you started having the nightmares. Do you remember what it was about?" Karen did remember but she had to be careful. She was treading in dangerous water, if she said too much. "What's wrong?" Catherine read her troubled face.

"I'm thinking."

"What is there to think about, you either remember or you don't? I'm betting you do, and you're just thinking of some story to tell me?"

"I do remember." Karen said slowly. "We were discussing Tammy's relationship with her mother. The topic came up somehow and I was curious."

"Mrs. Elsing? Why does that matter, you already know they were estranged?"

"I did, I should never have asked, I guess."

"Tammy doesn't usually get so upset about her Mother; I thought she had come to terms with it. I don't understand why she would react the way she did."

"I wasn't expecting it at all considering she was the one to bring it up in the first place." Catherine was eyeing her suspiciously.

"You're editing and I know it! Can we cut with all the bullshit now and can you just tell me what really happened between you two?" Karen took a deep breath; this wasn't going to go as planned after all.

"How do you feel about Mrs. Elsing?"

"What?" Catherine yelled back, startled at the randomness.

"Just answer the question," said Karen firmly crossing her arms as aggressively as she could manage. Karen waited and Catherine looked confused but gave in.

"I think she is a fair boss and is capable of her job but she chooses favorite's and may have questionable motives sometimes."

"If you could have her replaced would you?" Catherine answered right away this time and was willingly playing along.

"No, I value my job."

"Me too." Karen answered and reached into her bag. She took out the picture she was supposed to pass on to Tammy and slowly handed it over for Catherine to look at. Karen studied Catherine's reaction but it wasn't one of surprise. She seemed almost bitter and amused. She had to wonder again what Catherine and Mathew's relationship had been.

"Oh." Was all Catherine said and it was almost inaudible.

"This picture is the cause of Tammy's reaction." Catherine still hadn't looked up and was staring at the picture. Karen wanted to rip it back from her but restrained herself.

"How did you get this?" She said slowly.

"Mathew dropped it and didn't notice. I picked it up and obviously I couldn't just give it back to him. I also didn't think I should just leave it in the hallway either. This is so screwed up." Catherine finally looked up.

"We need to destroy this! It would cause a huge scene if this were to get out. You don't even know the half of it. In this town people judge everything! You did the right thing by picking it up; it could so easily have fallen into the wrong hands!" Catherine shoved the picture back to Karen.

"Actually I told Tammy that night that if I found it I would give it to her." Karen looked at her hands guiltily. Like a child expecting a scolding.

"You did what!" Catherine stood up quickly and talked with her hands. "You know that if she ever got a hold of this she would show the world!"

"I know. I was thinking of destroying it, maybe she forgot about it anyways."

"I doubt it. If you knew Tammy better you would know how much she wants to destroy her mother. Mrs. Elsing may not be the easiest to get along with but she doesn't deserve what Tammy wants her to have. It would ruin Mathew as well." Catherine sat back down and was attempting to calm herself.

"You like Mathew don't you?" Karen came right out and said it.

"I did, I used to. I still do, but what does it matter. He is with Mrs. Elsing." Her eyes shifted toward the picture solemnly.

"Actually, I'm not so sure they are still together. I've noticed that they have been avoiding each other and acting odd. I would almost bet money that they had a falling out. Even if they are still together Mathew has been acting strangely towards me. Is he usually the flirty type?"

"Uh oh," said Catherine and gave Karen a bitter stare.

"He creeps the hell out of me," said Karen answering the unspoken question. "Even if I wasn't married to the best man ever I would never and I mean never consider Mathew."

"Hey!" said Catherine slightly offended.

5

Maggie Elsing sat in the staffroom at lunch and picked her uneaten bagel into pieces. There were only five other teachers in the room and they were chatting in a couple groups at the farthest end from her. It was probably purposefully. Certainly she wasn't giving off a friendly vibe and it didn't take much for people to get the message. She already made sure Mathew wasn't there before sitting down. He took over Mr. Hull's lunch supervision duty and now Kevin was laughing at something someone said and was holding a coffee that looked as if it might spill if shaken any harder. *Why does everyone else have to be in such a good mood?* Maggie wondered if Mathew volunteered for lunch supervision because Karen had it as well. He seemed to have chosen her as his new crush and was rubbing it in Maggie's face at every opportunity. She wondered why she cared; she wasn't supposed to care anymore. But nonetheless it was eating at her and tearing her into as many pieces as the bagel.

Everything in the tiny staff room seemed to annoy her. Even with the crowd chatting mindlessly at the other end of the table, Maggie felt alone. Tammy called her on Saturday. It was the first time she heard from her daughter in a good part of a year. The conversation was short and ended abruptly when Tammy accused her of being a cheating whore unexpectedly and hung up the phone. This reduced Maggie to tears and left her punishing herself because her daughter was right. It was over, but somehow it wasn't. Perhaps it wouldn't be over until Maggie faced real consequences. Her mind went back to Mathew with the stack of pictures in her office. It was a while since that day back in her office and nothing had come of it. It was possible that he chickened out, or maybe he was just giving her more time. Maybe he found someone else and no longer cared. That would be the best option but Maggie didn't like it.

Something needs to happen, someone needs to make the next move and it should be me, Maggie thought. She sighed solemnly and looked around at all of what she created for herself. She thought of her husband and her daughter and knew she screwed up. It pained her to admit it, even just to herself but she had, and nothing would change that. Maggie was a believer in karma and sat with a newfound determination to correct what was wrong. Life wasn't worth living if it all was a lie. The next move would be hers.

Maggie left the staffroom and doubted anyone even noticed her absence. The hallway was silent except for the sound of her heels clicking on the linoleum floors. She stopped just outside of Mathew's classroom, his door was closed but Maggie knew he would be in there. She could hear the sound of his radio he kept on his desk spewing out classic rock music quietly. Maggie raised her hand to knock on the door but stopped herself short. She couldn't let herself talk to him, confront him. He might win. Maggie would be smarter than that, and she remained strong as she turned on her heel and walked back the way she came.

The air in her office seemed heavier than usual. For the first time since becoming principal she sat down at her desk without feeling the air of accomplishment. Her stomach was doing flip-flops and her heartbeat could be felt strongly in her veins working double time. Hesitantly Maggie picked up the phone and dialed her husbands cell phone number. It rang once and Maggie slammed the phone back down on the receiver. Then looking at the phone got the better of her and it wasn't enough. Maggie swiped the phone off of her desk and it landed a few feet away on the floor. She slumped down in her chair and put her face in her hands in frustration and anger. *What was I about to do!* She thought and pictured her husband's reaction to the truth. It pained her to think of how she would hurt him. She couldn't do it. Maggie heard her office door open and Mrs. Langley peaked in quickly with a look of concern.

"Is everything okay?" She asked. Maggie straightened herself up regained what was left of her professionalism.

"Yes, Mrs. Langley. Everything is fine." The secretary loitered at the door for a moment, her eyes dropping to the phone on the ground and the receiver off the hook. There was doubt in her eyes but she eventually left closing the door behind her. Maggie listened as her footsteps walked away and she knew the secretary had retreated all the way back to her own office across the hall.

Maggie picked herself up, fixed the phone on her desk and in a moment of stubborn determination redialed the number and heard the familiar voice on the other line. It went to voicemail. *Damn it!* She thought but then recomposed herself.

"Michael, we really need to talk."

6

"You look as if you could use a nap." Chase remarked as Karen practically sleepwalked through the front door.

"I just might do that," said Karen as she rubbed her temples and massaged her scalp.

"You have a headache?" said Chase, watching her with concern in his eyes. Karen nodded a reply and Chase noted she really did look a combination of exhausted and stressed. He led her over to the couch and switched on the TV and Karen fit into his arms. They both stretched out along the couch and Chase pulled a blanket over them. Within seconds Karen was sleeping comfortably cuddled up into him. Chase was careful not to wake her as he channel surfed with the TV on a low volume. He came across an old episode of something he enjoyed as a kid and watched that until he too drifted off to sleep not long after.

Chase began to dream about his plans for the future and a trip he was hoping to take Karen on in the summer. Soon the couple was no longer curled up on the couch in their living room; instead they were transported to Nantucket and biking along the shore. Karen was happy and smiling and he thought everything was perfect. As in most dreams Chase didn't question how he got there, he just knew he was content. The sounds of the waves and the birds chirping were trivial relaxing sounds in the background. He almost didn't notice when the sky began to darken and the sounds turned to undistinguishable ominous noises that interrupted the peace.

Chase noticed his bike disappeared from under him and the air had a bitter bite to it, the summer was over. Karen disappeared from his side and Chase started to panic. He turned in circles looking for her but all he could make out was endless darkness. He dropped to his knees and started feeling around hoping desperately to come across something, anything. His hands touched a sticky liquid and he instantly brought his hand to his face. The moon chose that particular moment to come out from behind the clouds and it was just enough for him to see the crimson color in the moonlight. Frantically Chase canvassed the ground but he couldn't turn up any sign of Karen. There was only a trail of blood.

7

Karen was sitting in her garden, it was spring and the sun was that perfect temperature, warm enough to feel on her skin without out being hot enough to make her long for the air conditioning. Her creation of flowers bloomed all around the backyard and Karen admired her hard labour of love. Chase sat beside her and they sipped fresh lemonade from wooden lounge chairs overlooking the yard.

"This is perfect," said Karen smiling, enjoying the tranquility of the weather. The stress of work was beyond her.

"You can almost picture a little child playing in the yard. Our little one. I can make a tire swing over there." Chase pointed to an old tree about twenty feet from where they were sitting. Karen smiled, envisioning the pretty picture Chase was painting of their lives. She pictured what it could be like in a couple short years.

"We'd also need a golden retriever to play fetch with in the park." Karen added to the fantasy.

"Well you never can forget man's best friend," said Chase giving her one of his famous lopsided smiled she loved so much.

"Please, somebody help me!" A voice startled Karen out of her reverie. She jerked her head up to the sound of the women's voice. "Please, help me!" Karen jumped at a clasp of thunder shuddered the ground and sheet lightning lit up the sky. In the few short seconds the beautiful weather had turned into a full-fledged thunderstorm. "I need help." The voice pleaded again. Karen looked over to where Chase was sitting but found his chair empty and already soaking wet with the rain. Karen followed the sound of the voice and found a brown haired women waving at her from behind the tree Chase had pointed out earlier. The women looked scared and beaten up and was soaked from the rain. Her clothes clung to her skin and Karen noticed hers were beginning to as well. Her wet hair stuck to her face and she brushed her bangs away and followed the women. As soon as Karen got half way out to the tree, she turned and disappeared.

"Where did you go?" Karen screamed into the wind. It was directed at both Chase and the women. Karen spun quickly in a full circle searching the horizons for a clue.

"Over here." The women materialized another thirty feet away as if out of thin air.

"What do you want?" Karen yelled at the women, but she just motioned for Karen to follow and turned and walked deeper into the trees, giving Karen her back.

"Follow me." She heard. It was only a whisper carried by the wind. Karen looked back at the empty chairs and then fought her way through the storm and mud deeper into her property. The women disappeared as soon as Karen began moving forward again.

"Where am I going?" Karen asked, ready to give up. Fear gripped at her, certain she was walking into some kind of trap but still she felt compelled to continue. Karen noticed with horror that there was blood in the grass under her feet. She was barefoot and now her feet were stained in a mixture of grass, mud and blood. Making up her mind she followed the blood trail deeper and deeper, until it felt like she ran forever. She fell twice in the wind and the thunder covered up her cries. *What am I doing?* Karen thought, nothing made any sense; but she knew she had to keep going.

The brown-haired women stopped at the end of the property line. She was silent and her back was turned to Karen. The sun managed to break through the clouds, and it illuminated the pond where Karen once skated on. Karen noticed the rain stopped without warning and the wind seemed too calm, everything was motionless. It was as if time just stood still. Karen got the feeling she was witnessing an emotional moment and remained back, silent herself. The fear was gone and replaced by empathy for the poor troubled woman.

Slowly the woman turned around to face Karen and they made eye contact for the first time. Karen could have sworn she could see right into the woman's soul from her eyes. There was despair and pain in them. They were the eyes of a woman who had long ago given up. Karen nodded in understanding and the women disappeared into the air as fast as she appeared.

8

Chase and Karen woke up simultaneously. Karen felt Chase's arm around her and realized she was dreaming. Only this time she remembered and wasn't frightened. The pain of the woman's tortured eyes engraved itself into her memory, it would not be easily forgotten.

"You're here," said Chase groggily from beside her. Karen swiveled around so she could see his face. He looked a mixture of concerned and relived and hugged Karen tightly to him. Something was wrong.

"What is it?" said analyzing his expression. She reached up to touch his face.

"I thought you were gone. You were there and then you were gone and there was blood. Horrible blood-"

"Chase!" Karen interjected. "You were dreaming. So was I...I saw the blood."

"How?" Chase mumbled, in deep thought. Karen didn't know why she said that. Yes, she had dreamed of blood but it wasn't the same blood, but yet she said it and it felt right.

"I don't know," she said seriously.

"Well, what happened in your dream, then I'll tell you what happened in mine." Chase offered. Both of them sat upright on the couch at opposite ends. The blanket fell to the floor during there nap. They faced each other, both feeling a little awkward.

"We were together in the backyard." Karen couldn't remember all the details of the beginning. "I think it was spring and we were happy. A woman called out to us…well to me. When I looked you were just gone and it was raining and the wind was strong. The storm came on suddenly. She needed help and I tried to follow her but she kept disappearing. I fell and I noticed there was a trail of blood on the ground; I got covered in some of it as I fought my way deeper into the yard in the storm. I wanted to turn back and give up but I didn't. Something wouldn't let me. I found the woman by the pond out back. Then the rain stopped and the sun came out. I felt the power of the moment, as if there was something greater to it, some greater meaning that was important and just for me to see. I can't explain it. Then the woman looked at me and she was gone. That's when I woke up." Chase remained silent but was focused on every word. Karen knew something she said caught his attention.

"In my dream we were biking in Nantucket, we were on vacation. Then without warning everything changed. You were gone and it got real cold. Everything went dark and I was scared when I couldn't find you. I'm not sure how exactly but I ended up crawling around on the ground to look for you. I couldn't see anything but I felt something sticky that got on my hands. Then went I tried to see what it was, a light manifested and I saw the blood on my hands.

There was blood all over the grass and I thought it was yours. Then that's when I woke up…What if the grass was the same in both your dream and my dream? Is that possible do you think?" Karen shrugged and held Chase's stare. Both of them had been considering the same thing. The same unlikely thing. It had to be a coincidence. But what if it wasn't?

"I've been having strange dreams all weekend, all of them have been nightmares and I didn't remember anything. It was almost to the point where I've been afraid to go to sleep. This dream was different somehow but I have the weird feeling it's connected to the other ones. I know how stupid that sounds. This almost felt like someone wanted me to see something, I felt like it was important."

"If they were connected, don't you think you would remember the other dreams?"

"Maybe I didn't want to remember the other dreams," said Karen without thinking. More and more things had been slipping out of her mouth lately.

The sound of Karen's cell phone broke the intense silence. She heard it vibrating and ringing from her purse that was on the table in the entranceway. Karen ran over to go answer it, relieved to get away from the oddly serious moment that Chase and her shared.

"Karen." She answered, quickly into the phone.

"Hi Karen, it's Catherine." Catherine said excitedly.

"What happened?"

"You didn't show anyone else that picture you found, right?"

9

Maggie sat alone at her kitchen table. She'd been there all night waiting for Michael to get home. It was getting late and she was getting uncomfortable. She faced away from the door and just stared blankly at the wall. Her cell phone was in front of her on the table, but it hadn't so much as rung since the voicemail she left her husband. She jumped as the front door opened and she listened as Michael removed his boots and set his keys down. She listened carefully to each of his footsteps as he walked closer to her and with each one she felt closer to tears. She hated herself for this weakness. Her hands were visibly shaking and she clasped them into fists that were so tight her knuckles had gone white. Her nails were cutting into the flesh of her palm but she didn't notice, but they were near breaking the skin.

"Maggie what did you want to tell me?" Michael rested his hand on her shoulder and she spun around to face him. She needed to give him the benefit of seeing her face as she destroyed him. A tear betrayed her as she faced him and it ran down her cheek. She swiped at it angrily. "My god, Maggie what's wrong!" He said, concern in his voice. Maggie removed his hand from her shoulder.

"I had an affair." Stunned silence filled the air, and then she continued. Confusion had boiled up in Michael's face, but not surprise. "It was with a teacher, it's over now. I ended it. I love you, but you don't deserve me." Maggie was full on crying now and quickly turned away to once again face the wall.

"Why?" It was all he could manage.

"I don't know."   Maggie got up and turned towards him again, no longer caring that her perfectly applied make-up was now streaming down her face, leaving behind betraying trails of black. "I think you should go." Michael remained silent as he retreated in his steps, picked up his keys and slammed the door loudly as he sped down the driveway.

10

"Of course not! I only showed you and told Tammy about it."

"Well Mrs. Elsing just quit her job."

Locked Door

1

"What do you think is going to happen?" Karen whispered to Catherine, Tuesday evening. The staff were arriving, prepared for a meeting with the head of the school board, Dana McMillian. The teachers were at a loss. The sudden disappearance of Maggie Elsing was a shock to everyone.

"This is probably just going to introduce us to the new principal. The meeting will probably be over quickly," said Catherine.

"I saw her crying in her office yesterday. I bet she had some sort of mental breakdown." Mrs. Langley was saying to no one in particular. Catherine just rolled her eyes and looked at Karen and back to the single empty seat in the room. Mathew had yet to show up for the meeting.

"Do you think he got fired?" Catherine whispered, her hand blocking her mouth from everyone's prying eyes.

"We can only hope," said Karen, mostly to herself. The thought of his odd friendliness was on her mind. Catherine, slightly offended said nothing and focused back on the group as a whole. Mathew walked in a couple minutes later and took his seat awkwardly in the empty spot across the room. He was smiling and Karen found herself noticing something about it seemed malicious. Karen didn't like his attitude and something about him was off. He seemed too proud, considering he was most likely responsible for driving away his former lover. His look was cold and calculating, almost cruel. Karen thought it almost seemed as if he imagined himself better than everyone else, which probably wasn't far from the truth.

"Hello everyone, as you know my name is Dana McMillian. I'm here this afternoon because a long-time employee of the school board Maggie Elsing has left us last night. Now it seems there is an opening in this school and I'm here tonight to introduce the new principal, Mathew Barry. I think all of you will appreciate one of your own teachers is residing over this school instead of hiring someone new." Karen felt as if her jaw could have been on the floor. She just sat there grasping at the idea. Catherine seemed equally surprised and even her biased position wasn't enough to over ride her sense of right and wrong of the situation and she looked shaken. Karen noticed the other teachers were clapping to congratulate Mathew on his new promotion. Karen tried to blend in but only managed to bring herself to put her hands together a couple times without producing any sound. She was still stunned.

"Thank you guys, this means a lot to me. I love this school and all the students and staff here. We all know how tightly nit this community is. I'd like to say everything remain the same as when Mrs. Elsing was with us and I hope that calms some of the nerves. As I was discussing with Mrs. McMillian before the meeting I will stay teaching the fourth grade until I can find a suitable replacement. The Spring Trip will be going off as planned for the weekend of May fourth." Mathew waited to see if there were any questions before taking his seat, there were none. Most of the teachers just wanted to go home to their families.

"You are dismissed," said Mrs. McMillian. The room quickly emptied except for Mathew and the school board director. Karen waited patiently for Catherine to exit the school; she waited by her car far enough away their conversation would not be heard from any of the others nearby.

"Oh, my god!" said Catherine, excitedly.

"Calm down," said Karen, noticing a few curious teachers, including Melinda staring at them from across the parking lot.

"I know! It's just so insane, so completely stupidly insane." Catherine was fuming.

"What are the chances that the one person most likely responsible for Mrs. Elsing quitting without notice, would be the one promoted to be principal? Anyone and I mean anyone would be better for the job. What about Kevin Hull?"

"Well who else has spent so much time inside that office?" Catherine laughed, a coping mechanism for the seriousness of what just happened. Karen joined in and sighed.

"This town is like high school all over again." Karen stammered.

"Amen sister." After that Catherine started walking towards her car. Karen called to her, stopping her in the middle of the parking lot.

"Has anyone talked to Tammy?"

"Good idea," said Catherine and practically jogged over to her van where Karen assumed she would be calling her friend. Karen was about to leave but was stopped when she noticed Melinda, now alone, making her way over to her.

"Karen?"

"Yes." Karen replied, confused. Melinda never talked to her outside of work and the spring trip meetings.

"I noticed you didn't seem happy about Mathews promotion. I can't say I am either." She said with her voice was full of implication. Karen knew she wasn't alone when it came to the truth.

2

Chase was working late waiting for Karen to get home. The final third of his novel was slowly making its way down on paper. Not that he wouldn't go back and change it all later but right now he was happy with his work. Chase pounded out another two pages of text before saving his word document and staring blankly at the screen. He watched the cursor blink at him repeatedly for a few seconds before closing the window and committing to his work being done for the day. Chase looked at the computer screen and saw that it was already almost six in the evening and Karen should have been home long ago, but she did say that there would be an important meeting after work. Chase quickly picked up his phone and ordered a pizza to be delivered, Karen couldn't possibly be much longer.

After hanging up the phone and spending a few minutes contemplating the quietness of the house Chase turned back to his computer screen. He opened his search engine without thinking about what it was he wanted to look up. He searched for the town's newspaper and went looking for information on any possible archives. It turned out he was in luck when he found an online version through a library website. He mentally thanked the Internet gods and hoped they would remain in his favor. Chase typed April 1998 as the search date and started scrolling through old newspaper articles. It didn't take long to spot what he was looking for. The story must have been about the only real news at the time.

Wednesday, April 8, 1998

Jennifer St. Claire remains missing after two days of searching, said police chief Henderson this morning. Richard St. Claire, her husband of eighteen years, was the last person reported to have seen her.

"I woke up on Friday and I found a note she left on my pillow. She said she left and wasn't coming back. I don't know what happened. She was just gone," said Richard St. Claire. During his interview he was clearly distressed over his wife's disappearance and repeatedly mentioned his worry over their sixteen-year-old daughter Molly.

Police are still attempting to locate and contact Jennifer St. Claire but all attempts have failed. There is no evidence of any foul play or any reason to suspect Jennifer has been taken against her will, according to police.

Richard kept scrolling through the articles and stopped at one about six weeks later.

Friday, May 29, 1998

What happened to the St. Claire's? Not only is Jennifer St. Claire missing but now the rest of the family of three are too.

The friends and neighbors have not reported any information on the whereabouts of the family, however it may be possible they joined Jennifer St. Claire into hiding. No one seems to have any idea why they left or where they have gone. It is like the family just disappeared into thin air.

Every person seems to have a different idea of the events that transpired to cause the St. Claire's absence.

"I believe that the St. Claire's were a part of some kind of secret cult and they were discovered and forced to leave." John

Doggitt had to say, one of the more far-fetched theories sprinkled around town.

"If you ask me, there's some deep dark reason those people are gone. I think it may be caused by a crime that occurred. It makes no sense to me why they could just be gone, there's no reason not to tell people unless there was something to hide," said William Peterson yesterday. This is the most widely accepted theory around the small town.

Police say nothing has been found to give reason for the claims.

Chase read through a few more articles but most of them just followed up on the main two stories. One article about three months later announced the house was to be foreclosed and another one was on the condition the house was found in. Chase nearly gagged a few times at mention of the gas masks that needed to be worn. He remembered the disgusting old carpet he had ripped out himself. The condition of the house prior to the sale wasn't disclosed and he believed it should have been. The report claims garbage built up everywhere, including dead rodents and un-cleaned up vomit stains around the house. Chase wasn't so sure he wanted that pizza anymore. The last article he could find was published only a few years earlier covering a debate about reselling the house or condemning it. Chase skimmed the article already knowing what the result of the vote was.

The doorbell rang and Chase shut down his computer and went to pay for the pizza. As he was doing so, he saw Karen pull up into her side of the driveway. *Perfect timing,* Chase thought. He saw Karen smile in appreciation when she noticed the pizza in his hand and she watched the pizza guy walk back down the driveway and pull away.

"You're a genius." She said, hugging and kissing him quickly at the door. Chase wasn't sure if he should tell Karen about his research, it would just give her more cause to pursue the meaning behind her dreams. She was beginning to consider the idea that maybe there was some kind of importance and meaning to the gory vision's they had every night. Chase thought she may just be right, but he would rather not prove her theory. This was their house they had bought together, their first house. He didn't want to ruin the dream they had of starting a family in it, he wasn't prepared to move again.

3

Tammy Elsing called and cancelled all of her hair appointments she planned for the day. The coffee maker finished brewing a fresh pot of coffee and she pored two mugs of it, both of them were black. She handed one over to her father who had shown up at her door at two that morning and crashed on her couch with no explanation. She didn't really need one then, the smell of alcohol and self-despair said it all. There was only one person who could have triggered that reaction. Her mother.

"Are you going to tell me what happened?" said Tammy as she took a seat across from her father atone of the bar stools by her center island. He met her gaze with glazed over dead eyes. The situation had clearly not hit him to the full extend yet and he was in shock. An awkward silence passed between them, no one daring to speak for a long stretch of time. Tammy was wondering if it would be best if she left him for a little while to gather his thoughts but eventually he spoke.

"She cheated on me?" He framed it more as a question than a statement. Tammy having waited for this moment her entire adult life; didn't know how to respond.

"How do you know?" The words sounded funny coming out of her mouth, she had known.

"She told me. I was at work and she left me a message saying that we needed to talk and when I got home…I never expected–I couldn't even begin to think it. When I got home she was sitting at the table and she told me right to my face that she had an affair. An affair can you believe it, right under my nose the whole time!" Michael was getting angry now. Tammy decided it was a good thing. He was getting over it his own way and learning how to deal with the news.

"What happened after that?" Tammy wondered and she was trying to bridge the gap of time between the confession and her father at her door with nothing but what he had on and his truck.

"I left, she was crying and I left. I didn't know what else to do. How did she expect me to react?" Tammy was angry, it would be just like her mother to expect to get her way in the end. At least she didn't beg him to stay, but she didn't leave him herself. She should have left him years ago, before she hurt everyone. She broke up the family and she did it years before now. "Do you know who it is?" Tammy went back to her drunken night at Morgan's.

"I've got an idea."

4

She saw it. Fear took hold on her. She understood the full extent of it as she once had shortly after she was killed. Her death was not an accident. It was not simply the result of a crime. No, her death was for a carefully crafted purpose. She was destined to die that day, her fate had been decided the day she was born. Everything that transpired happened for a reason. There were plenty of unseen forces working beyond the capabilities of humans to understand. Knowledge of them and understanding them were impossibilities until after death. Now she knew everything, she understood everything.

This was why on that late April day in 2012; she was able to sense it returned. The evil lying dormant for years had been set in motion. This town was a cursed place—a place that housed many dark secrets in the shadows that even the oldest of the town's residents had omitted from their stories over the generations. An evil that was the town's very foundation, and it was no longer dormant.

5

"There's something you're not telling me." Karen accused before stuffing her mouth with another mouth-watering slice of pizza.

"I don't know what you're talking about," said Chase, but even he knew his voice was too high. Karen finished chewing and swallowed her pizza while giving him a bemused look from across the dining room table.

"I did some research," said Chase and Karen immediately made the jump to their house. The excitement showed in her eyes, but it was tinged with fear.

"Well what did you find? Anymore skeletons in the closet…or in the backyard." Karen regretted the words before she finished speaking them. Chase didn't look pleased and the reality of her fears suddenly felt more real. Her dreams were nothing more than dreams concocted from her vivid imagination. *But then what did Chase find?*

"I don't know about the yard, but this house was a lot worse off than we were led to believe." Karen made a disgusted face. She understood why Chase didn't want to tell her all the details about the state the house was in. The information wasn't what she had been hoping for but she was glad that he didn't find any red flags.

"Remember that note we found?" said Chase after a little bit of silence as they both finished eating.

"How can I forget? That was a pretty bad night," said Karen and pretended to stick a finger down her throat to prove her point.

"I found a reference to a note that Jennifer St. Claire left her husband before going missing. It turns out she left a couple months before the rest of the family abandoned the house and went missing."

"It was in the house the entire time. It's hard to believe that no one touched it since then and we found it after all these years." Karen couldn't believe it. "It's creepy."

"Definitely creepy. If I didn't know better I would say it's like a clue from one of my crime novels." Karen and Chase both laughed at that but Karen resisted the urge to run up stairs and find the note. She was developing a new theory, but Chase was not ready to hear it just yet. She pretended to brush off the information and changed the topic back to her day at school–omitting the Mathew drama part–and to Chase's progress with his manuscript.

6

It was late as Mathew found himself pacing in his apartment. Morgan's closed its doors for the night and Mathew knew he didn't have too long before he was expected to start his first day as principal. He tried to sleep but it was impossible and the horrible insomnia kept him up. It was nerves, he decided. Mathew found a bottled of Gravol in his medicine cabinet and swallowed a tablet with a sip of water. It would help him sleep as much as he hated to do it. The stress of his new promotion was getting to him more than he cared to admit even to himself.

Mathew knew he was under qualified and undeserving of his new title and pay increase. He worked hard to seduce Dana to secure his position and his efforts paid off well. He wanted to lash out against Maggie. It was a shame she wasn't around to watch him tear apart her accomplishments. No one knew where she was but it didn't matter, he knew she would be drawn to check up on her precious school eventually. Her inability to let go of anything would make her do it, and Mathew would wait and laugh in her face.

It wasn't just Maggie that prompted him to his new position. Karen Williams was a bigger inspiration than he originally realized. He felt compelled to get closer to her from the first time he laid eyes on her back in February. It was Mathew himself that brought her resume to the attention of Maggie. He felt an attachment and wanted the challenge. She was cold and shut off to him despite she was candid and open to everyone else. Karen was married and appeared to be one of the rare cases where she was actually happy. Mathew knew women well enough to know that as much as they appeared to be happy, somewhere deep inside they loathed their lives and longed for freedom. Mathew was all too willing to provide them with the freedom they all wanted, even if they didn't know they wanted it. Karen was different; she wasn't like all the women he had grown accustomed too. She wasn't so easily read and manipulated. Mathew longed for her; he wanted to meet the challenge. She would be the next notch on his belt.

Mathew collapsed on his bed; he could feel himself fighting to stay awake against the influence of the Gravol. He ran through his game plan before he went to sleep, it was beginning to become a habit. He would seduce Karen on the New York trip. He would get her alone during the lunch break and make his move. Karen wouldn't be able to say no to him once he turned up his charms. *Yes, of course that will work!* Mathew thought as he worked out the details to his new plan. Once he had Karen alone in New York he would finally taste of the forbidden fruit.

The trip was in a week's time and the plan was so close to being executed. He just had to get through his first week at being principal first. What could go wrong? Mathew drifted off into a drug-induced sleep.

7

"Chase?" Karen whispered and waited to see if he would reply. It was late and they went to bed but Karen had too much on her mind to sleep. "Chase, are you awake?" She tested again. When still no reply came Karen lifted the covers off of her body and found her slippers by the bed. She quietly tiptoed to the door, slowly turning the handle and she let herself out of the bedroom without being noticed. Karen breathed a sigh of relief as she ducked quickly into the office and powered up her laptop. She sat at Chase's desk and imagined herself to be a detective working on an important case. The clock on the laptop read 2:13 a.m.

Karen typed the name Chase had mentioned earlier into Google–Jennifer St. Claire. A couple promising results popped up. She clicked on the first article and rejoiced when she saw it originated from the local paper. The date was from early 1995. She skimmed the article, which was about local arts. At the top was a picture of a young child of about eight, wielding a violin standing beside a women sitting behind a piano. They were both smiling. Karen's breath caught in her throat as she recognized the women in the picture. It was the women that often starred in her dreams and invaded her head at night. Karen stared in dumbfound disbelief at her computer screen. After recomposing herself she read the cutline below the picture: An excited Amy Tomlin practicing for her upcoming violin solo with music teacher Jennifer St. Claire at the piano.

Jennifer St. Claire, the same women who lived in her house. It was the same women behind the note that she found under her bed. Karen felt weird about looking at the picture. She was clearly happy and smiling in the picture, and it touched her eyes. Karen decided she was beautiful and music must have been a passion. Karen felt like she caught a glimpse of the past, before whatever it was that happened took them into a downward spiral. There had to be something major that took place that changed the happy women in 1995 into the emotionally ruined women that haunted her dreams.

Karen thought of Suzie Martin from her girls' night. She worked in the music store downtown. Was it possible that she might have known Jennifer before she went missing? If music was her passion, as it seemed, it wasn't a far stretch to say she probably frequented the music store. Perhaps it was time to take the detective work for the next level. Karen knew what she would do after school let out tomorrow. It was time to give Suzie a friendly visit.

"Karen, are you up?" Chase called from the bedroom.

"Shit!" Karen muttered under her breath and slammed her laptop down and darted out of the office careful not to be too conspicuous.

"Just getting a glass of water, go back to sleep and I'll be in, in a minute." Karen assumed Chase went back to sleep when there was no reply and she went down to the kitchen and poured herself a glass of tap water. She drank it quickly and went back up to attempt to shut down her mindful of swirling thoughts long enough to get some sleep.

She stood in the doorway of their master bedroom. Chase was already unconscious again and snoring soundly in the bed. He was being a cover hog now that she had abandoned her place beside him. Karen was glad to see that the nightmares had left him alone for now. She wasn't as lucky herself but at least they had let up in frequency in the last week. Mostly her dreams didn't frighten her anymore. They intrigued her and drew her further into her obsession. She was convinced her dreams were being manipulated by something that wanted her to know something important. Chase didn't believe it yet, but she would prove it.

Tomorrow she would talk to Suzie.

8

Karen knocked on Catherine's door just after the final recess bell rang in the afternoon. Her students already vacated the classroom in a rush, but Karen could see Catherine was still chatting with a couple students by her desk. Catherine met her gaze and smiled at her as if telepathically apologizing for the hold up. Karen nodded and waited for the two young girls to chat themselves out and run outside to join their little friends. The weather had thankfully warmed up enough to only require a light sweater and jeans. It wasn't short weather just yet but it was close and Karen loved it. Spring was here and flowers and leaves returned from the bitter winter's grasp for another year.

"I called Tammy," said Catherine before Karen could pull a chair up to her desk. It was the first time the two of them had a chance to talk since their meeting the night before.

"And?" Karen prompted when it became clear Catherine was not going to offer any more information.

"Tammy doesn't know what her mother is up to any better than we do. She's not answering her calls or returning them and hasn't talked to anyone. Tammy is not even sure Mrs. Elsing is still in town or not. For all anyone knows she could have taken off, for how much she has shut the world out," said Catherine and it was clear something had to have happened that drew Mrs. Elsing to uproot her entire life. Karen wondered if Jennifer St. Claire was in the same state of mind when she wrote the note she found.

"Did anyone try her husband?" Karen didn't know why she asked that, it just sort of came out of her mouth.

"Actually, that's the funny thing. Tammy said her mother left her father right after she quit her job. Mr. Elsing is living with her in the city, she wouldn't tell me any of the details but I gather it probably relates to that blackmailed picture. I guess that means nothing now."

"In a way it makes sense. Mathew was blackmailing her, probably because he was aiming at her job. Then he got what he wanted." Karen was thinking out loud.

"No, that doesn't work at all." Karen gave Catherine a confused glare, but Catherine was deep in thought that Karen could almost see the gears in her head churning out a new theory. "No, why would she give Mathew what he wanted and leave her job if she was just going to leave her husband anyway? Why let Mathew win that way?"

"Maybe Mathew didn't win." Karen added.

"Then what did he want?" *That is a good point, if not his new promotion, what were Mathew's intentions?*

The bell rang once again to signal the end of the break and Karen started to make her way back to her classroom. She hesitated at the doorway.

"Do you know if Suzie is working tonight?" She asked Catherine quickly, she had nearly forgotten she meant to ask.

"Um, yeah. She should be working until five." Catherine looked as if she was considering asking a follow up question but some of her students started making their way back to their seats and she dropped it.

"See you." Karen mouthed as she rushed down the hallway to beat her students back from the break. Karen made it to her doorway just as the first group of students made it from outside tracking globs of mud from their shoes. *Spring is here!* Karen thought as she picked up a piece of chalk and started writing textbook pages on the blackboard. She heard a few protesting groans as her students all took out their math workbooks and partnered up. At least the day was almost over. It turned out to be a pretty good day, Karen managed to avoid Mathew completely and she got to talk to Catherine. Soon she would even get to feed her investigative obsession and talk to Suzie. Karen smiled as she finished writing the instructions on the blackboard. *Today was not half bad.*

9

Karen was glad to be out of her classroom and into the fresh spring air of late April. She bypassed her car in the parking lot and decided to walk the three blocks to the music store. As she neared the sidewalk in front of the elementary school Melinda drove by with her new SUV and slowed down by Karen and rolled down the passenger window.

"You need a ride?" She asked.

"No thanks, my car is in the parking lot. I just thought I would enjoy the weather for a bit before it starts raining again."

"That's probably a good idea. Nine more days till NYC!" said Melinda excitedly before driving off towards the outskirts of town in the opposite direction than Karen lived–the wealthier side of town. Karen hummed as she walked and people watched. It seemed lots of people were out and about downtown. There were preteens on bikes making their way home from school; Karen recognized one as Braydon from her class. She waved but neither of them saw her. On the other side of the street there was a bus from high school that just made it back from the city. A bunch of teens were chatting loudly amongst themselves. One of them was wearing the uniform from the pizzeria and she assumed he was probably on his way to work. Karen crossed the street at the single intersection in town big enough to have stoplights and a cross walk. An older couple of about seventy were purchasing ice cream from a booth attached to an Italian restaurant. Karen mentally made a note to stop there with Chase sometime soon. Karen finally got to the music store and when she opened the door a little bell rang and signaled a new customer.

"Karen?" said Suzie in surprise as she noticed her. She was standing behind the counter with a trumpet and some instrument cleaning supplies. She put it down as Karen approached. "I didn't know you were into music. What made you drop by?"

"I do play piano," said Karen, answering the first question but ignoring the second. She had to wait for the right moment to bring up the tough subject without sounding completely crazy.

"Oh right. I did hear that from somewhere but I guess I forgot."

"Well that's alright." Karen smiled. "It's a nice place you got here." She meant it. The shelves were lined with rows of every kind of instrument as well as the usual guitars. There was a new drum set for sale off to the side and a couple keyboards. Behind the counter were the smaller supplies: tools for instrument repair, guitar strings, and reeds for different woodwind instruments. Karen saw into the back room where she could make out an older piano and a bulletin board with various music related colored posters. It was the same piano that Jennifer sat behind in the newspaper photo of her back in 1995. Karen realized that she stopped playing the piano since her full time job and decided to try to get back into playing it again. It was doing nothing but collecting dust in her living room.

"The place isn't mine, I just work here but I feel like I probably do more with the shop than the owner does. Mr. Bantting has owned this place since the 1970's but he is getting up there in age and is practically retired. He comes in once a month to check up on things, but besides that it's just me and the weekend girl."

"Do you teach any lessons?"

"Sadly no. There hasn't been anyone qualified to teach in a long time. It's a shame really, the store was set up to do lessons." Suzie thought for a moment. "Hey! You just said you play piano?" Karen didn't like where this was going.

"I studied music but I'm probably not qualified to teach in a professional shop like this."

"Why not? You have a degree and you are an elementary school teacher. Sounds perfect to me. You could get a couple extra bucks and only work a couple hours a few days a week." Suzie was a little too enthusiastic. "It would be great working with you."

"Maybe I would consider taking you up on that in the summer, but I don't have time now." She saw Suzie's expression drop slightly, but she was serious about considering the summer. She would just be bored anyway.

"Oh well, it was worth a shot. So why did you come in here today? I doubt it was a random drop by."

"Your right. I had some questions I wanted to ask you, and I'd rather not have to explain myself." Suzie looked apprehensive.

"Ohh-kay." She dragged out the word.

"I was just wondering if you knew a Jennifer St. Claire? I believed she worked here?"

"Yes I knew her. She used to give me piano lessons when I was just a kid. Of course I can hardly play a note now. She disappeared in 1998, when I was only eleven and I quit piano after that. I really wish I could still play." Karen couldn't contain her excitement. She didn't expect Suzie to know her so personally.

"What was she like?" Suzie thought back to her childhood.

"I remember I liked her. She made music fun to learn and didn't push me too hard. I was sad when my lessons ended. At the time I didn't realize what really happened since my parents didn't say anything. Eventually I learned the St. Claire drama is big news in this town. Honestly I thought people would have let it go by now, but I guess not or you wouldn't have found out about it. Seriously, how did you find out?" Karen should have known that she couldn't expect people to not be curious in this town.

"I live in her house." Karen watched as Suzie's jaw dropped; there was a silence, as she comprehended the information. Apparently not everyone was privy to all the gossip in town after all.

"I think that answered about all my questions. What! You really live in her house?" Karen sighed.

"Yes, and I was just curious. People have been telling me stories and I'm not sure what to believe anymore. What's your theory, you must have one?"

"There's something I knew as a kid that I didn't tell anyone," said Suzie. She was whispering but there was no one else in the shop to over hear. "I knew that Mrs. St. Claire's husband hit her sometimes and I knew she was scared. The fact she ran away never surprised me."

10

Karen picked up the lid to her ancient piano. It was a long time since she bothered to even look at it longer than to wipe the dust off. She sat down and riffled through her sheet music before deciding on her favorite piece, *Claire de Lune* by Debussy. She hummed along as she played, the music felt good after all this time. After a while she became aware of Chase watching from the doorway, he was smiling. The sheet music came to an end and she paused to smile back at her husband.

"I forgot how much I loved the piano." She said gleaming.

"That was beautiful," said Chase as he walked over to her. He didn't want to disturb her earlier. "I wonder how long it would be before you rediscovered your baby." Karen giggled.

"I forgot all about the piano when I started teaching. I was too busy I guess. I ran into Suzie today at the music store and it reminded me." Chase looked quizzical.

"Why did you go to the music store?" He said slowly. Karen got a sense that Chase knew more than he was letting on about her true motives.

"Suzie works there and I wanted to say hi." Her voice rose a little too high at the end, and Karen noticed it. *Busted!*

"Right," said Chase. He was staring at her making her feel incredibly guilty but she couldn't tell if he bought it or not. She really wished he would stop staring at her like that.

"Alright, alright!" She cracked. "I wanted to talk to Suzie to ask her about Jennifer."

"I knew it!" He accused. "What is so important, that you can't stop thinking about it? You are not a detective, why does it matter what happened here?" He was serious and it scared Karen.

"I feel like Jennifer wants me to know something. I think she has been leading me to clues. It was no accident I found her note, and it was no accident that I keep dreaming about her."

"How do you know that it's even her? It's probably just gotten drilled into your head because everyone talks about it around us. It's nothing more than that, just your crazy subconscious mind," said Chase, he was attempting to sooth her but it wouldn't work this time.

"No, it's her! I saw a picture of her, and the person I keep dreaming about is with no doubt Jennifer St. Claire!" Karen was defensive now and jumped up from the piano bench and slammed down the lid, it made a horrible crashing noise that echoed through the entire house.

"Whatever. Are you saying this house is haunted?" said Chase, backing down a little bit.

"No, yes. I guess it could be in a way. I mean something clearly is using me for some reason and I want to figure it out, but haunted? I'm not saying I've seen a ghost or I think there is anything in the house. It's just a house, ghosts aren't real." Chase took a deep breath.

"So you don't want to move?"

"No, I love it here. What would make you think that?" Chase looked relived and he hugged her.

"It's nothing. I just thought something but it's stupid." They embraced for a while longer. Karen's brain was still on other things. Chase brought up a topic she had not considered until now.

11

"Hmmm, Chase, stop it." Karen muttered sleepily and rolled over taking her pillow with her. She was fully awake now and she became aware of the sound of her piano being played downstairs. It was a slow piece she didn't recognize but it was beautiful. Karen sat up and regarded Chase snoring softly in a deep sleep beside her. The piano continued and Karen felt like she was in the middle of a horror movie, as she felt drawn to the source of the sound. She would be in the part where she would be screaming at herself to stop. Regardless Karen made it to the hallway and started down the stairs. The house appeared to be empty; it was silent except for the piano's excellently played chords. The air felt still around her, but she didn't feel threatened. She actually felt rather peaceful and it had a calming aspect to it.

Karen continued down the stairs slowly and carefully, not wanting to draw attention to her presence. She considered grabbing a weapon briefly but realized it was too late for that. If it were an intruder, she would just get herself discovered sooner. Karen tiptoed slowly to the door of the living room; she was standing in the exact spot Chase had stood earlier that evening. Karen stood mesmerized as she witnessed what she thought was the most realistic dream yet. Jennifer St. Claire sat on the bench and was playing the ivories. She wore nothing but a white housecoat, her hair was damp and brought back into a bun with a clip, as if she had recently gotten out of the shower.

Jennifer turned her head to notice Karen before a look of panic crossed her face. Her mouth gabbed open like she was screaming but no sound came out. She reached one arm to Karen as if she was desperate for help. The air started to feel heavy and Karen stood paralyzed in fear, it kept her rooted to her spot despite her brain yelled for her to run. Jennifer disappeared and the keys played themselves for a few moments more, as if an invisible force was there. Karen did scream as the basement door flew open and smashed into the opposite wall. The same force that through open the door flung Karen to the ground like a wave of energy passed through–almost like a sonic boom. Karen looked up in time to see the smear of blood on the wall, and drops of it on the floor. There was a horrible nails-on-chalkboard screeching sound and Karen gapped in horror as a handprint of blood appeared out of no where and continued down the length of wall leading to the basement as if an invisible person were being dragged against their will. The basement door flung closed and the house was silent again.

Karen slowly got up and forced herself to resist the urge to run and scream. She pulled herself together with her last bit of courage she could summon and walked to the closed basement door. She tried the handle and it was locked tight. Giving up she backed away a step, watching the door, afraid to look away. A moment passed and the doorknob slowly turned and the basement door creaked open noisily. Karen felt compelled to walk into the doorway, one step then another. She just reached the second step when the door slammed closed and locked behind her. She clawed desperately at the door willing it to open as it had before but it stuck.

She was engulfed in darkness and fumbled around for the deadbolt. It was stuck tight and she couldn't move it. Crying, Karen slumped down on the steps and curled herself into a ball.

12

Karen woke up when a light started shining in her eyes. The sun had risen high enough to be coming through the small window high in the wall. Karen rolled off her old beanbag chair she slept on. The basement was damp and depressing, Karen routinely avoided the space except for laundry. As she stood up, pain ran through her back and neck from sleeping on it wrong. Karen stretched and grumbled before making her way back up the stairway. The smears of blood from the night before were gone and she knew she must have imagined them. *Maybe I was sleepwalking?* Karen questioned as she brought back faint painful memories of the night before. Karen tried the handle and was overcome with relief that it was unlocked.

She did a quick check of the piano and the walls, she flashbacked to the blood and hand prints. Now the walls were clean but the memories wouldn't fade from her mind anytime soon. The clock on the oven said it was only six in the morning and Karen would have to be at work in only two and a half hours. No point in going back to sleep. Karen brewed a fresh pot of coffee and threw some bread in the toaster. Today was going to be a long confusing day.

Reflection

1

"Are you all packed?" asked Chase, watching as Karen was stressing out, looking for anything else she might need on her trip. She was rushing up the stairs with a big bag of assorted candies and snacks she bought for her students. They were meant as trivia prizes for the game she planned for the bus ride to Manhattan. Karen had to admit she was nervous. She'd never been in the position of entertaining and being responsible for three classes of preteen students in a huge city. She could tell she was on the brink of a fit of anxiety.

"You're working yourself up for nothing. Relax. Breathe. Everything will go fine." He stopped her before she could make another pointless trip down the stairs in search of her cell phone that she already placed in her bag an hour ago. His hands were on her shoulders and he started massaging them. Karen felt herself finally beginning to relax and think for a second on more than just pleasing everyone and not forgetting anything vital.

Wait! Suntan lotion! Karen started to rush to the bathroom, but only made it a half step before Chase's solid arms locked her in.

"And where do you think you're going?" He asked before sighing and reluctantly letting go. Karen picked up on his mood and sensed something was off.

"Okay, what's on your mind?" Karen walked past him and sat down beside him on their bed, forgetting the lotion for a moment.

"It's just you have been a little distant lately and now your going away. I miss you." Karen was surprised and confused. She hadn't been aware of anything different between them.

"I'm not even gone yet and it's just for the day." She said, slightly concerned. The seriousness in Chase was real; Karen slipped her hand into his on the bed and held it in her lap. Chase managed a half smile, but it just came off like her was trying too hard. Karen waited.

"That's not what I meant." He took Karen's free hand in his and they faced each other. "Lately when I wake up at night I noticed you gone, and last week you didn't come back to bed all night. You spend long hours at your computer and I can tell something is bothering you but you wont tell me what it is. I haven't asked because I'm afraid and you clearly don't want to talk about it. Just tell me. Is it me?" He looked upset.

"What! It absolutely, positively is NOT you. But you're right, there is something I should tell you but I'm scared how you're going to react." Chase looked unsure, but his mood noticeably picked up.

"Try me." Karen did not want to be having this conversation but it had to be done.

"That night I didn't come back to bed something happened, and I didn't say anything because it sounds crazy." Chase gave her a patient look, which encouraged her to go on. "I woke up because I heard the piano, when I went to check it out I saw something. I mean I thought I saw something but I couldn't have. It's impossible. I must have been sleepwalking and dreaming the whole thing, but somehow I ended up in the basement and I thought I was locked in. I slept there all night and by the time I got out it was already morning." Karen looked down, ashamed and humiliated and waited for Chase to tell her how clinically insane she was being. Instead he burst out laughing a deep bellowing laugh that was usually reserved for drunken nights out with friends.

"That's where you were! Wha-what did you sleep on?" He continued to laugh between syllables. Karen didn't know how to react; she was at a loss for words so she answered truthfully.

"On the bean bag chair we had in our old apartment." She said in embarrassment. Chase eventually calmed himself down but he was smiling now and he meant it this time.

"So what do you think you saw."

"Jennifer St. Clair's murder."

2

"Thirteen…fourteen…fifteen."   Karen muttered silently as she completed the head count. Melinda and Mathew were still tallying their classes as they lined up on the sidewalk. The parent volunteers were standing by the coach bus watching the group excitedly. No one travelled to New York City before and the energy was high. Melinda moved her sixth grade class onto the bus first since they were oldest and would sit in the back. Karen's class was next and her students ran past her to claim their seats.

"Hi Mrs. Hunter," said Karen as she approached her parent volunteer. She hadn't been pleased when she discovered it would be Sarah's mother but was not surprised. Mimi Hunter appeared to be pleasant and easy to talk to in person but Karen knew it was an act. She forgot about the brutal phone incident and extended the woman the best smile she could fake as they talked briefly about expectations of the day.

The sidewalk in front of the school emptied of students and Karen and Mimi were the last to board the bus. She cringed as Mimi took the seat beside her daughter Sarah, leaving Karen to sit in the last seat available beside Mathew. She sighed in frustration as she settled in for a long ride. At least the bus driver already had been given a pile of movies to allow her a reason to be silent.

"Are you happy to be going home?" *Oh no*, he's *talking to me.* Karen thought before turning in her seat to look at Mathew, he was smiling and looked his usual friendly self.

"Kind of, I haven't been back to the city since me and my husband moved out here, but this town is my home now," said

Karen, but as soon as it was out of her mouth she realized that she wasn't completely over the city just yet. Manhattan will always be the familiar of home to her.

"Don't you miss it?" It was clear Mathew was set on having a conversation so she decided to make the best of it.

"Parts of it, but there are parts I don't." Karen did miss the high-energy atmosphere and she missed going out and buying something without the entire town knowing about it, but she also liked the slow pace of the country too. Manhattan certainly had its flaws. No one trusted one another and everyone led very private lives. Karen had more close friends in the small town than she's ever had in the big city.

"So you really don't mind the small town. It always seemed like your husband dragged you out here." Karen was stunned at Mathew's bluntness. Who was he to make observations on their marriage? How did he even know anything about their home life? It just struck Karen as very odd. Mathew always was giving her the creeps. She couldn't help but be a little snippy in her answer.

"No, I like the country and we both decided equally to move here." Mathew, knowing he struck a chord turned back to look out the window, finally leaving Karen to pretend she wasn't sitting beside the person she quite possibly hated most in the world. The bus pulled away out of the parking lot and Melinda got up and made her way to the front of the bus.

"Hey! Listen up everybody! Yes, that means you Derrick!" She said and sounds of excited students began to die down. "We have about two hours before we get into the city—" Melinda was cut off by sounds of cheering. "So that's about time for one movie. The choices are Grease, for those that don't know it's a musical, like one we will be seeing later on today. The other movie is The Wizard of Oz. So raise your hands when I hold up the movie you want to see." Melinda took turns holding up both movies and took a tally of the hands. It was clear more students wanted to watch The Wizard of Oz. Karen thought it was a good choice because they had tickets to see the musical Wicked on Broadway later.

A few minutes later the mini TV screens above their heads were playing the song 'Somewhere over the Rainbow' and the students quieted down a few pegs. She was just settling down for a nap when Mathew nudged her in the side.

"What?" She said and Mathew held out a bag of jellybeans for her.

"Want some?" Jelly Beans happened to be Karen's favorite candy and they were impossible to say no too.

"Yes, thank you," said Karen as she grabbed a big handful out of the bag. She looked over at Mathew to see if she was taking too much but he was smiling.

"Your welcome. Just help yourself if you want more. I never travel light on candy." Mathew laughed. "Just make sure you don't let any of the pint-sized see." Karen nodded and looked around. Most of the students were enjoying the movie and a couple had already started napping, which was to be expected for six in the morning. *Maybe this won't be such a terrible ride after all.*

3

Karen fell asleep within the first fifteen minutes on the road. She looked peaceful and Mathew didn't want to disturb her. Despite the rocky start to the day, Mathew felt he was doing well in persuading Karen to give him a chance. It was luck that she sat beside him on the bus–he planned it that way but so many factors were involved he hadn't counted on it working. He was surprised at the coldness in her since she was always warm and friendly to everyone. He even noticed she was friendly to Mimi, even if he could tell it was feigned. That didn't surprise him; Mimi was not an easy to deal with parent. She was over protective and very involved in her daughter's life. He dealt with her regularly the year before when Sarah was in his class.

Mathew got a hint that Karen might not like him, and he feared it would be a problem. Mathew was liked by everyone, he didn't know how to deal with this scenario. The Jelly Beans were a great ice breaker like he hoped and Karen softened a little towards him. He would have to tread carefully. Baby steps.

"Jennifer," mumbled Karen softly in her sleep and she stirred slightly. The name instantly peaked Mathews attention. What was Karen dreaming about? Maybe there was a deeper reason she didn't seem to like him and thwarted all his advances. Karen moved a bit more in her now restless sleep and rolled onto him. Mathew didn't try to move her back and enjoyed the new closeness.

When they reached the tunnel into Manhattan Melinda once again made her way to the front of the bus. The movie just finished playing and the screens returned to black. Many of the students that drifted off to sleep began waking up. As Melinda passed Mathew and Karen's seat she gave Mathew a reproving look before stopping to address the students. The coach bus stopped as it hit traffic entering the city and it jolted Karen awake. She opened her eyes quickly and sat up before looking over at Mathew horrified.

"I'm sorry, how long was I sleeping on you?" said Karen apologetically after getting her bearings.

"Not long. No worries." Mathew replied, Karen wasn't hiding her disturbed look very well and he frowned realizing he was only giving her more reasons to build up her wall further. "Really it was only like thirty seconds, I was about to wake you up." He lied but it seemed to calm Karen down slightly.

"Sorry," said Karen again and turned to watch Melinda who was waiting to speak. The traffic was increasing and it took Melinda's whole speech before they came out of the tunnel into Manhattan. The buildings took him by surprise and awed many of the students. Mathew couldn't help but notice Karen's smile and the way her eyes lit up with pure joy. He could really see her as the city girl now that Karen was back in her natural environment.

4

As soon as Karen made her way onto the street the feeling of home engulfed her. She missed it even if she denied it to herself up to this point. The students came off the bus in groups and were pushing their way onto the street in front of a Starbucks. They couldn't get into New York fast enough. Many were looking up in awe over the height of the buildings.

"Does this feel like home yet?" asked Melinda coming to stand beside her. Mathew was the unfortunate one that was tasked with rounding up the students. He wasn't helping as he just increased their energy level with jokes but Karen didn't protest. She felt just as excited as the kids.

"Yes, and I'm so glad to be back. I never did thank you for inviting me to join you on the trip." Melinda got an uncomfortable look on her face and Karen knew she had stepped onto awkward territory. She'd forgot she worried about Mathew's involvement once before but it was a thought that slipped her mind.

"Um…I thought you knew that Mathew was the one who wanted you. We were originally planning on asking Kevin to help chaperone." Melinda looked down at her feet. Karen felt weird as she noticed Mathew watching her, and she got angry as it clicked in her head. Suddenly it made perfect sense. "Um, I'm sorry I shouldn't have told you. You're not mad at me are you?" Melinda asked.

"No, I'm not mad at YOU." Karen clarified between gritted teeth. She was still glaring angrily at Mathew, who now had wrangled the kids into three lines and was chatting with the parents. He didn't seem to notice Karen's evil stare, which just aggravated her further. "We probably should get some food into these kids." Karen said, and turned to see Melinda was about to say something. Melinda looked a little troubled but after a few seconds of silence she went on as nothing was exchanged between them and took the first group of students into Starbucks for breakfast, leaving Karen confused.

Melinda definitely was about to say something important and Karen wanted to know what it was. She pushed the thought out of her mind and temporarily forced herself to forget her troubles and enjoy the day. Karen took half of her class into the café. *Coffee, that's what I need.* Soon all the teachers and parent chaperones had taken their group to get food and everyone was seated at the tables. It was quiet as the students ate quickly and the adults sipped at their long awaited caffeine fix. After ten minutes the noise level went back up and Karen knew the class was ready to move on. It was almost time for their Top of the Rock adventure. It was the first big event on the day's itinerary.

She was excited. Chase and her went to the Top of the Rock on their third date and it was full of good memories. The view from there was fantastic and the weather was perfect and not too cold or windy.

"Time to go!" Mathew called and pointed to his watch. Karen started to gather students and usher them out the door and back onto the busy sidewalk, while trying hard to not block anyone from passing. It was a losing battle. They crossed the road at a crosswalk and made it down into the tunnels with Karen leading the way. She explained to the group how the Rockefeller building worked. They quickly saw Rockefeller square, her and Chase had just been there last Christmas. It was their last big Manhattan event before the move into the smaller town.

They went in groups up the large elevator; Karen's group of eight was first this time round since Karen was acting as tour guide. At the top her students immediately ran towards the edge and looked out. The view was as spectacular as she remembered. The wind picked up at the top, which made one of the girls in her group nervous. Mimi's seven students were next up and soon the class was reunited. Mimi produced a camera and they all got a group photo of everyone jumping at once. It turned out pretty cool and looked like they were flying. Karen took out her digital camera and got a couple scenic shots overlooking central park. She didn't take many because this was far from her first time. Karen ran into Mathew on the second level and he noticed her right away.

"Want to take a picture together?" He asked and pointed to his brand new digital camera that looked expensive.

"No thanks, I've already got lots," said Karen politely.

"But I bet none of them have this smile in them?" said Mathew and wittingly pointed to his face, which dawned a cheesy grin and dimples. Karen giggled not knowing how to react.

"No they don't." She agreed.

"Come on, just one picture," said Mathew once more and one of the students overheard him.

"Come on Mrs. Williams, get in the picture." Karen couldn't say no to the young boy and stood uncomfortably beside Mathew and smiled her fake camera smile.

"Say cheese!" Mathew pointed the camera at them, holding it at arms length away. It flashed in Karen's face, blinding her temporarily and made her see black spots.

"That's bright," said Karen, squinting her eyes.

"That it is," said Mathew, as if blinding her was a good thing.

"Can I get my picture with you?" The boy that had spoken earlier asked and that sparked an interest in the other students. Soon the Top of the Rock turned into a photo studio. Luckily they were the only ones there because of the early hour of the morning.

They made there way down to the gift shop and students bought some cheap souvenirs to bring home. Karen didn't buy anything for herself but just looked around at what there was to offer. Nothing seemed to catch her eye.

"Okay, time to get back on the bus." Mathew called once they had all got what they wanted from the gift shop. Karen almost giggled when she noticed Sarah and Mimi sporting matching t-shirts. Once all of the six groups of students were present they made there way back onto the street and Karen got her class together for yet another head count. Next up was going to be a tour through the Natural History Museum. She had shown her class the movie 'Night in the Museum' the week before to get her class excited and even Karen was looking forward to this portion of the day.

5

Melinda didn't like what she was seeing. Karen was confusing her and it kept taking her mind off of the wonderful trip they were having. It was only a week or so ago that Karen had told her she didn't like Mathew and she was so relieved to have someone on the same page. Melinda was suspicious of the inner goings on of the school board and knew something wasn't right. Maggie Elsing left her job with no explanation to the staff, which was odd but not unrealistic. Maybe she was under a lot of stress? She had been distant and possibly colder than usual in the weeks before. Melinda was willing to overlook Maggie's departure but something about Mathew struck her funny and set off her women's intuition.

Everyone loved Mathew and yes, he was easily likeable in a boyish way. He was fun with his students and a great teacher. He was certainly never principal material, but Melinda completely detested the way the teachers just accepted him as the new boss without question. Catherine and Karen were the only ones visibly angered by the developments and Melinda was glad not everyone was fooled. She liked Karen and hoped they would get to talk more, but now she couldn't help but notice Karen was chummy with Mathew. It kept gnawing at her mind. *Were they together?*

First it was Karen sleeping on Mathew's shoulder and then she saw them take a picture together at the Top of the Rock. They seemed on more than good terms. Nothing made sense anymore. What was going on? Melinda didn't put Karen as the type of girl to fool around, she always pictured her the conservative professional type. She just didn't like the way Mathew looked at Karen.

Melinda decided it was probably best if she shut her mouth and tried to enjoy the rest of her trip. Karen and Mathew's relationship meant nothing to her. She just thought she found someone on her side, but maybe Karen was more complicated than she pictured. She did hang out with drama queen Catherine after all. A part of her wanted to confront Karen about Mathew and ask her why she told her she was on her side when it seemed now she really wasn't. She almost did once before when they were at Starbucks but Melinda never got her chance and at the time but it was probably for the best.

6

"This is cool!" One of Mathew's fourth graders said once they reached Central Park. One of the parent chaperones offered to bring blankets and they quickly spread them out in a quiet grassy area. Earlier the students had a chance to choose a place to get lunch and now they were sitting down and quietly eating. Karen was happy the day had been a success so far but it was starting to overwhelm her. She was tired already and needed a much-deserved break. After scarfing down a burger she had purchased from her favorite corner stand she left her students with Mimi and went for a walk along Central Park. They were close to a fountain she really liked and you could see the skyscrapers when you sit along the edge.

Karen watched the people walk by and relished in the moment she created. This was New York. This was home. She closed her eyes and let the sunbeam down on her shoulders and chest as she relaxed. She knew the students were just beyond the trees and if anything happened she would hear it. Footsteps approached and stopped just before her and Karen snapped alert. Mathew momentarily escaped his students and must have been watching her leave the others.

"You know we shouldn't be here," said Mathew taking a seat beside her. Karen forgot he was her boss until that moment and had a second of panic until she saw the kind look on his face.

"Your not going to fire me, are you?" She joked, already knowing that she was safe. Mathew laughed.

"No, I just came to see what you were up to. Are you okay? It must be overwhelming coming back like this. I know you haven't been here since you moved out of the city." Mathew was being genuine and for once Karen felt comfortable speaking to him.

"Really I'm fine. It's great being back here and all and it definitely will always feel like home but I like moments like this." She looked around at the empty section of park. "It's quiet and peaceful and you can even hear the birds. I realize now that I miss it but I needed an escape. I'm living right where I need to be for the moment." Karen smiled, her thoughts poured out of her before she really had a chance to think about it. She knew she was right. The city was amazing but what she needed and wanted was an escape. Central Park was always one of her favorite places. She liked to go to a quiet and deserted section and just take a break to think for a while. Karen knew this trip was good for her in more ways than one and she was thankful to Mathew for recommending her, even if his motives were not to be completely trusted.

"This place is nice," said Mathew and that's when Karen noticed he moved closer to her when hadn't been paying attention. Their legs were now touching and she could feel his breath on her shoulder when he talked. How could she have missed that? Karen grew uncomfortable again. Her first instinct was to jump up but she fought it not wanting to insult him. She pretended she didn't notice. "There isn't anyone around to see us," said Mathew softly and as he did so his hand moved to graze her inner thigh. Karen instantly grabbed it and pushed his hand away before jumping up infuriated.

"What the hell do you think you're doing?" She screamed at him, shocked. Mathew looked surprised and to Karen's relief remained seated on the fountain. Karen wanted to say more but she stormed back to her students flabbergasted and disgusted. Mathew didn't follow her.

7

After Karen stormed off Mathew sat alone on the fountain and recollected himself. Just where did he go wrong? Mathew was foreign to rejection and despite knowing Karen was not an easy target he had not expected her to reject him. This was somehow different than when Maggie left him in the very public scene at the restaurant. When Maggie dumped him he had grown tired of her and was ready to move on. Mathew knew he didn't handle the situation well because he allowed the tables to be turned. Mathew let the relationship go on because he enjoyed the power behind the affair. It was his fault it ended badly, it was a mistake.

The blackmailed pictures were a ploy and nothing more than a fun desperate game. He did originally intend to use them for leverage if he needed something, same as he manipulated his way into yet another position of power. They still sat in the bottom drawer of his desk that he kept locked and to his knowledge only him and the custodian had the key.

Karen didn't take long to garner his attention, she was the new girl and fresh meat but yet his attraction was deeper than that. He genuinely liked Karen unlike he ever felt for any other woman before. He didn't know how to deal with his feelings and Karen's cold attitude both frustrated and confused him. Now he screwed up and Karen was never going to trust him again. He felt sure of it.

It felt like hours passed as he sat in Central Park after his plan failed. In reality only minutes ticked by but it was still long enough to require Mathew to resume his supervising duties. He was the principal and he needed to set a good example, even if he was growing to despise his new job title.

8

The theatre was packed with people going every which way waiting for the doors to open so they could be seated. Karen took the time to buy herself a mug that said 'Wicked' on it. She had a collection going from musicals she had seen on Broadway. Karen never saw 'Wicked' but was very familiar with the story line. Her students were excited but the long day had worn most of them out and everyone was starting to crash. It was a good thing they would be sitting down for the next few hours. Times Square at night was next and then the two-hour bus ride back into town. With all the excitement of the days events Karen couldn't help but want nothing more than to crawl up next to Chase in their bed and sleep for hours. At least tomorrow was Saturday.

After what seemed like an eternity of waiting, the doors opened and the group of students was led into the breath taking theatre, towards their seats. They were seated together on the second tier and everyone had a good unobstructed view of the stage. The thick curtain was drawn and besides from the chatter of the other audience members the atmosphere was calm. Karen waited until all her students were seated where they wanted to be and left her aisle seat to go on search of the washroom. Melinda got up from the other end and got Karen's attention, she pointed towards the exit and Karen nodded and waited for Melinda to get by the group of students.

"Your going to the bathroom?" She asked when she finally made it into the aisle.

"Yes, I think we have a while before the show starts."

"Twenty minutes," said Melinda after checking her watch.

"Good because I've been waiting all day!" said Karen and started up the stairs to the closest exit sign.

"Me too." The two teachers made it back out to the now nearly empty lobby and it didn't take them long to find the women's washroom without swarms of people blocking entranceway.

"Can I ask you something and you give me an honest answer?" said Melinda timidly but serious. Karen was washing her hands and didn't notice Melinda came out of the stall before her. She walked over and took a paper towel to dry her hands.

"Sure, ask anything?" said Karen concerned, the heavy mood made her uncomfortable and she didn't like how Melinda watched her every move.

"What's up with you and Mathew?" said Melinda, more demanding than she had been two seconds before. The question took Karen off guard; she was not prepared for that. Karen's mind instantly turned to the blackmail picture. Melinda couldn't have known about it did she?

"Me and Mathew. Well I don't like him that much. Actually hate may be closer to the word I'm looking for. Especially after today." Karen's anger was once again boiling over as she found herself back on the fountain in Central Park, spilling her guts openly and giving Mathew the opportunity to think it was acceptable to make a move on a married women. Karen watched Melinda cautiously and knew she wasn't convinced. *What the hell does she want?*

"It's just I've been watching you two together all day and it doesn't seem like that to me at all! You have a husband Karen!" Karen almost snorted. Now she was well past angry. Who was she to accuse her of infidelity? Mathew! God, she hated Mathew! "That's all I have to say. I didn't mean to upset you. I'm going to go now." Melinda awkwardly started towards the door and Karen still furious took a moment to realize if Melinda left now, she would never believe the truth. Karen caught up to Melinda and grabbed her shoulder harshly and spun her around.

"No!" She practically yelled in the poor woman's face. "You are going to stay here and hear the truth." Karen was still talking very loudly and firmly, unaware that she was terrifying Melinda.

"Um, excuse us." Karen noticed the parent volunteer from Mathew's class and a very shy girl; she believed was named Samantha standing in the doorway. The volunteer gave Karen a disapproving glare and she was suddenly embarrassed.

"Sorry Pamela," said Melinda. She was faster on her feet than Karen to save the situation. Melinda, now having regained her composure led them outside the bathroom and into a corner of the lobby. "Okay, I'm listening," said Melinda, clearly expecting Karen to start blabbering of her affair, which did not exist. Karen didn't let it bother her again and took a deep breath to calm her nerves. This would be a civilized conversation for the sake of the students.

"Melinda there really is no affair. I can't even stand being around Mathew, the whole idea is ridiculous!"

"I saw you sitting on the bus earlier and you were sleeping on his shoulder. Then later you were taking pictures together and you looked like you were getting along. Then what finally convinced me was when you disappeared at lunch and I saw Mathew go after you. I assumed you planned on meeting. It's just too suspicious Karen! What am I supposed to think?"

"First off, I didn't want to sit with Mathew earlier, I even suspect he may have worked it that way on purpose! I fell asleep on the bus and I must have rolled over and ended up on his shoulder but he told me it was only for a minute. I don't know how you could have seen that! At the Top of the Rock Mathew asked if he could take a picture with me and I denied him. I only did it when a student wanted me too. It was impossible to say no! The park was a surprise to me. I left because I needed time alone away from the students. Mathew followed me and we did talk. He asked me about living in New York and for some reason I opened up to him. I realize now I shouldn't of because he took that as a sign it would be okay to try to make a move on me. I freaked out on him and he left me alone. I can't get that moment out of my head! Mathew has always made me feel uncomfortable and after today he scares me a little. Please don't let me have to be alone with him again! Karen was starting to get emotional as she divulged her feelings to Melinda. She wiped at her eyes that started watering against her will.

"I'm sorry," said Melinda kindly seeing Karen's genuine reaction. "I was way out of line earlier."

"I wont hold it against you, I believe you were just trying to help," said Karen, and she checked her cell phone for the time. "We only have a few minutes left."

"Okay, but I think we should probably talk more later. Mathew can't keep getting away with this!" Karen was glad Melinda now sat planted firmly on her side.

"Thank you," said Karen and she hugged Melinda before they went back through the theatre doors. Just as they entered the theatre lights dimmed and spotlights illuminated the stage. Karen easily made it back to her seat without attracting attention but Melinda had more difficulty making it to the other end of her row. Karen checked that

Pamela and Samantha both were already back in their seats. Pamela caught her glance and made eye contact. She clearly still didn't approve of the scene she inadvertently walked into. Karen ducked a little deeper into her seat in embarrassment and tried to empty her mind and watch the show.

Background music was playing and the curtain was opened as the audience watched in silent anticipation.

9

Times Square was stunning at night and was almost overwhelming to his over tired brain. Mathew was ready to call it quits and her couldn't push himself out of his funk since the lunchtime failure. He looked around and most of the students appeared as exhausted as he felt. One day Mathew was going to come back here again and enjoy the sights without his chaperoning duties. At least he was being paid for the day unlike the parent volunteers who probably dealt with the same problems he faced. The never ending class head counts were beginning to annoy him but had saved him a few times. Conner got lost when he got distracted at a particularly intriguing exhibit at the museum. The others moved on without him, which caused for a few minutes of panic.

Karen was on his mind and she was sure to keep her distance. Mathew didn't even blame her. He would call it a win if she kept the incident to herself. Now that he was principal he really couldn't face that kind of gossip as he did when he was a teacher. Now he understood Maggie's reasoning and she loved her job. He found new respect for the woman and almost felt bad for the troubles he caused her. The nagging feeling he was the reason for Maggie's departure was another thing to repress in his mind. Mathew felt as if he was destroying more things than ever lately and it may have started to get to him. He used to feel he helped people but what was he really doing?

It was a relief when the coach bus was in sight and after a quick talk with the driver; he was able to load all the students. They sat in the same places as the morning and Mathew hoped he would get a chance to at the very least talk to Karen about what happened. He needed to know she wouldn't tell anyone. Mathew didn't picture Karen for the gossiping type, she was more secretive and the most genuine person he knew.

Mathews hopes were dashed when Karen brushed past him on the bus to sit at the very back in Melinda's old seat. Melinda replaced Karen beside him, she bore a serious expression and Mathew didn't bother trying to make conversation. He leaned on the window and tried to get comfortable as the bus pulled away from the side of the road. The movie 'Grease' came on the TV screens and the students found enough renewed energy to sing along to the songs they knew, or tried to by mumbling along to the words.

Once the traffic out of Manhattan thinned Melinda softened her demeanor a bit and gleefully sung along to many of the songs. Mathew guessed she supplied this movie, since it appeared to be a favorite of hers. Mathew knew Karen must have had to orchestrate the seat switch up and he wondered how she managed it. It was possible that Melinda was doing Karen a favour because she knew of his mistake. He wondered but doubted it. Karen wasn't a friend to

Melinda and they didn't exchange words often. Pamela even said that she walked in on the two women arguing in the washroom. Certainly they didn't get along. He became increasingly confident that Karen would stay quiet as the drive went on. If she did say anything it wasn't going to be to Melinda.

As the bus drove through the neighboring cities Mathew feared Karen would immediately go to her husband. He couldn't have that and didn't want to deal with it. Plans began to form to intercept the problem before it left the premises, a new challenge with less of a reward as the lunch one did. Hopefully this challenge would prove more successful.

10

The bus stopped in the parking lot and Karen watched happily as a swarm of excited parents waved to their children. She was relieved that her day was almost over. By the looks of it most of the parents were waiting to pick up their kids and she wouldn't have to stand around in the dark for long. It was only eleven-thirty but the day of stress and the early morning did her in. She looked over at her car in the parking lot and longed to be able to drive it back to her home and crawl into bed beside Chase. It was only one day but she already missed Chase. It occurred to her that she was going to have to tell him about Mathew. He already knew that he made her uncomfortable but now she had something major to tell him. Karen didn't know how Chase was going to react.

Karen watched as one by one her students found their parents and left the grounds. The chaos was finally fading away. The lights from the streetlights illuminated the parking lot but it was a little eerie as the people left. Mathew and Melinda both stood with the remains of their classes. Karen was still waiting on three parents to show up, a look at her cell phone told her it was five to midnight. *Hurry up!* She mentally screamed at herself in frustration. As if on cue a minivan sped into the parking lot and two students left. One of them was from Karen's class. *There's only two more to go.* By midnight Melinda had gone home and she was left uncomfortably with Mathew.

A few minutes of awkward silence passed, neither one of them looking at the other. Karen's remaining student sat at the curve and looked a little nervous. She felt for the poor kid, being the last to be picked up was never fun. Mathew's student was next to leave and finally Karen's remaining student jumped up in excitement as a very apologetic woman opened the door and gave Karen a quick wave. She looked embarrassed and drove off quickly. Karen would have done a happy dance if she could muster up the energy. Mathew, even now relieved of his chaperoning duties didn't head immediately towards his truck. Karen felt uneasy and pulled out her cell to tell Chase she was on her way home. He quickly replied back with a smiley face, which meant he was still waiting up. Karen smiled but it was short lived because she noticed Mathew watching her.

The parking lot seemed to grow longer and longer as she walked away. Mathew's eyes bore into her back and he started walking in the same direction. It seemed as if he was following her, but his truck was parked near her so he probably wasn't. Mathew was just going home. That had to be it, no reason to be paranoid. Karen didn't even believe herself and she jumped as one of the streetlights flickered and nearly burnt out. *Nothing is going to happen, nothing is going to happen,* she played on a loop in her mind. Mathew's truck was up ahead and Karen slowed down to make sure he was going to get in. Karen breathed a sign of relief as Mathew unlocked his truck and opened the driver's door slowly. Karen stood alone in the parking lot hoping to watch as he pulled away but instead the truck stopped in front of her car blocking her exit. The passenger window rolled down and Karen tensed up and her feet felt welded into place, betraying her instinct to run.

"I need to talk to you," said Mathew coldly, and it was an order, not a request.

"There is nothing to talk about! Can you please move your truck?" said Karen firmly, and she was amazed at how steady her voice felt.

"I'm not leaving until you get in the truck so we can talk." Mathew leaned over the seat and pushed his passenger door open towards her.

"I'm not getting in," said Karen angrily. "I told my husband that I'm on my way home. If I don't show up soon he'll come down here." She threatened.

"This will only take a moment. I want to apologize." For a brief moment Mathew softened and became less intimidating. Karen accessed the situation, not liking where this was going. Mathew took advantage of her hesitation and became the deciding factor as he shut off his truck and took the keys out of the ignition. He put them down on his passenger seat. "You don't trust me." He accused, and looked genuinely hurt. Karen didn't buy it but against her better judgment she stepped up into the truck, making sure that she sneakily slipped Mathews keys in her pocket before closing the door.

"Mathew this isn't right, you know that?" Karen scolded as if talking to a student. Mathew looked around awkwardly as if he wasn't comfortable with this anymore. *Good!* Karen thought, at least this wasn't his normal. She took in her surroundings and noticed the truck was clean, an unexpected surprise. The only garbage was an empty cup of coffee in the cup holder and a pair of sunglasses on the dashboard. It wasn't what she expected of a man's car. Everything was almost like brand new.

"I'm sorry you feel uncomfortable now. It shouldn't be that way between us. It really doesn't have to be. I was wrong and I know that but can we start over? I mean start over as friends?" To Karen his apology seemed sincere but she wasn't going to ever allow herself to trust Mathew. Not now, not ever. Karen's cell phone vibrated in her hand. She was clenching it tightly in her right fist, out of Mathew's line of vision. Her knuckles went white and as it went off it startled her. She tried to ignore it but she wanted desperately to check on the message. It had to be Chase.

"Mathew we can't be friends. You made sure of that."

"I need to know what I did, and I know earlier in the park I was in the wrong. What was it that I did before that to make you not like me?" Mathew seemed vulnerable, and he shocked Karen by the outburst of honesty.

"I know about your affair!" It slipped out. She clasped her hands to her mouth and she dropped her cell onto the floor by her feet. She dared to glance at Mathew and couldn't tell what he was thinking, but he almost looked angry. Mathew moved closer and Karen quickly jumped towards the door, preparing to attack if necessary. She was quickly embarrassed as Mathew merely bent down and handed her the phone. The screen turned on and claimed the unread text was from Melinda and not Chase. Mathew and Karen shared a look, a mental apology on both sides.

"How?" Mathew questioned after the awkwardness passed. He was calm but unpredictable.

"You were walking down the hall and dropped a paper on the ground. I went to pick it up for you and was meaning to return it. That was until I saw the picture." Mathew exhaled and seemed to be working hard to maintain his composure.

"You didn't show anyone?" He questioned, an edge had leaked into his voice.

"No." Karen answered without thinking, "I mean yes, but no one that would have caused Mrs. Elsing her job, I swear!"

"Well, who then?" Mathew was angry now and no longer trying to hide it.

"Chase and Catherine are the only ones who have seen it. I told Tammy about it but she hasn't actually seen it?"

"Tammy who?" This stumped Mathew; guess they weren't as close as she thought. Karen decided to play it safe.

"She's a friend from out of town." Mathew softened a little.

"Are you one hundred percent sure Catherine didn't go to the school board?"

"Yes, I destroyed the picture after that so there was no evidence. Mrs. Elsing quit her job on her own terms. If you cared so much about that, I probably wouldn't have brought that picture to school in the first place!" Karen accused.

"Can I have my keys back?" Karen stepped out of the truck and backed a few paces away before throwing them at Mathew. She watched as Mathew turned his truck around and was about to leave the parking lot. As he passed her the second time she caught a glimpse of something in his side mirror that sent shivers down her spine. Where it should have shown Mathew's reflection was something with almost solid black eyes.

Something she would not soon forget.

Broken Glass

1

Mathew mentally cursed himself as he sped off towards his apartment. *Stupid! Stupid!* He realized the moment he left the parking lot of the school that he let himself get distracted from his goal. Instead of threatening Karen to keep her silence, he let his emotions get the better of him. Karen must be headed home right now to go tell her husband what happened, no sense turning back now. Even if by some miracle she were still there he would look like a bigger idiot than he already felt. For once in his life, Mathew realized he might have real repercussions to his actions. That was his second failure of the day.

"It's too late now," said Mathew to himself as he parked outside 'Morgan's.' The bar crowd was in full swing and for a moment Mathew considered letting his sorrows drown at the bottom of a glass of scotch. The bar called to him but the drunks arguing by the doorway were a sufficient deterrent. The bouncer was nowhere to be seen and it looked like a fistfight might start at any moment. Instead Mathew started up to his second story apartment. The back of Morgan's was empty except for a young couple smoking marijuana. They watched as Mathew unlocked his door and retreated to his bachelor pad.

<h3 style="text-align:center">2</h3>

Karen sped home still fuming from her interaction with Mathew. She also worried about Chase; he had a right to know what was going on. Mathew went way too far this time and he wouldn't get away with it. Karen put her car into park and slammed the door angrily on her way out. The house was unlocked and the outside lights were left on waiting for her. Karen hoped Chase was still awake, but she didn't expect him to be. The conversation with Mathew held her up another fifteen minutes and it was getting closer to one in the morning.

Before Karen managed to get inside her cell phone buzzed again and Karen remembered Melinda texted her earlier which was very odd. The first message read: *R U OK?* Karen didn't understand but assumed it probably had something to do with being left alone with Mathew. Melinda's second message was even more confusing. *We NEED to talk ASAP!!* Karen felt a twinge of uneasiness in her stomach. Surely Melinda wasn't texting her at this time to have a calm discussion about how their boss was a psychopath. It had to be something more important; Melinda was a reasonable woman who wasn't into the gossip scene nearly as bad as the rest of the town. Something must be wrong.

Karen texted: *tomorrow ok?* It was less than ten seconds later the reply came: *Tonight if possible. Doesn't matter how late.* Karen felt the seriousness of Melinda and her stomach dropped. *OK just got home, will call at 2.* This better be important. Melinda hit send and put her phone back in her purse. She jumped as the door swung open before she looked up.

"I thought I heard you out here. At least I hoped it was you," said Chase happily. So he did wait up for her. "What happened, you look like your dog just died or something?" said Chase, with a serious tone. Karen looked at his concerned look for two seconds and instantly lost control. The tears welled up in her eyes then the sobs came and Karen had no energy to fight them back. Chase said nothing and pulled her inside closing the door before they woke up Shannon and Jim across the way. Once inside Karen dropped to a ball, not caring about her dignity anymore. Chase didn't know what to do and he sat down beside her on the floor and tried to put his arm around her. Karen just shrugged it off which worried Chase.

"I'm sorry," said Karen eventually and wiped tears from her face. She looked at Chase and she felt horrible for making him worry. The conversation they had the night before weighed on her mind. What if Chase thought she wanted to leave him? She had to say something soon, but the words wouldn't formulate. Her brain just jumbled up all the problems up into one big super problem. She exhaled deeply and focused on calming herself. Chase waited patiently, scared by the outburst and knowing there was nothing he could say or do to help the situation, what ever it may be.

"Mathew tried to seduce me today." She began with, Chase didn't say anything and it made Karen feel worse. He couldn't possibly think something was going on, would he? "I yelled at him but he terrifies me! I'm so scared he is going to do something. He followed me to my car and he said things to me…I…I think something isn't right about Mathew. I saw something. Something evil." Karen started to feel her emotions well up inside her again threating to burst out. Remembering the dark shadow and its coal black eyes was making her nervous just thinking about it. The hair on the back of her neck was standing up. *Evil was the right word*, Karen thought.

"I'm going to kill him!" said Chase through gritted teeth. "How can he do this to anyone? How can he do this to you?" Chase jumped off the ground and began to pace across the floor fuming. He eventually stopped and leaned on the table, his mind was clearly working on something. "Evil?" Chase questioned and looked back at Karen. She thought once more of the image in the mirror but it became too much and she broke down again. Chase rushed towards her and held her and Karen let him this time.

"There's something else," said Karen and looked up at Chase. "Melinda texted me with something urgent. I told her I would call her a soon as I could."

"No!" said Chase firmly. "You have enough on your plate at the moment, just forget about anything else for a while."

"You are probably right. I need to get some sleep. I want to forget about today." Chase understood and they both cautiously stood up and slowly got ready for bed. Neither spoke much, and they didn't have too. Karen wanted space and time to process and recollect herself. It seemed everything around her was off and maybe she was just going crazy. Karen thought back to all the questionable things she'd seen in the last month, maybe the closest solution was for her to simply question her sanity. Chase tucked her into bed and was noticeably avoiding anything that might draw on another outburst. Karen would have protested but her energy was depleted, as soon as the lights flicked off Karen was unconscious.

3

Chase couldn't sleep. The image of Karen at her emotional breaking point was fresh in his mind, and he couldn't banish them. Chase wondered if he was to blame for this, after all it was his idea to move out to this small town. Karen hadn't been her usual light-hearted self in months. She claimed to see things, hear things and she believed that whatever it was had a message meant just for her. Chase wanted to believe Karen, but even his creative mind couldn't truly believe that she was locked in the basement forced to witness Jennifer's murder all over again. Chase did check the door and the lock was working fine. Nothing in the basement jumped out to him as strange. If Jennifer was murdered down there, whoever cleaned up did a good job. There were no signs of a struggle.

Chase remembered his dreams and his did seem similar to hers. In them he never once saw Jennifer St. Claire like Karen claimed. Chase did believe that Karen wasn't lying to him but he did wonder what was going on. His wife slept soundly in bed beside him, she seemed at peace and looked as innocent as a child. *What is going on in your mind?*

4

History repeating, always misleading.

The circle was nearly complete and the events escaladed to a new high. The action was occurring much faster than it previously did and followed the pattern to a T. The length between appearances was decreasing and the electricity in the air was almost palpable.

The darkness would spread and poison whatever it touched, usually people and sometimes places. Evil feeds on despair, anger and greed and sucks the life out of its victims slowly, making them beg for salvation. She had seen first hand the perils of the darkness and what it can do to a person. She witnessed the horror and felt it's wrath, she was the product of the curse.

Death would be left in the wake of darkness and only death can mark the end. Sacrifice, willing or unwilling, known or not. The stakes were raised and she did not know if the warnings would be enough to spark the battle. The circle must reach an end and its destructive time has come. Anyone could be infected and soon the plague would win.

5

Mathew sensed something was wrong the moment he locked his apartment door behind him. He was being watched. He made a dash for the light switch and bathed his small apartment in light as he quickly searched the obvious hiding places. Nothing was touched, and he was alone. Still, even without a sign of an intruder Mathew felt a presence. The air around him was heavy and he paranoia took over. He double-checked the lock on his front door and on the few windows. Then he quickly got inside his bedroom and barricaded the door. It was nonsense but it made him feel a little better. Then for the first time since his childhood Mathew checked under his bed. He still heard the faint sound of music coming up from the bar. It would soon come to an end but the sounds of life nearby comforted him.

Mathew rested on top of his blankets and closed his eyes. He didn't dare turn out his light and he didn't bother getting undressed. He let himself concentrate on the bass line and he began to drift off into a restless sleep. Mathew only slept for a few minutes but he was startled awake by a buzzing sound that kept increasing steadily in volume. The light in his light bulb was growing brighter and then burnt out completely. The sound was humming like an overflow of electricity and the volume increased steadily until it was too much to bear. Mathew clasped his hands to his ears. *This isn't happening, this isn't happening,* the mantra wasn't helping.

The darkness made him wish he were under his covers, in a blanket sanctuary. He forced himself a quick look but couldn't tell if the barricade in front of his door was still there. He thought it was, but never in his life did his bedroom seem this dark. The air was growing heavy and Mathew felt a pressure in his lungs and his eyes burned as if there were smoke in the air but it didn't smell like smoke. He was suffocating! It felt like someone had just released mustard gas into his room and Mathew knew he was going to die. He felt it, and knew it with utter certainty. The pressure he felt increased and started near the top of his head and push down. It soon felt like it was tearing him limb from limb and the pain. Mathew begged for it to just kill him already. Death would be better than this agony.

Silence. The end came on so suddenly Mathew knew he must be dead. He sat in the nothingness for a while before he dared to open his eyes. The room was still dark but now he could see a little. The barricade was untouched and everything looked normal. Mathew tried to move slightly and felt nothing, the pain was gone and he felt fine. As he made the leap and tried to stand he was overcome with nausea and barely made it into the bathroom before hurling for five straight minutes. He was very much alive or this was what hell must be like. He was shaken and made no effort to question what happened. The bathroom light remained functional and he checked himself in the mirror. However pale, Mathew found he was intact. He opened up the medicine cabinet behind his mirror and dug out two Advil and took them with tap water. He closed the cabinet and was startled by the reflection. He moved closer to the mirror and used his fingers to open his eyes further. They were very bloodshot but the most surprising thing was the mist of darkness that fluttered around in his eyes before moving out of sight. It wasn't obvious but it was there. Mathew backed away quickly. This had to be a dream.

6

Chase woke on Saturday morning to the sound of the doorbell. He rolled over in bed and checked the time, which proclaimed it to be only seven in the morning on the nose. The sound of the rain was audible on the house and he wondered who would be here at this hour on a Saturday. Chase unwilling to leave the warmth of his covers fell back onto his pillow and tried to drift off to sleep again. Karen was still motionless next to him except for the rhythmic sounds of her breathing. He hoped if he waited long enough the brave sole who woke him on a Saturday would just leave. He finally got comfortable again just when the visitor grew impatient and started knocking heavily ignoring the bell.

"All right, I'm coming, I'm coming." Chase grumbled to himself and swung his housecoat on to cover his boxers. He trudged down the stair in a half-asleep stupor and looked out the peephole. It was an unrecognizable woman wearing a yellow rain slicker. Another round of violent knocking pursued and Chase opened the door halfway. The woman was stopped with her arm still raised. She appeared phased by him, clearly not expecting to see a person. "Can I help you?"

"Oh, you're Chase!" The strange blonde woman said. She was older than him by at least five years and was soaking wet. Her expensive looking SUV was parked behind his truck in the driveway. It was covered in mud and looked like it had seen a few puddles on the potholed dirt road, which was Bentley Street.

"Yes, Can I help you?" Chase repeated rather confused. The women looked rattled and seemed almost hyper which contradicted the gloomy weather. She had too much energy for the morning.

"Um, yes. I really need to talk to Karen. She was supposed to call me last night." The woman said rapidly. She kept peering around Chase into their house as if she was looking for something. "Do you think I can come in?" Chase remembered Karen mentioned she needed to call someone. He couldn't remember the name exactly.

"You must be Mel- Melanie?"

"It's Melinda actually." She gave him a half smile and looked around him again.

"Karen's sleeping right now but I can tell her you dropped by."

"Yeah, that's not going to work for me. I REALLY need to speak to Karen. Can't you wake her up?" This woman was stubborn. It was too early for him to deal with this.

"Um, Okay I'll see what I can do." He left the woman outside in the rain, and climbed the stairs to see Karen was already awake. She was sitting up in bed waiting for him.

"Was someone here?" said Karen, a puzzled look on her face.

"Melinda's outside, she said she really needed to talk to you. I get the feeling she is not going to leave until she does," said Chase and he watched the flicker of worry cross Karen's face. "What do you want me to tell her?" The question didn't need an answer because Karen already jumped out of bed and was going for her housecoat and slippers. Chase sensed there was something in the air but he tried to stay out of it.

7

Melinda was pacing along the William's front porch nervously. It was part because the cold air had chilled her to the bone and her jacket was soaked through, and part because she was about to explode if she had to wait any longer. The rain had died down to a slow drizzle but it was pouring when she left the house.

"Melinda?" Karen answered, her hair was disheveled and she donned nothing but a housecoat. Melinda almost felt bad about waking her so early and a pang of jealousness because it was clear that Karen slept.

"You didn't call me!" Melinda complained, and a look of realization crossed Karen's face.

"Sorry, do you want to come in?" Karen asked and backed away from the door. Melinda followed her into the kitchen. She slipped out of her wet coat and instantly felt so much better. Karen offered her a seat at the table. Melinda instinctively took in her new surroundings. Karen's place was nice and cozy and not anything like she expected. The house suited Karen but she was expecting it to be spookier because of the reputation. It was a stupid expectation really. "What did you want to talk about?" said Karen almost robotically.

"I think something is really wrong with Mathew." Said Melinda quickly.

"No shit. He's a lying psychopath that manipulates people to get everything he wants." Karen started to get angry, and it wasn't Melinda but the mention of Mathew. Just the thought of him mad her blood boil.

"No, I mean more than that. I sensed it when I sat next to him yesterday. He scares me," said Melinda and her eyes began to water at the very thought of sitting next to him. Mathew said nothing the entire ride back to the school and he had this look in his eyes. It was a cold calculating stare and there was this horrible feeling she had right down to the pit of her stomach.

"He scares me too but there's not much we can do about it," said Karen and she balled her knuckles into fists on the table in frustration. Melinda sensed she was annoying Karen, maybe she had been wrong to come here. She shouldn't have bothered; it was a stupid idea in the first place. Karen wouldn't understand, but she deserved a warning.

"Maybe not." Melinda answered, "but I think you shouldn't be alone with him. What I felt yesterday reminded me of something my grandpa used to tell me as a child. He used to warn me about a darkness that existed here and that I needed to be careful or the darkness would be able to poison my soul. I never really took my Grandpa's tale seriously. I always thought it was a ploy to keep me out of trouble but what I felt from Mathew can only be described as an evil that consumed him." She waited for Karen to say something, the glazed over look was scaring Melinda. She was afraid Karen would kick her out and get angry. It sounded so stupid, but why did it feel so right saying it?

"I know what you mean, I've had that feeling myself," said Karen slowly. "I'm not really sure what to believe and I sure as hell don't know what to do next?"

"I don't know what to believe either. I don't exactly think my Grandpa was a genius but I couldn't just ignore this. If I'm right, Mathew is very dangerous, particularly for you," said Melinda, she was grateful Karen seemed understanding. She wasn't sure if the roles were reversed if she would have done the same.

"Is there anything else to the story?"

"He said this town was built on blood and suffering and it's the pain that started the curse and set the darkness in motion. I don't really know what it means." Melinda admitted. The town has always been a safe, sheltered place. It was hard for her to picture anything that could have ruined that image.

"Did something happen here? Anything that might give merit to the story?" said Karen thoughtfully. She was being way more open-minded than Melinda expected her to be and it was freaking her out a little bit. This all felt so serious. It was so far-fetched, so absolutely crazy but they were really talking about the possibility of a curse in the small town.

"I don't know. I don't think anyone has ever been murdered here." Melinda remembered the house she was in. "At least anything that has ever been substantiated." Karen looked behind her purposefully but Melinda didn't know what she was looking at. She turned back around with a frown on her face.

"Every place has its secrets," said Karen and Melinda had to agree. If the gossip told her nothing, small town life was no different from the city, except here things were done behind locked doors. Secrets were swept under the proverbial rug and kept from the knowledge of the town. Everyone wanted to maintain the image they had forged for themselves. They were not immune to the horrors of the bigger cities, not completely.

"Can I ask you something?" said Melinda curiously.

"Anything?" said Karen.

"I never expected you to believe me this easily. You can feel it too. You can sense it?"

"I saw something in Mathew. Something I can't explain. I feel something has shifted. Something dark." Karen spoke purposefully and Melinda could see the fear in her eyes as she spoke. She believed what she said, it was clear.

"Karen?" Melinda looked over to see Chase standing just outside the room. He looked uncomfortable and deeply troubled. When Karen didn't speak, he made eye contact with Melinda and she noticed the disapproval in his eyes. He was concerned for his wife, and rightfully so, anyone who listened in to their conversation would have believed them crazy. Melinda hoped they were crazy. She got up and grabbed her coat, which thankfully had dried up during their chat.

"I have to go." She said, Karen awkwardly followed her to the door and they hugged briefly on the front step.

"I'll see you soon," said Karen and Melinda managed a half wave before she got in the driver side of her SUV and backed out of the driveway.

8

Karen watched as Melinda sped awkwardly away, she avoided looking at Chase but she could feel him standing silently behind her. Many emotions started boiling up to the surface, Karen couldn't process what she was feeling. She was reeling from what Melinda brought forward and confused on where she could draw the line from fact to fiction. It was evident on Chase's expression that he was worried and she couldn't face him. Karen couldn't bring herself to look into his judging eyes, knowing he was questioning her mental state. She didn't notice it before but now she was knew without a doubt that she had lost Chase's confidence. It was heart wrenching.

"It's cold outside," said Chase eventually and reached around Karen to close the door, she still wouldn't look at him. They both stood in the entranceway for a while longer awkwardly.

"We need to talk." Karen gave in first, Chase nodded and both moved into the living room and sat down on one of the couches.

"What was that about?" said Chase, and Karen could tell it wasn't what he wanted to say. He was choosing his words carefully. It hurt Karen even more. She wasn't as fragile as he seemed to believe her to be. She wasn't crazy!

"Melinda was just warning me to stay away from Mathew. I agree with the advice," said Karen, "you should too." Karen was making it impossible for Chase to disagree with her, and she needed to make him understand her side. She needed to prove herself.

"Don't patronize me! I know you understand why I'm upset." Chase accused angrily.

"I'm not. I know you think I'm crazy and emotionally unstable and you may even be right," said Karen. "I'm a little stressed and overwhelmed and I don't understand why everything has to happen to me." She realized she was dangerously close to tears. "I do know some things for certain. Mathew is dangerous! He's manipulative and doesn't give a shit about anyone but himself. Melinda is right about that at least."

"Mathew is scum." Chase finally agreed, "But I'm worried you are reading too much into this. You are seeing things that simply aren't there! You are playing detective in a case that doesn't exist and you are really worrying me. Can't you let it go, please, for me?" said Chase, the look on his face ripped Karen to shreds. She could tell how much he was hurting and she could end it. All she had to do was let go, avoid Mathew and pretend nothing else mattered. *Could I do it?* Karen asked herself.

"It will be hard." Karen admitted truthfully, but it wasn't an answer. Chase gave her a serious look and Karen knew he noticed too. Then he squeezed her thigh and she knew for now they would be all right. She hugged him slowly and whispered in his ear. "I'll try" The hug broke and Karen noticed for the first time that she wasn't dressed yet. Melinda had only been there for forty-five minutes and it wasn't even eight O'clock.

"Coffee or back to bed?" Chase asked, getting up from his spot on the couch.

"I don't think I can sleep now," said Karen. "There's too much on my mind." Chase understood and headed into the kitchen to put on a pot of coffee. Karen followed and started putting together ingredients for pancakes on the counter. She needed busy work.

"I'm sorry Karen," said Chase suddenly and he meant it.

"It's okay. I would have been worried too," said Karen while pouring the pancake batter mixture into her frying pan. "I think you scared Melinda, she left fast enough." They both laughed, and it felt good to finally break the tension between them.

"Since when are you two friends? You never really mentioned her much before."

"We bonded over our mutual hatred of Mathew during the trip," said Karen. She remembered the bathroom conversation. *Poor Melinda,* she thought. Karen got the feeling the woman was involving herself in something she would be better off avoiding.

"I still want to kill that guy," Chase muttered.

"Me too." Karen had never hated anyone in her life as much as she hated Mathew Barry right now. Chase went to grab a clean glass from the dishwasher but he fumbled it out of his hands. It shattered on the kitchen floor in a bang. Karen wondered if she was broken like the glass. She decided she wasn't, not yet. She was changed, battered and cracked but she was still whole. However it would only take one more fall and she would shatter. Maybe Chase was right. It was time for her to let go. It shouldn't be hard. Starting Monday Karen would go to class, avoid Mathew and forget about darkness, and possible homicides. Starting Monday, Jennifer St. Claire did not exist.

Part Three

Darkness Rises

1

Maggie decided it was time to return to reality once again. Her vacation was over and she didn't feel any better about herself. Running away from her problems wasn't the answer, the pain she felt never left. Maggie wished she could be one of those people to drown away their problem with copious amounts of alcohol but that wasn't in her. Instead she would harbor the pain and let it eat away at her spirit. Florida wasn't a complete waste of time. A change of scenery was welcomed as it helped her to forget if only temporarily, and best of all she was a stranger to everyone she met. She befriended a couple that welcomed her into their group, and she had a few friendly dinners and nights out. She pretended to be someone new, a total stranger and called herself Tammy, taking on a totally new identity. It seemed like such a simple escape but now back home, she knew no amount of reinvention would see her through this turmoil. The judgment and knowing glares would follow her around indefinitely. Maggie was certain the truth would have come out over the past two weeks. Everyone would know her horrible dirty little secret.

Maggie pulled up to her house during the cover of night. She was exhausted from her flight home and she sluggishly popped her truck and carried her luggage into the house. Everything looked the same as she left it. Michael never returned home, and the thought left Maggie feeling empty. She would be forever alone. A part of her believed her husband would be sleeping in bed, waiting for her to return but she should have known better. Michael's possessions were all in place, as if he was still living there which only added to Maggie's pain. He hadn't even come home to pack yet.

The red light was flashing on her answering machine; at least someone called to check in. She missed three calls in the last week. The caller-id declared two of them were from Tammy. At least now she knew where Michael fled too. The third was from the school board. She deleted the last one. She didn't care what they wanted. Maggie wasn't going back and she wouldn't let herself have anything to do with the elementary school ever again. It was all too painful, too fresh. Maggie pressed play hoping the call might be from Michael using Tammy's phone.

Message one, the high-pitched robotic voice declared. *Mom, I know you're there. Pick up! Dad's here. What the fuck, were you thinking? He's better off without you anyway.* BEEP. *Message two,* the machine said before Tammy's voice returned on the line. *Mom, where are you? It's been three days and you haven't called me back. We need to talk!* BEEP.

The machine went silent. Maggie deleted the rest of the messages, disappointed and a little relieved Michael hadn't bothered to call. It saved her from hearing him angry and hurt but still she wished she could hear his voice one more time. She wanted to know everything would work out, knowing full well that it never would be the same again. She ruined the possibility of any reconciliation when she told him to leave.

Maggie didn't like the sound to Tammy's voice in the last message. She seemed angry, but also worried. It was unlike Tammy to go to her with a problem, even if she was the cause of the problem. She fought back the urge to call her back. It was too early in the morning, and surely her daughter would be sleeping by now. She could wait until tomorrow.

Maggie went back to her bedroom and thought about going to sleep. She looked over at the king-sized bed and she could almost picture the ghost of her husband sleeping peacefully on his side. It looked wrong without him there. Maggie walked up and ran her hand over the comforter. She wouldn't get any sleep here tonight, just painful memories. Abandoning her bed, she quickly dressed in her nightgown and got a stray pillow and blanket from the linen closet before passing out on the living room couch.

2

Mathew jolted awake from a bad dream. It was windy and too cold to be his apartment. He took in his surroundings in horror, finding himself on the muddy forest floor of a small clearing. *How did I get here,* Mathew thought as panic started to cloud his mind. Pine trees surrounded him in all directions, making it impossible to know which way he was facing. It made Mathew dizzy to look up at them. His head pounded with a massive headache and he closed his eyes and put his hands to his head. The pounding negated slightly but there was a wet stickiness that seemed wrong. He quickly drew them away and gapped in horror at the crimson viscous liquid that covered both his hands almost down to the elbow. It was too much blood! Mathew struggled to take in a breath and pressure started to build up in his head painfully. Panic enveloped him and he found he couldn't think straight. Something happened, the blood wasn't his own. Someone had to be dead or dangerously injured. He forced himself to look around. He was alone, and the source of the blood still remained a mystery. Minutes passed and reason replaced the panic, as Mathew's survival instinct became first priority. If something happened it wouldn't matter if he were dead.

The wind blew furiously through the trees and Mathew noticed he was shirtless and covered in dirt and blood. He needed to get out of here or he would likely die of exposure or starvation, whatever happened first. He stood slowly and was overcome by a wave of dizziness. His head was sore as if he had been struck by something and he realized he probably had a concussion. The clearing looked man-made, so there must be a way out. There was a rock slab in the middle stained by something rust-like. It resembled a table and was too perfectly shaped to be a product of nature. There were also scorch marks in the ground as if someone held a big bonfire surrounding the rock slab. This place had seen people before. His fears were dulled slightly. There was hope for escape. Mathew stumbled over to a tree that was attracting his attention. The bark had been carved to reveal a strange symbol. On closer inspection Mathew found five trees with different carvings engraved on them, none of them he recognized and none of them clearly marked his way out. He was doomed to be lost in this forest forever.

Determined not to make this strange place his grave, he picked a direction and stuck to it. If he walked long enough in one direction he would come to something eventually. All he had to do was survive that long. The sun was rising in the sky and warming up the ground, he was thankful the summer was soon approaching. Maybe he would have a chance if his head injury allowed him to get far enough away. He would deal with the blood on his hands later.

3

Karen's students were preoccupied all day with watching the clock on the wall. She didn't blame them, the last day always seemed to drag on and on, no matter what fun games she could invent. She finished with the curriculum a week before and now her job was starting to seem more like babysitting than teaching. Keeping fifteen young preteen minds on her was a challenge during the last days of school, now the last hours. The bell would ring for lunch any minute and Karen could sense her students were bored of the movie she plopped them in front of. They were too excited about the prospect of the endless summer they saw before them, full of warm weather and outdoors. Karen was looking forward to the break too. She was even considering teaching piano lessons again like she promised Suzie she may consider. Things with Chase were going well and she was surprised how easy it was to forget everything that happened and start fresh. The obsession was behind her.

Mathew avoided her just as much as she avoided him and the two hadn't crossed paths in days. Melinda was becoming a good friend even though Karen got the feeling Catherine was a little apprehensive about their new camaraderie. Karen never told Catherine what happened during the trip, it was better that way. Melinda never spoke about Mathew or mentioned anything that was spoken during their morning meeting. It was a silent agreement between them that the incident of minor craziness would be forgotten. Chase was right when he thought she needed to relax and that was exactly what she planned to do when the day was over. The lunch bell rang signaling noon hour just as the final credits came up for the film. She switched on the lights and it wasn't long before the sleepy kids started chatting loudly and crowding the door and hallways as they found their lunch in their lockers.

Karen stayed long enough to be sure her class was settled before taking her bagged lunch from the bottom drawer, before heading to the staffroom. Catherine and Melinda were both sitting in the far corner chatting happily. Melinda was waiting for the microwave. Both women seemed to be getting along, and maybe they would all be a group after all.

"Hey Karen!" said Melinda, when they spotted her in the doorway. Karen smiled squeezed past the others gathered around the table. The mood was jovial and everyone was on their feet and moving around in the excitement.

"Hi guys," said Karen.

"Check out what Billy made me!" Catherine gushed as she held out the most adorable of homemade cards. It was written with crayon on red construction paper and said, 'Thank you for the best skool year yet!' The card came with doodles of a stick figure at a chalkboard pointing to a math problem, which was comically but probably accidentally inaccurate.

"That is possibly the cutest thing I have ever seen!" said Karen smiling. "I got a few gift cards, and a plastic apple figurine that says 'Best Teacher.' Sarah gave her the latter. "Looks like the next teacher might have some work to do." The look on Catherine's face was priceless. "I was kidding." Catherine seemed appeased and looked at the math problem and giggled.

"It does add to the cuteness factor." Melinda added. "You guys are lucky. All I got were a couple Starbucks gift cards given to me by students who were obviously forced to by their parents."

"Sometimes I wish I taught the younger grades again, they are all so cute and appreciative. Then I remember what it was really like and realize I'm happy where I am." They all laughed at that one. Karen finally got to her leftover pizza and soda for lunch and they were quiet for a while as they finally sat down at the tables and ate.

"Do you know if you're coming back next year?" Catherine asked between mouthfuls of her own salad.

"I was supposed to find out today but I couldn't find Mathew this morning. He was a no show to our meeting." A nervous knot made its way into Karen's stomach as she recalled the ordeal. She was an anxious mess all last night dreading her seven a.m. meeting with Mathew of all people to find out if she would be returning full-time next school year or if she would end next March after the previous teachers maternity leave was over. There was even a chance today would be her last day, but she was fairly confident with Mathew as principal that wouldn't be the case. It was one of the things she liked about Mathew as her boss-the only thing she liked about it.

"I haven't seen Mathew today either?" said Melinda.

"Me either," said Catherine. "That's a little weird. I wonder where he is?"

"Hmm, I call good riddance," said Melinda, giving Karen a meaningful side look.

"Still I wish I knew what is happening with my job. At least I told Suzie yesterday I might teach piano lessons during the summer. I think that'll be fun."

"Ooh, I bet Suzie loved that!" said Catherine approvingly. The bell rang signaling the end of lunch and the beginning of recess. Karen and Catherine both had outdoor supervision duty today. Karen didn't mind, and it was absolutely gorgeous weather. The summer seemed to start early. The flowers in the gardens were in full bloom and the trees sprouted the beginnings of baby leaves.

"I guess I'll see you two later!" said Melinda before Karen and Catherine reached the door. The two of them hurried out to their posts. As soon as they opened up the big doors leading to the playground they were overcome by the sounds of children's laughter and screams. Karen heard a few students from her class teaching younger students an inappropriate song about teachers to the tune of 'Joy to the World.' She smiled and ignored it.

"I'll see you in a bit," said Karen and walked towards the junior end of the schoolyard, which was mostly a big field. Some of the older boys started a game of kickball and a gathering of students were watching and looking to join in. Karen decided that would need her attention so she could make sure they played fairly. She was pleasantly surprised to find they were including younger students and running a quick tutorial on how to play. They split into two teams: girls verse boys, which Karen decided was fair enough. She already stopped them from splitting the teams by grade, because it was clearly going to give the older students an advantage. The students agreed with her and changed their minds and a friendly game began. Karen watched for an inning and then started walking the field. She looked around and saw Catherine was up by the play equipment talking to a few students.

"Mrs. Williams'?" a young girl called. Karen looked up to find three fourth grade girls running towards her. She believed the one who spoke was Maggie. They were in Mathew's class.

"Hi Maggie," said Karen curious as to what started the mob.

"We are going to be in your class next year!" Maggie started, clearly the boldest of her shyer friends. Karen wondered once again if she was guaranteed a job, and where Mathew was.

"Is that so?" She asked hoping the girl would elaborate.

"Yeah, I saw it on my report card earlier. I can't wait!" The girl said happily. Karen was relieved. If it was printed on the report cards she was coming back for September for sure. Mathew was probably going to tell her she could stay until at least next spring break. That was a weight off of her shoulders.

"I can't wait for you all to be in my class," said Karen smiling. "Fifth grade is a lot of fun." The girls giggled as if what she said was the funniest thing in the world.

"School can't be fun." One of the quieter girls said, Karen believed her name was Laura.

"Why not." Karen argued, although she had a similar opinion.

"Because it's hard work like math problems and reading," said Cindy, the girl who hadn't said anything up to that point.

"What's wrong with reading?" Karen challenged.

"I like reading," said Maggie happily, as if she was bragging.

"That's good, reading can be fun if you find the right books." Karen added. "Don't you like gym, music or art?" She asked the group.

"Music and art are fun. I hate gym though," said Cindy, getting more confident in the conversation.

"Want to know a secret?" She said to the girl. She then lowered herself to whisper in Cindy's ear. "I hated gym too!" The girl smiled pleased to share a secret.

"I guess school is sort of fun, sometimes." Laura finally concluded. Karen took it as a win. When the girls left Karen headed towards the middle ground between her and Catherine's supervision duties. With one last glance of her area, she concluded that her students were playing nicely enough she could spare a few minutes. Karen was giddy with the knowledge she would be returning in September with yet another fifth grade class. She hadn't realized how much the stress of her uncertainty weighed her down.

4

"Ten, nine, eight, seven, six, five four, three, two, one!" RING! The class counted down the final seconds until summer break. At the bell they all jumped out of their seats, and Karen made a half-hearted attempt at controlling them before decided *what the hell?* She let them run wildly through the halls. It took less than five minutes for the hallway to become a ghost town leaving only the teachers still in the building and a few lone stragglers. It was a whirlwind of action and then silence, peaceful silence. The school suddenly felt very empty and it couldn't have been more perfect. It felt like the end. Catherine came rushing out of her classroom and did a little twirl in her joy as she made her way over to Karen, which inspired a fit of giggles from both of them.

"I swear every year this moment keeps feeling sweeter!" said Catherine happily.

"It's the first time I've got to experience it," said Karen. It didn't occur to her before that she never supplied for a class on the last day. She suddenly felt more like a teacher.

"That's right!" said Catherine who also forgot Karen was never full-time. "I hope you come back as the official teacher next year. These past three months have been awesome, it seems like you've been here longer." Karen smiled.

"I was thinking the same thing."

"Hey, what are you two fine ladies up too?" said Melinda as she joined them in the hallway. Catherine's expression fell slightly at her appearance and Karen knew they wouldn't be friends if it weren't for her. It made her feel a little awkward but she pushed it to the back of her mind. At least they could play nice.

"We were just talking about how awesome this day is," said Karen.

"I never expected anything else," said Melinda. "I was wondering if ice cream sounds good to anybody. My treat?" she said. Catherine instantly perked up.

"Sounds great to me," she said. Catherine agreed quickly, so Karen went to retrieve her purse from her desk and locked her door. The three of them walked towards the main entrance and out into the parking lot. The opted to forgo the cars and walked the short walk to the small outdoor ice cream kiosk Karen noticed earlier.

"I've been meaning to try this place since it opened," said Karen. She instantly met by two shocked faces.

"You mean you haven't had it before!" said Catherine incredulously.

"It was closed for the winter until recently." Karen defended.

"Your in for a treat," said Melinda.

"I can't believe I get to be with you when you lose your Jackie's virginity!" Catherine cooed.

"I don't think it can be THAT good," said Karen, but her curiosity was peaked. They reached the small Kiosk, which was manned by a young teen with jet-black hair and an eyebrow piecing.

"I'll have a double scoop of Caramel Twist, in a sugar cone." Catherine ordered. Melinda ordered a flavor called Barry Blast, which Karen never heard of before. She looked over the handwritten chalkboard of flavors and selected the safest one.

"I'll have a double scoop of Chocolate Fudge," said Karen and watched as the girl scooped it for her. Her mouth was already watering in anticipation. Melinda true to her word paid for the lot. "Thanks Mel, your awesome," said Karen, which was followed by a 'thanks Melanie,' from Catherine. The two women stared at Karen as she went in for her first taste. They hadn't been lying about Jackie's. All she could taste was the rich chocolate fudge, which was heaven in her mouth. She nodded her approval and muttered the word 'good' but it was muffled by another mouthful of ice cream. Some dripped on her chin and she wiped it away with her hand quickly before anyone noticed but it was already a lost cause. Catherine laughed.

"I bet it's better than anything in New York!" said Catherine smugly, "I knew you'd like it."

"I never said I wouldn't," said Karen, she manage to already finish half of her ice cream, which was good because the sun was melting it quickly and it began to make her hand sticky. They started walking back towards their cars in silence, all trying to finish before they made a mess. Karen reached her car first just as she finished the rest of her cone. "See you guys soon," said Karen and waved goodbye.

"You can count on it! Girls Night is next Friday!" said Catherine and got into her van. Melinda looked confused and Karen wondered if Catherine purposely said that because Melinda never got invited. She signed, hopefully she wouldn't always be the glue forcing the two together.

"Bye Melinda!" said Karen before closing herself into the small car and pulling away. She stopped behind Melinda's car and rolled down her window. "By the way, Girl's Night is next Friday at Morgan's. I'm sure everyone would like it if you showed up." She said and Melinda perked up again.

"Sure I'll think about it," said Melinda. Karen drove off so she wasn't blocking the parking lot and was happy to find she didn't get stopped at her usual red light. Today turned out fantastic.

5

June 26, 1872: Willis Morgan knew the time had come. The sun was low behind the trees and cast the sky with orange and pinks. It was both beautiful and eerie. He sighed heavily, nerves getting to the better of him as a heavy lump churned in his stomach. Everyone needed him tonight and turning back wasn't an option. Willis forced himself out of the tiny shack and saddled his black gelding Ebony. He quickly filled the saddlebags with supplies trying to push the dark thoughts out of his mind. The sunlight was quickly fading as he spurred the horse into a gallop and ran down the vacant dirt road. A few curious onlookers watched from their windows in the safety of their homes for the night. They were given away from movement in the curtains. Willis flew past them until reaching the nearly unmarked trailhead. He slowed his horse to a trot and cut through the dense brush onto a much less travelled trail through the woods.

The trail narrowed even further as he got closer to the meeting place. This would be as far as the horse could take him. He pulled up, dismounted quickly and hitched Ebony to a nearby tree. With his supplies in tow, he struggled through the forest. There were only subtle clues to reveal anyone walked here before. The ground was mostly untouched and overgrown since their last meeting. A renewed sense of anxiety overcame Willis as he broke the tree line into the natural clearing. His eyes lay on the sacrifice altar and wouldn't leave. The place was well chosen, and he could feel the power emanating from the circular pattern of the trees. The sky was bright orange over the forest and he got to work on the important task, he couldn't let himself think about anything but what he was doing in the moment. Backing out wasn't an option when they came so far. First he carved marks of the five trees at different points in the circle, the symbols stood for fire, water, earth, wind and spirit. They were the elements needed to access the hidden power on the sacred grounds. He then placed candles around the circle and altar and lit them one by one. He completed his work by connecting the trees with lines drawn in the sand with a stick. Once he was done they formed a pentagram pattern in the earth.

The air was still and the power of the setting got to him. He felt uneasy as if someone was lurking unseen watching him and accessing his work. Sounds of footsteps moving in the brush which startled him from his reverie and he changed into his dark purple robe before walking out down the forest path to greet his followers. Two people already arrived on foot, both donned in matching robes. No one uttered a word but stood solemnly awaiting the others. A woman was screaming in the distance, and a galloping horse was fighting its way through the narrow path. The screaming woman began to weep as she came into view and saw the three men awaiting her. Willis pitied her but she was the chosen one and she deserved this fate and at least she could serve a purpose now. Bruce had plucked her from the brothel and she was nothing but a washed-up prostitute. She brought this on herself in a way. The woman was young, early twenties, maybe even late teens. She would be a fitting sacrifice. The remaining council member, Henry, followed the horse, which carried the restrained prostitute. Everyone just called him 'The Doctor'. The Doctor wasted no time in taking a needle from his bag and plunging it into the veins of the screaming girl. She fought it for a few moments and slumped over unconscious in the saddle. Still no one had spoken a word since they arrived. The ritual had already begun.

The girl was stripped naked then laid out on the sacrificial stone in the centre of the clearing. The robed men slowly turned and walked to different corners of the pentagram to represent their respective element. Willis was spirit and took his place to complete the circle. The drugged girl stirred and he feared they needed to hurry. The moon was full and high in the sky but it wasn't yet directly over the clearing. He could hear the breath catch in the throats of his followers, each fearing the same thing. The candlelight was dim but enough to see the silhouettes and shadows of everything. The candles held in the palms of the men illuminated the hooded faces, but he could only make out the bottom portion and no one was easily identified.

Twenty minutes later Willis plunged his dagger into the heart of the young whore while his followers repeated a chant in Latin. Willis's didn't focus on what they were saying and it became background noise, which raised the level of energy. The power worked through him as a vessel and released as it got what it wanted. His focus was pinpointed on the girl under him and as he raised his dagger above his head he witnessed her eyes open, pleading with him before he plunged his dagger into the heart. He pushed past the ribs, which snapped under pressure. He found the heart and ripped it free from the body and offered it up to the savior in exchange for another fourteen years of protection for his town. He held the heart high above his head and liquid dripped down his arm, soaking him through with blood that looked purple in the candlelight. His followers were silent, the chanting having reached an abrupt end.

"It had to be done." He said and ended the ritual by taking his hood off and abandoning the circle. The others did the same. He could see the uncertainty in their faces and would be lying if he could say he didn't feel it the same way but they needed to see his firm leadership.

"It'll be dawn soon enough, lets get this cleaned up," said The Doctor and started pouring gasoline down into the lines drawn on the ground and all around the altar. Willis did the honors and using the candle meant for spirit, he set the pentagram into flames and watched as the whore burned. The offering was accepted.

"I'll see you again in fourteen years," said Henry as everyone dispersed into the darkness. Willis was left alone once again in the secret spot. He could see the smoke billowing up into the sky and was horrified to notice the moon looked to be blood red through the smoke. For the blood sacrifice he guaranteed the town another profitable fourteen years. The town would be able to remain against any challenge put forth by it. They were protected.

6

Mathew was relieved to see a dilapidated old shack in the distance. He was overcome with exhaustion and his body desperately needed to stop moving. He ached to his core. The place was and old timey house that looked like it would have been nice in the previous century. Now the porch had caved in on its support beams and there were big gapping holes in the roof, with over half the shingles missing. The windows were broken. Off to the side was a two-stall stable that looked to be in slightly better condition than the bungalow. Mathew tried there first because the roof still covered the entire structure and seemed sturdier. He found a bale of straw in one of the stables, gave it a quick rodent check before sitting down.

His body wanted to sleep and shut down but he fought the urge to close his eyes. He found his cell phone in his pocket and checked it. There was no signal. *Damn it!* Mathew thought as he slammed it shut and whipped it against the wall. A horrid groaning noise radiated from the roof and the structure battled to keep standing. Mathew held his breath waiting for the thing to cave in on him. When it didn't happen, his attention went back to his phone. The light had gone off and he wondered if he broke it, not that it would matter anyway. It was useless and he wasn't sure if he would make it back home. Even if he did, he had the suspicion something very wrong happened. He probably shouldn't return home until he knew what he would be returning to. There might be trouble awaiting him and a mess to clean up. *Who did I hurt? What happened?* He thought. He knew he needed to get back somehow. If he did something, justice needed to be served.

Mathew didn't remember a thing from the night before and the thought scared him immensely. Would he keep losing time like this?

***

Mathew jolted awake. Somehow he fell asleep sitting against the wall. He checked outside and could see it was late afternoon judging from the position of the sun in the sky. He picked up his phone and knew he would soon need to get moving. There might be a long walk involved to getting back to civilization. Curiosity got the better of him, as Mathew was about to go follow the old dirt road he found. He entered the shack, stepping carefully around the door, which was now off its hinges. He could see the sun from the roof. This place hadn't been loved in a long time. There were minimal signs of life. He toured the rooms and only found a living room and a kitchen, which housed a stove that was more a fireplace than stove and made of cast iron. Everything was covered in a thick layer of cobwebs and dust. He could feel it tickling his shoulders and clinging to his skin. Fighting the urge to leave he forced himself onward and past an empty room and Mathew assumed it must have been the dinning room. Then the last door led to a bedroom at the back of the house.

This room appeared to be the most sturdy–the house collapsed forward but was still standing in the back-but nothing prepared him for the shape the room was in. He pictured this to be what the inside of a mental patients room must be like. Only someone with a serious disease would have been capable of the mindless writing and scribbles on the wall. He ran his finger over a gash in the wood, it seemed to have been made by a knife tearing at the wall in someone's fit of rage or anguish. There was no blood, but the knife hole pattern was one of many. The writing on the wall was written in black paint and was considerably more legible in the far left of the room, but as it went around it slowly got all jumbled up as its author plunged deeper into madness. He tried to read some of the words but found it hard to make out. Some appeared to be written in a foreign language, maybe Gaelic or Latin.

English portions were written in lone words, EVIL was by far the most repeated word, and he could see different variation of "We're all going to die." "We are doomed." "Kill" "Death." "Murder." Mathew found it hard to peel his eyes away. These are the ramblings of a sick man. Maybe Schizophrenia. A gust of wind blew against the house, which started another unnerving groan. Mathew backed out of the haunting room and made his way out of the old house. If he stayed much longer he would risk getting squashed beneath the wooden beams should they collapse with him still inside.

Mathew looked down the road he was following and noticed sadly that it ended past the house. He didn't want to get scratched up again by the trees but what else was he to do?

A short bushwhacking session later Mathew stumbled on a fallen branch and as he was grabbing for his scrapped ankle he was pleasantly surprised to find himself in someone's backyard. He was still in the country but at least he could go up to the house and find out where he was and ask to borrow a phone. His day finally began to look better. There was a nice pond nearby and remembering his bloody hands he washed up as best he could. He really wished he had his shirt. His bare chest was badly ripped apart by stray branches and spots of dried blood and scabs had formed. He wasn't going to be well received. Mathew upped his pace to a slow jog as he ran to the house in the distance.

7

Melinda knew something was wrong the moment she pulled onto her street. The vibe was off and there were no people around enjoying the day. Kids newly released from school should have been playing on bikes and beginning games of road hockey, but instead the street was a ghost town. *Where is everybody?* Melinda rounded the corner to turn on her street and immediately got an answer to her question and she wished she didn't. A group of people had formed and began gathering around Mrs. Elsing's house, which was only a few houses separated from her own. She counted five city police cars and the town sheriff's old beat up cop car. Police tape sectioned off the property and was surrounded by the people she expected to see earlier. A few reporters were among those closest to the yellow tape but no one was talking to them. As she watched another news van appeared and parked a little down the street by her own house. Melinda slowed her SUV down to get a good look at what was going on. There wasn't an ambulance so it couldn't be a medical issue, which was hopeful but the cops seemed serious. It wasn't good. Maggie parked and ambushed the reporters as they were carrying cameras and equipment out of the van.

"What happened here?" She asked.

"It's to early to say, but we are following up a lead about a potential homicide." One of the men carrying the camera said to her and walked off, too busy to bother with conversation. Melinda ran up to the scene but it was already crowded with onlookers. All she could make out was a hysterical women being comforted by one of the female officers. Melinda stepped away and pulled out her cell, immediately calling Karen and Catherine. Whatever happened shouldn't have happened in their small little town. Crime scenes like this were expected of the big cities, but never here.

8

Karen answered the phone just as she was paused at a stop sign. She slammed the phone down and tried to throw it back into her purse but it ended up falling under the passenger seat. Karen executed a U turn as best she could on the narrow dirt road, nearly driving into the opposite ditch in the process. She sped back towards town in a fury. *A potential homicide,* she thought. It didn't sound right in her mind, especially paired with, *at Mrs. Elsing's house*. Karen sped through the yellow streetlight earning some unhappy looks, from the still oblivious couples checking out the antique shops. It wasn't hard to find the right place. People were gathering quickly, the news of the crime scene spread like wildfire and everyone in town tried to get a piece of the action. Karen parked a block away and started looking around for Melinda. Her eyes fell first on Catherine, who was waiting by her car. She was parked a little further down the street keeping her distance from the main crowd. The small subdivision was becoming Grand Central station today, at least in small town standards.

"Where's Mel?" Karen asked as she jogged towards her friend.

"I haven't seen her, but I only just got here five minutes before you did. Isn't that her SUV?" said Catherine, and pointed towards the vehicle parked in Melinda's driveway.

"Maybe she's in her house. We probably should walk over there." Neither of them really wanted to get pushed around in the crowd. The women made there way towards the mess of police cruisers, news vans and pedestrians.

"There she is!" Karen spotted the blonde right up by the police tape; she was having a heated discussion with one of the police officers. A reporter was beside them scribbling furiously on a notepad. The two of them were stuck at the back of the crowd and couldn't quite make out what was going on.

"Get back!" One of the uniforms yelled and Karen's stomach dropped as a coroners van pulled up by the house. Onlookers were scrambling to get out of the way. A mother with a couple young children noticed the new arrival and coming to her senses seemed to realize the gravity of the situation and dragged her curious boys back into their home. A few others decided to leave, and Karen wasn't sure she should stay around to see what might be going into that van. She hoped Mrs. Elsing wasn't the one in the house and was about to appear alive at any minute. The concept of the obvious possibility was beyond comprehending. *Did she commit suicide?* She was under stress and was acing weird for weeks but was she a woman who would have wanted to end it all. Karen didn't quite think so but it was more likely than a homicide like Melinda suggested. All Karen knew for sure was there was a body in her bosses house. Nothing else was clear.

"Karen." Melinda was trying to get her attention and made her way over to meet them.

"Sorry, this is all so crazy," said Karen.

"I know, just think there is a dead person in that house right now. Should we really be here? I don't want to see…" Catherine trailed off, and said exactly what Karen was thinking. It would only be a matter of time before they wheeled the body out.

"Did the cop tell you anything?" Karen asked.

"He didn't tell me anything, although he wanted to know if I saw anything suspicious last night. They are definitely treating this as a homicide. Do you really think it could be? Mrs. Elsing cut contact with everyone do you think it's possible maybe she…"

"It's possible," said Karen.

"Oh my god! Tammy!" Catherine yelled. Karen's looked up in time to see the woman escorted out of the house by three officers.

One of them appeared to be F.B.I. and it was clear there was no doubt this was a murder. Tammy was a mess. Her face was blotchy and swollen from tears and stress and she had something in her hair that made Karen's stomach churn. Blood never bothered her before but this was way to close to home. She hoped more than anything Mrs. Elsing wasn't in the house. Tammy covered her face and allowed herself to be led under the police tape and into the back of a police car. Reporters were firing off cameras everywhere until Tammy was hidden away again. Their attention was then directed to the emerging stretcher. A black body bag was strapped to it and Karen was glad she couldn't see anything. Another round of pictures were fired and one reporter was standing away from the mob shooting video.

"Lets get out of here," said Catherine. Her eyes were fixed on the car that Tammy was sitting in.

"Should we go over there?"

"No, leave her be," said Karen. The car left in the direction of the police station anyway. Karen grabbed Catherine's arm and directed her friend away from the crowd. Melanie stood watching with concern and followed them.

"Who was that?" She asked once a safe distance from the reporters.

"That was Mrs. Elsing's daughter." Karen answered. Melanie said nothing and led the group into her house, and the quiet seemed to contradict the chaos that was just outside. Karen was taken by surprise by her home. Everything was white and clean with an edgy modern design. Catherine and Karen both took a seat one of her bar stools pulled up to her center island. Karen admired the contrast of the sparkly black marble countertops, it was a look she was more accustomed to seeing in Manhattan than in the small farming town. Karen wondered just how wealthy Melanie was.

"Who do you think did it?" Catherine asked, coming out of her daze.

"Assuming it was Mrs. Elsing, and she was murdered there are only thee people I would suspect," said Karen. She was afraid to give her real thought away. Karen was contemplating the idea Tammy looked a little suspicious. She was covered in blood when they saw her come out of the house. She clearly was on the scene before the police even knew about it. It was odd for her to be there at all, Karen didn't think Tammy visited her mother. Why would she have gone today? On another note, both Mathew and Maggie's husband had motive.

"You think Tammy did it?" said Catherine accusingly.

"Do you?"

"No, she might not have been on the best terms with her mother but she's not a murderer!" Melinda stayed out of the conversation but listened intently, feeling left out and wondering just how involved her new friends were with their old bosses life.

"Who are the other two?" said Melinda. Both the woman turned to her, as if they forgot she was in the room. "You said there were three suspects."

"Her husband and Mathew," said Karen.

"Karen!" Catherine protested. Karen wasn't sure if she didn't want Melinda to know about the affair or if she didn't like that Mathew was included on the list. Melinda cringed at Mathew's name and gave her a look. It was clear that Melinda was thinking about that evil supposedly in the town.

"I don't think Mathew is capable of this either," said Catherine with a snarky edge to her voice. Karen understood she was only defending him because of her ridiculous crush, or maybe it was defending herself for having feeling for him in the first place.

"I wouldn't be so sure about that. If anyone in this town is capable of murder I would think Mathew would be," said Melinda.

"Not you too!" Catherine snapped.

"I'm not saying he did it. I can't think of why he would want Mrs. Elsing dead. I just think he's capable."

"Oh, he has a motif," said Karen.

"You two are fucking unbelievable," said Catherine flabbergasted. She threw up her arms and marched towards the door.

"Catherine wait!" Karen yelled, feeling guilty for angering her friend. A part of her just wanted Catherine to leave so she could talk openly to Melinda but she still felt compelled to smooth things over.

"Karen, I'll talk to you later, but a lot has happened today. I think I should go." She didn't wait for a reply. Catherine let herself out of the house and stormed away.

"What's wrong with her?" Melinda asked. The whole exchange confused her.

"She might be a little too close to the situation. Tammy and her are close and she has a thing for Mathew."

"Someone should warn her about that one."

Discovery

1

Tammy didn't know what was happening with her father. He wasn't himself and she feared he might be clinically depressed. Most of the time he stared at the TV in a near catatonic state and she fought to get him to perform the simplest tasks. Getting Michael to put down any food was a difficult chore and sleep was another matter entirely. No one heard from her mother since the incident and it looked like she fled town. The situation was ten times worse than she ever expected it to be, and she mentally prepared for this day. Lately her father was scaring her and it was uncomfortable. She was tiptoeing around her own house, avoiding anything that might trigger a reaction in him. Something just wasn't right and after a couple weeks, when no improvement came Tammy worried it might be more than depression. There was a terrible feeling she got whenever she looked at her father. It gave her the creeps and was enough to make her hair stand on end.

She called and left desperate pleading messages on her mother's voicemail and tried to track her down. The project was a lost cause. It was rare for her to leave town and no one who knew Maggie could get in contact. When Tammy got a call from the school board, she decided to visit her mothers place. She drove to town expecting to find the house abandoned and was shocked to find her mother's car parked in the driveway. It looked like she was home but there wasn't any answer at the door. She stood outside for fifteen minutes before scavenging around for the hollow plastic rock they used to keep the spare key. It was a slim chance but on the fourth try she found the one with the false bottom and sure enough uncovered the key. Her mother was a creature of habit. Tammy opened the door and instantly knew something was wrong. The tidy and well-kept house was uprooted. A black frame with a picture of her parents on their twenty-fifth wedding anniversary was smashed on the floor in the entranceway beside two abandoned suitcases. It seemed her mother did return after all.

"Mom?" Tammy called nervously. She was greeted with silence. Tammy ascended the stairs slowly to her parent's bedroom. If her mom arrived back late into the night she may just be sleeping from the jetlag. She reached the top and found the bed looked undisturbed and still perfectly made up like her mother liked it. *That's odd,* Tammy thought and the calmness was getting to her. Everything was so empty and untouched. The house seemed empty and lifeless while remaining unchanged and it made her jumpy.

"Are you home?" She attempted again, but still not a sound from the empty home. It didn't seem like anyone was around but her mother couldn't just disappear so soon after she got back, could she? Tammy tried the kitchen and noticed the answering machine by the phone was cleared. Her mother must have checked it recently. The last message she left her was less than twelve hours earlier. Where was her mother now?

"Oh shit!" Her eyes went to the sliding door that led to the backyard. The glass was broken and forcibly unlocked and still left partially open. An intruder was in the house. An intruder might still be in the house. Tammy spun around on her heels, panic taking over and she couldn't decide whether to escape or grab the nearest weapon. She swiped a butcher knife from the counter beside her and quietly concealed herself in a corner. She listened for any sign of movement, but there was nothing but silence; the pounding sound of her heart and her own muffled breathing. She ran into the living room and the knife clattered to the floor by her feet.

Her mother was on the couch. Her throat slit and lifeless eyes stared out at Tammy. Her head resting a pillow soaked through with blood with her body wrapped in a blanket.

"No! This isn't real. This isn't real. I'm dreaming," She screamed and took her mothers body into her arms. "Mom." She shook her, hoping to find some signs of life. It felt like a rigid plank in her arms, already cold but still Tammy hoped she would move or make a sound. The blanket fell away onto the floor. Tammy shrieked a blood-curdling scream and dropped her mother and crawled quickly back a few paces, horrified. A hole was in her chest, where the heart should have been and Tammy could see the white of broken ribs, which were ripped apart cruelly. She stifled her gag reflex and backed away as far as the kitchen before hurling twice in the sink. Tammy reached for the phone and quickly dialed 911 and waited. The voice of the operator came over the line and Tammy went numb and the phone slipped through her fingers onto the kitchen floor. She could hear the faint voice asked her what the emergency was but she froze. Tammy was too weak to retrieve the phone and all coherent thoughts came to an end.

2

Chase was having difficulties containing his excitement. It didn't matter how many manuscripts he completed, the final pages were always the best to write. The story was wrapping up and soon he could do a final edit and read before passing the remainder of the job over to his editor. Dan was getting annoyed with him since he went a few weeks over deadline but it wouldn't matter now. The book was nearly complete, just a few more sentences. Chase typed in a blur, knowing exactly how to finish his work having planned it detail by detail in his head for months. He couldn't type fast enough. Almost...DONE. He admired the words on the screen for a few seconds before clicking save and slamming down his laptop until tomorrow. He wouldn't look at the novel for a few more days to give it time to settle. He'd be able to pick out more mistakes if he distanced himself. Chase sat in his comfy computer chair contemplating what he should do next. Free time seemed like a foreign concept and he was in the mood to go celebrate. Karen should have been home by now.

BAM!   Chase heard something banging from downstairs. Going to investigate, he left his office, and was surprised to find someone frantically pounding at the patio door. Chase wasn't sure if he should answer but whoever it was seemed to be desperate or confused. After a moments hesitation he unlocked the back door and stepped to a safe distance from the stranger.

"Can I help you?" He said. The man was a mess, half naked and covered in mud and scratches. It looked as if this guy hiked here through miles of dense forest. He was too clean cut and his jeans hinted subtly at designer origins but he could almost pass for one now.

"I got lost in the woods. Yours is the first house I came across. Please tell me I can use your phone. I've been walking all day!" The strange man was slightly winded and just oozed desperation.   Chase not knowing what was appropriate for the situation took pity on the straggler.

"I have a phone you can use, it's in the kitchen. There's a bathroom upstairs and your welcomed to clean yourself up a bit," said Chase.   If this happened in Manhattan Chase never would have opened the door but small town life must have left more of an impression on him than he realized.

"Thank you!" Chase knew the man meant it. He pointed out the direction of the bathroom and watched as his new friend climbed the stairs leaving behind a trail of footsteps in his wake. The tap water turned on and Chase felt good about his good deed of the day. He poured two cups of lemonade for his guest.   Karen freshly squeezed it herself before leaving for class. It was already nearly five and Chase was getting worried. She hadn't texted or tried to call and it seemed unlike herself to disappear without warning. Something must have held her up at school. Chase wondered if it had to do with her job being on the line. Maybe she was signing a contract or something. Mathew was supposed to meet with her today and Chase knew she was worried about her future employment. He didn't want to admit it, but he was nervous for when her job ended at the school. He wasn't sure what Karen was going to do if she wasn't able to teach.

"I'm Mathew Barry by the way," Chase jumped as the man approached from behind him, he hadn't even noticed he left the bathroom. Mathew? It couldn't be the Mathew that terrified his wife. The same one that only two weeks ago left her curled up in a ball on the floor in the middle of the worst breakdown he'd ever witnessed. Chase froze. It couldn't be, Karen was talking to that Mathew right now.

"I'm Chase Williams," said Chase watching Mathew's expression carefully for any clues.

Mathew eyes opened in recognition. It was unmistakable. Mathew knew his name. "Aren't you my wife's boss?" Chase was using all the mental strength he had to not punch Mathew out, right then and there. He wouldn't do it, not yet but he wanted to badly.

"Karen is your wife?" Mathew backed away a few steps, clearly understanding the dire situation he inadvertently placed himself into.

"Yes, I thought she was supposed to be talking to you right now. You wouldn't happen to know where she is would you?" He spoke through gritted teeth but was impressed he was doing a better job at controlling himself than he expected.

"I swear I don't. I wasn't at school today. Why would you think she would be talking to me?" Mathews voice was getting defensive but he wasn't lying.

"She was supposed to find out about her job today."

"Oh, right. She has her job. The teacher she is replacing quit but I haven't told her yet. In case you haven't noticed, I never made it in to class today."

"She's probably freaking out right now," said Chase but mostly to himself. Mathew squirmed uncomfortably. He was mentally calculating how long it would take to hike back into town without help. He kept eyeing the door, and seemed to be waiting for an escape.

"I'm sorry. I should have told her earlier." He sounded like a robot, monotone and emotionless.

"Here, Karen made this before she left for work," said Chase and shoved a glass of lemonade into Mathew hands. He nearly fumbled the cup, expecting a punch instead of a drink. He looked up at Chase confused, his look full of questions.

"I know what you tried on my wife." The elephant in the room finally acknowledged.

"Why are you helping me?"

"Who says I'm helping you." Mathew non-discreetly placed his lemonade down on the counter untouched.

"I think I should go," said Mathew, having enough of the awkward situation. "How far of a walk is it to town from here?"

"I wouldn't know," said Chase, and he would be lying if he claimed to not be enjoying watching Mathew struggle. The man was making an easy target of himself, having gracelessly shown up at his door.

"Any chance I can borrow your phone now?" Chase sighed, he wanted to continue the torture this man so deserved but he wasn't one to pick on people when they were down. Mathew was terrified and seemed to have been through a rough day. Now might not be the time to unroll his punishment, and at least he was allowing Karen to keep her job. That was an action deserving of some mercy. Chase handed over the receiver from the countertop beside him. Mathew ripped it from his hand quickly before he could change his mind and walked into the furthest corner of the room to make his call.

"Oh, I'm glad you picked up. I really need your help." There was a pause. "Yes, this is Mathew. Can you please pick me up and give me a ride to town. I'm at the William's place." He looked frustrated. "Yes, that is Karen's house. I'll explain when you get here. Please hurry!" Mathew ended the call, and looked stressed. Chase wondered who was on the other end of the phone. Was it another girlfriend? Suddenly Chase remembered the picture Karen showed him a few months ago, of the blackmail picture of him and

Karen's old boss. Mathew pitied the thought of another one of Mathew's victims.

3

"Why would Mathew have anything to do with Mrs. Elsing?" Melinda asked.

"I think the better question would be why wouldn't he. For starters Mathew and Mrs. Elsing had an affair but they broke up a couple months ago. Haven't you heard the rumors or sensed the tension between them. Those New York trip meetings were so intense you could cut the tension between those two with a knife," said Karen. They were both seated at the center island again after Catherine angrily stormed out.

"I never really thought about it much. I mean I heard the rumors like everyone else but I usually never pay attention to them. With the way the town talks, most of what comes down the grapevine is completely made up, or so altered the truth is masqueraded behind some crazy story," Karen laughed.

"Yeah, that's probably for the best. A couple weeks ago someone tried to tell me I was in a relationship with Mathew." Karen narrowed her eyes accusingly.

"Um, right. I am sorry about that," said Melinda.

"Its alright. The point is Mrs. Elsing was cheating on her husband with Mathew for real, and it wasn't just a rumor. There was photo evidence of the affair. I accidentally came across it and Mathew found out. I think it has a big part to play in Mrs. Elsing's resignation. She must have been protecting it from getting out or something. Either way both Matthew and her husband could have a reason for wanting her dead. Although they would have to be mentally unstable to follow through with it."

"Mathew," said Melinda, and Karen saw the image of his reflection with the black eyes in the mirror. The though was enough to give her chills.

"He's definitely my first pick for a suspect. I know he's capable. I also know her husband has been living at Tammy's house because he found out about the affair."

"Mathew disappeared. I wonder if the police know about their connection. He's certainly looking pretty guilty to me."

4

"I really hate to ask but you don't suppose I could stay here until I my ride comes?" Mathew asked. Chase bit the inside of his cheek. This guy was really testing his limits.

"Wait out front," said Chase. Mathew didn't protest and Chase escorted him to the front step and closed the door on him and locked it. Chase watched from the bay window as Mathew took a seat on the step and put his head in his hands. Chase sat down in the living room and flicked on the TV and put it to something mindless and dumb. He wanted to forget about the day. Somehow finishing his manuscript was meaningless and he wasn't in a celebratory mood any longer. He really wished he knew what Karen was doing and where she was but at least he knew she was safe from Mathew temporarily.

Chase couldn't focus on the show, his mind kept wandering aimlessly back to Karen and Mathew's presence out on the porch. He wished he could punch the guy, Mathew deserved it but something seemed off about him and Chase couldn't put his finger on it. He seemed afraid and not just because he inadvertently walked into the house of a man he tried to cheat but something bigger.

5

Mathew felt light-headed, and there was this horrible pressure that took over the moment he sat down. He should have taken the lemonade when Chase offered it, but the chance it was tainted wasn't worth the risk. However he didn't truly believe Karen to be homicidal. Mathew was thankful Chase had more grace than he ever did. If the situation were reversed Chase would have a black eye and a sore jaw by now.

A wave of nausea passed over Mathew and his vision blurred; everything around him was a different shade of grey. He was never this dehydrated before in his life. His ride better appear sooner rather than later or Mathew feared he would pass out by the time she arrived. He grimaced as a sharp burning pain started behind his eyes. He clawed at his face in attempt to end the pain but it just kept building up in pressure to the point his head felt like it would burst.

As suddenly as the pain came on it stopped and Mathew found he could think clearly again. He could see things better than before and he knew Chase was trying to kill him via lemonade. Chase was going to keep attacking him and in order to save himself he needed the man dead. It was only a bonus that the results would also end in Karen being conveniently single.

Mathew stood up, no longer paralyzed with dizziness. He walked around the house, knowing Chase locked the front but probably never thought to also lock the back. The backdoor led nicely into the kitchen and if he remembered correctly a knife block rested right on the counter, close to his fingertips. Mather slinked around the building and found the back porch. He carefully tried the door and was relieved to find Chase was in fact dumb enough to leave it unlocked. He was thankful that aspect of small town life caught on to the hard New Yorkers. Mathew slowly slid the door as silently as he could manage, while checking for signs Chase was nearby. The TV was playing loudly and Chase was chuckling at something under his breath from the living room couch.

Mathew let himself into the house, keeping the door open for an easy escape route. He was afraid the slamming of the sliding door would alert Chase. He carefully navigated himself to a spot against the wall, out of sight from the living room. The knife block was where he remembered and within reach. He went for the largest handle, the butcher knife. He heard the sound of metal against metal as he quickly pulled it out of the slot. The knife was definitely kept sharp enough and felt good in his hands. He wielded the weapon behind his back, clasped carefully in his right hand. He tiptoed closer to the living room and peered inside. Chase was sitting on the couch focused on the TV but it would be easy for him to turn his head and see Mathew standing in the doorway. It wasn't going to be simple to sneak up on him, and he didn't like relying on the power of the TV as a diversion.

Mathew tried to formulate a new plan but was startled by a buzzing sound from the coffee table. He quickly backed up a few paces and clung to the wall as cover. Chase looked around and frowned towards the kitchen, then picked up his cell from the table. He double-checked the kitchen again before swiping the screen on his phone to check his text. He looked suspicious and Mathew feared he would be discovered. Chase got up and walked towards the bay window, he had his back to Mathew momentarily and it was tempting to cross the distance between them and make himself known. Tempting, as it was it would have failed and he kept his patience and pushed his body deeper into the corner by the stove. Mathew listened as the footsteps quickly led closer to the door, now that Chase was out of his line of vision. One…two…three. Mathew emerged from the doorway and immediately noticed the sliding door left ajar. Mathew took the moment's pause to regain his dominance of the situation and moved in behind Chase, readying the knife ready to bite into his flesh.

"Looking for me?" Mathew whispered into Chases ear and he flung around faster than anticipated. Mathew was thrown back a couple paces.

"You!" Chase gapped in horror and was frozen in place, his eyes catching sight of his knife in Mathew's hand. Mathew lunged at Chance using the knife as a sword. Chase dodged just in time and made a move to grab his arm but missed and he instantly felt the bite of the blade slicing through his flesh. He recoiled and nearly fell backwards, his arm stinging from the pain. Mathew was high on power and the glint of fear in his victim's eyes lifted him up and left him wanting more. Mathew ran at Chase, knocking him to the floor. Chase crawled backwards towards the wall and kept out of reach of Mathew. He watched as the desperate man eyed the open door, contemplating a run for it.

"I don't think so," said Mathew and slammed the door closed, making sure to correct Chase's fatal flaw and locked it in place. Suddenly there was an abrupt pain in his head and his vision blurred and went black, then he hit the floor.

6

Catherine barely made it out the door of Melinda's house before her phone rang. The caller id told her the call came from Karen's house, but she knew she wasn't home. Who could be calling her? It was doubtful Chase would be phoning but maybe he was wondering where Karen was, and why she wasn't home yet. Karen's disdain for Mathew bothered her and Catherine wasn't in the mood to talk.

As much as she knew he wasn't to be trusted and admittedly contained numerous flaws Catherine couldn't help but feel slightly defensive when her friends berated him. Mathew wasn't a murder. Arrogant and narcissistic? Yes. But homicidal? No way! It angered her Karen understood her feelings on the matter but continued to publicly side against Mathew and confided way too much in Melinda.

To Catherine, the sixth grade teacher was always a bit quirky and an odd ball. She couldn't understand why Karen suddenly seemed to enjoy her company. She was friendly and surprisingly tolerable but wasn't quite able to fit into the group. It was childish of her and she understood that but she was hurt Karen actually seemed closer to Melinda than her in the last few weeks.

Catherine wasn't always drawn to Mathew, but when he showed interest in her at the staff Christmas party last year she fell victim like many other woman to his charms and boyish looks. She went home with him that night and she woke the next morning to a pounding headache and empty bed. Worse still, January classes started again and Mathew carried on as if nothing was ever exchanged between them. Catherine hated herself for caring that much but the feeling never quite went away. She should hate him, she would have a justified reason to but something inside her just couldn't let go. Finally deciding she was mentally ready to deal with a Karen related problem she answered the call just before it was about to go to voicemail.

"Hello?"

"I'm really glad you picked up. I need your help!"

"Is that you Mathew?" Catherine was dumbfounded. Mathew didn't sound like his usual cheery self. He seemed off.

"Can you please pick me up and give me a ride to town. I'm at the William's place."

"Um, why are you asking me for? Isn't that Karen's house? What the fuck are you doing there?"

"Yes, that is Karen's house. I'll explain when you get here. Please hurry!" Mathew hung up the phone before she could protest. Karen's house was a 15-minute drive from Melinda's. She thought about ignoring him but he seemed so frantic and desperate, the curiosity got the better of her. Maybe if she pulled through for Mathew he would stop ignoring her. Catherine didn't even know what she wanted any more.

Catherine drove the distance to Karen's house and slowed as she turned onto the dirt side road. She wasn't ready to face the source of her problems and she was stalling. Catherine drove closer and finally parked along the road opposite of Karen's house. Looking around she didn't see Mathew anywhere. She really hoped it was possible to avoid the awkwardness of Chase and Mathew together. Catherine had no idea the two men even knew each other, never mind hung out in their spare time. She didn't quite get the feeling that was what was going on here, if that were the case Karen would have known where Mathew was earlier and she most certainly would have said something. Catherine was sure Karen would be forbidding any kind of social interaction with her work nemesis.

She slammed down on the horn in frustration after sitting in the car for a few minutes. Still there was no sign of life from Karen's house and there didn't appear to be any movement from inside. The bay window was drawn and she could see the living room was empty, and it didn't look like anyone was home. Catherine tried the horn one more time in a desperate attempt to not have to leave the van. She contemplated just driving away, in fact she sort of thought it was her best option. Catherine worried the implications of the strange call.

Nothing about the day seemed right, and everything was turned upside down. The front door of Karen's house slowly swung open and a shirtless Mathew emerged. Catherine's stomach clenched with fear, the sight was unsettling as she noticed dark crimson colored stains on Mathews jeans and nearly dried blood that looked to come from a wound on Mathews head. He noticed the van and jogged over to the passenger side and slid into the seat.

"I'm sorry about this," said Mathew solemnly. He didn't look at her, just stared straight ahead like an emotionless robot.

"What the fuck Mathew?" Catherine screamed at him, he flinched at her unexpected outburst but remained emotionless and still. "Are you going to answer me? You promised you would answer me!"

"I got lost."

"It looks like you've been in a fight!" Catherine worried about the blood and dirt on her seats. Luckily her van was in need of a good cleaning, but this was unacceptable and scared her.

"Chase hit me over the head with a frying pan," said Mathew, still speaking in a monotone like daze. He wasn't fully invested in the present. Catherine could see why Chase might want to hit him. She was restraining the same urge.

"Why did he hit you?"

"It's not important. Can you just drive please? I really want to go home." Mathew was pleading now and he seemed surprisingly on the verge of tears, so much so that it shocked Catherine and she reversed into Karen's driveway to turn around. She wanted to ask so much more but she feared the response she would get. Maybe she should give Karen a call. She had a mind to drop Mathew at the police station or the hospital. He wasn't in any condition to be home. She wondered if he had a concussion. She drove in silence until she reached the main road of town.

"Sure you don't want to get that checked out. It looks bad," said Catherine and reached over to get a closer look at Mathew's head. He grasped her wrist tightly and didn't let go.

"Mathew you're hurting me!" She shrieked.

"I'm fine!" Mathew yelled and released his grip. There was a ring of red impressions on her wrist and she knew it would bruise. She looked down into her lap and refused to make eye contact.

"Mathew, get out!" Catherine said as calmly as she could

"You said you'd take me home," Mathew said firmly but he exhausted her level of patience for the day.

"I said get out!" He looked over at her to access the situation but reluctantly stepped out of the van and slammed the door closed. Catherine made sure to lock it the moment it shut. Mathew knocked on the window. He was trying to tell her something but it was muffled through the glass. Catherine signed and opened the passenger window a crack.

"Don't tell anyone you picked me up okay?" Catherine noticed the light was green in front of her and she sped off leaving Mathew waving furiously at her from the corner. She thought she saw him give her the finger in her rearview mirror. Catherine turned towards her home contemplating what her next move should be.

Something didn't feel right. She decided Karen was probably on her way home. She should check up with her later.

7

"Have you seen anything like that before?" Deputy Anderson asked Police Chief Grierson.

"I've never seen a murder never mind what that was. It looks like some sort of ritual killing. There hasn't been a serious crime in this town since before I became a cop and that was a good twenty years ago now," said Grierson.

"It's a good thing you called the F.B.I. in, there's going to be lots of questions and I have no idea how we are going to handle this. The media are going to dig up some facts sooner or later and we could have a panic on our hands," said Anderson.

"I know. This cannot get out."

"Do you think the daughter did it?" Anderson asked.

"I know Tammy, I busted her with marihuana a few times when she was a teenager but I doubt she's capable of murder. I just can't wrap my head around it."

"The husband then? It's pretty clear the couple recently separated."

"There may be something there, but the F.B.I. are handling the questioning for now. I think we should let them deal with this, quite honestly I don't want to think about the possibility someone from our town could commit such a heinous crime," said Grierson. Anderson brewed a cup of strong coffee and took it over to his desk. There was endless paperwork to fill out and his mind kept wandering back to the sight of Tammy covered in blood sitting on the kitchen floor staring motionless at the phone in a near catatonic state. All his training for the police force never prepared him for that moment and nothing could have prepared him for what they found next. Anderson had a nagging feeling they were missing something but he couldn't figure out what it could be.

"Were you with the police when the St. Claire's went missing?" Anderson asked. It slipped out of his mouth before he'd put much thought behind the reasoning.

"I was the deputy then, it was over fourteen years ago now. Why do you ask?"

"I was just thinking. That case was probably the last big thing to happen in this town," said Anderson. Even he wasn't entirely sure why he asked.

"Yup, it was. I still remember it like it was yesterday. That case never sat right with me for some reason. It caused a bit of a panic in town but turned out to be for nothing. At least that's how the official story goes but sometimes I wonder. I questioned Richard myself when Jennifer was reported missing and I got the feeling the man was hiding something. I was still young then and there was more evidence to prove he was telling the truth than lying. Still I wish we spent more time investigating."

"You think something happened to Jennifer?" Anderson never heard his boss talk about the case so openly before.

"Jennifer, her daughter. I don't know. I like to think not but we need to remember just because this is a small town doesn't mean we are immune to bigger issues. Just look at what happened today," said Grierson. Anderson searched the St. Claire case report on his laptop and saved a copy on his desktop. He was curious about what else the town had been victim of and cross referenced any case report for murder and missing persons cases, expecting it to turn up blank. After buffering for what felt like forever, the results were in and Grierson wasn't wrong. They may be small in numbers but they weren't immune to murder. There were four homicides reported on file at the station since the year 1900 and there were other major cases of missing persons who were never found according to their reports. They were still listed as suspected homicides and their cases ran cold. Anderson was horrified, his image of the town he called safe forever shattered. Something about the files felt wrong in his gut and Anderson was compelled to figure out what it was.

"What are you reading?" Grierson asked taking in his expression.

"Its nothing." Anderson replied sharply and quickly minimized the files after making sure he had them in a folder on his computer. He wasn't sure why he didn't feel comfortable explaining himself to his boss but he didn't expect the older man to understand.

"You're not looking up the St. Claire case are you?" He seemed suspicious and by the tone in his voice Anderson could tell he wasn't going to be helpful.

"You caught me." Grierson grumbled loudly from across the room.

"Take my advice, just leave it be otherwise it will eat you up inside. Trust me I know." After that nothing was said on the subject, and Anderson returned to finish his report of the homicide of Maggie Elsing.

8

The sun was already half down by the time Karen left Melinda's house and reached her car.

"Shit!" She said, realizing she forgot to tell Chase what she was up to, but he would have to understand under these circumstances. She sped towards her side of town and managed to just make it through the light without having to stop. Karen pulled in beside Chase's truck but hesitated for a moment, as she caught sight of the front door slightly ajar and moving in the wind. It was unlike Chase to leave it open and a bad feeling crept into her gut. She slowly walked up to the front porch and nearly fainted at the sight of a half handprint left behind in a red substance that could only have been blood, it still looked slightly wet.

"Chase!" Her heart skipped a beat in her chest as she heard faint mumbles coming from the kitchen. "Chase!"

"Karen?" The voice sounded weak and far away. She dashed across the room, dropping her purse on the floor.

"Oh my God, what happened?" She shrieked and dove towards the floor where Chase was laying squished up against the side of their kitchen table. He held his left arm tightly and Karen fought another dizzy spell as she could see blood oozing from a wound. A small puddle had pooled on the floor and coagulated already.

"Are you okay?" She wrapped her arms around her groggy, husband and started to cry.

"Mat-Mathew." He stammered and his head nodded as if he was going to pass out again.

"Mathew did this?" Mathew nodded but more deliberately, then his eyes fluttered and he passed out.

"No, wake up. Chase?" She shook him gently and he mumbled in his sleep. BAM! Karen jumped as the telephone tumbled off the counter and crashed into the floor spontaneously. Without thinking she picked the phone up and after finding a dial tone punched in 9-1-1.

"9-1-1 what's your emergency?" A woman's voice declared from the other end of the line.

"My husband's been stabbed." Karen said as her voice started to betray her and break into a sob. She fought back the growing lump in her throat and gave the woman her address. She hung up after being promised the police and paramedics were already on the way.

"I'm fine!" Chase protested from the kitchen floor. He was awake again and was trying to prop himself up with his good arm, but slid back down.

"Don't move." Karen instructed, giving him a reproachful look.

"I was stabbed, I didn't break my back," said Chase sadly, as he managed to finally garner the strength to push himself into a sitting position, leaning against the table leg for support. Karen took a seat beside him, and the sun caught the glint of a tear running down her cheek. Chase wiped it from her face with his good arm and Karen half smiled, but it dropped from her face as soon as it appeared.

"I'll be fine. Its just blood."

"Do you remember what happened?" Karen asked, making as much effort as possible to keep her eyes off the puddle of blood on the floor.

"All I remember is Mathew was here and he tried to kill me. He managed to stab me with that knife." Karen followed his gaze to the horrifyingly bloodied knife on the floor where it fell. The bastard had the gull to use her own knife. It angered her now she could tell Chase would be fine and wasn't as badly maimed as it originally appeared.

"So he just let you go?"

"I hit him with a frying pan and it knocked him out. That's when I must have passed out, because last I remember he was lying right here. That's all I remember, although I'm glad I woke up to you and not him, and I'm glad he didn't find you. He was dangerous. He's a sick man." Karen heard siren's getting closer to the house and she stood up and walked to the window. A police cruiser stopped behind her car in the driveway and there was an ambulance not too far behind. Two police officers greeted her at the door.

"I'm Officer Grierson and this is Deputy Anderson. I heard there was a stabbing," the chief was eyeing the bloody fingerprints left on her front door. Karen knew Mathew must have left them as he fled the scene.

"My husband is inside." She told Grierson. Two paramedics came rushing up the driveway with medical supplies. "He's in the kitchen." She told them and they quickly pushed past her and made their way over to the kitchen. The police followed and she watched as the paramedics spoke with Chase and got him seated in the kitchen chair. Karen was glad to see he seemed weak but was fully alert and his personality was showing now the shock of the ordeal was fading into a memory. Karen gave her statement to the police chief with as much detail that she could remember, and a description of Mathew. Her phone buzzed in her pocket and it made her jump.

"Are you nervous?" Officer Grierson asked giving her a sympathetic look. Karen didn't answer and checked her phone to see Catherine was calling. Maybe she would be apologizing for her behaviour later, or maybe she got a hold of Tammy, however doubtful that was.

"I have to take this," said Karen and made her way up stairs so she could be alone from the bustle of activity in the kitchen.

"Hello?"

"Hey Karen, the strangest thing happened after I left Melinda's house. I got a call from your house and it was Mathew calling me. It was odd, he wanted me to pick him up and he didn't look good. Karen, he scared me."

"Why didn't you call the police?" Karen tried to refrain from screaming at her friend. The anger was boiling over and she needed to sit down, her breathing was coming in short bursts.

"Um. I guess looking back at the situation I probably should have." Catherine voice went weak.

"Catherine. Mathew tried to kill my husband. I've got the paramedics and police at my house right now. Mathew stabbed Chase and you were his escape route!"

"I'm heading over there right now. I'm so sorry Karen." The line went dead and Karen knew Catherine was panicking and probably jumping into her car. She didn't get the feeling she knowingly escorted Mathew from the crime scene, but she was acting very foolishly.

"Karen." Chase called from downstairs, he seemed to have his strength back. She dashed to meet him and found Shannon and Jim in her living room. "They wanted to know what was going on." Chase helped, when it was clear she was surprised to see them.

"I saw a man get into a van about an hour ago." Shannon told the cops.

"Did you recognize the vehicle?" Anderson questioned.

"It was Catherine's." Everyone turned to stare at her. "She just called me and told me Mathew was here today and she drove him home. I told her Chase was stabbed and she said she's on her way over."

"Uh, I thought it looked like Catherine's van but I didn't want to say anything. I didn't think she would be involved in something like this."

"I don't think she knew anything but she should have," said Karen sadly. This whole Mathew ordeal was going to strain their friendship and Catherine was the first real friend she made in this town.

They all turned to the sound of a car door slamming outside. Catherine was true to her word and rushed over, probably exceeding all the speed limits in the process. Running footsteps ran up the driveway and Catherine poked her head in the door, which Karen still left partially open. She looked stressed, and apologetic.

"You're the Catherine who picked up Mathew Barry from here?"

"That would be me," said Catherine sadly.

"I have a few questions for you." The two police officers led Catherine into the kitchen. This was going to be a long night.

Origins

1

The events leading up to the demise of her family were unavoidable. Jennifer saw it soon after her death. Everything was connected in a big vicious cycle that would continue to take lives from the town one by one until someone was able to put and end to it. Jennifer saw the damage first hand and felt its wrath, the task certainly wasn't going to be easy. She saw the evil in Richard's eyes when he dragged her to the basement that April night. It wasn't her husband but something else, something nefarious. The deaths taken during the spring of 1998 were the price the town paid for some long forgotten debt, and a greed that existed in the hearts of the original founders. It was a chilling tale, and one no longer remembered by most the living and a story the dead still feared. Jennifer was able to communicate with the others like her who met with similar ends. The other victims. They were the Lost Souls.

There was only one soul Jennifer wanted desperately to hear from but Molly still remained silent, a dark void in her existence. She couldn't sense her presence whether living or dead, the girl was simply gone.

2

It came to Willis in a dream and it wasn't long before the seed was firmly planted in his brain. It beckoned him towards it, with promises of wealth and status. In the year 1844 Willis had needed and desperately wanted to forge himself a path to be better than his father and his father before him. Willis craved independence and the image the dream showed him offered a way to achieve even the dreams so ambitious he feared to admit even to himself. Then there was the bearded man. Willis was drinking at the pub when he first saw him out of the corner of his eye. The figure caught his eye from across the room with a knowing glare. They never spoke but the feeling that came over Willis was so powerful he would never forget that moment. It was nearly a fortnight later when Willis, drunk with beer was stumbling back to his mothers shack with the help of friends Bruce and Harry. The bearded figure stood motionless across the street as if he was waiting for something and Willis took his opportunity to get answers.

"I can get back from here alright," said Willis but he was preoccupied with the mysterious stranger. After his friends left him alone he called to the man. "Hey you!" The stranger beckoned him to follow without turning to face him. He started walking down the dark alley and quickly disappeared from sight. Willis gave chase and followed him into the dark abyss. "Who are you?" He demanded.

The question remained unanswered. The dream replayed in his mind the farther they walked, the city limits were nearing and the trees were growing thicker. "It's you isn't it?" Willis finally asked.

"I've been waiting for you." The figure replied and the walking stopped. They were far from the city now.

"I don't know you."

"You will," said the stranger. Willis couldn't shake the feeling that overcame him in the presence of the stranger. It only seemed to be intensifying and left him with the hairs on the back of his neck upright. His instincts screamed for him to run and get away, but his inquisitive mind was curious. Despite everything Willis stayed, if only to figure out what made this man so different.

"What do you want from me?" Willis demanded, his voice was oozing with unfound confidence.

"You already know why I'm here. You've dreamt about this many times over. You are chosen."

"My dreams, you've got to be kidding me." The man stared, frustrated. Willis began to get nervous as the energy of the situation changed. It was odd how he suddenly felt so connected to everything and noticed every change.

"I have a proposal for you. I know you want power and respect, I can give it to you, but there will be a price to pay. There is always a price."

"I don't have much," said Willis.

"I'm not interested in money. I will give you a new life, all I ask for is the same in return."

"I don't understand."

"You are chosen, so you will in time. All you need to do now is accept my offer." The bearded stranger extended his hand to shake. Willis hesitated, but good manners insisted he shake an offered hand. Something seemed fundamentally wrong about the situation but at only twenty-two Willis craved power and he truly believed he would get it. Willis offered his own hand but the man grabbed hold of his wrist and he tried to thrash away. He got a good look into the stranger's eyes and he could see a black mist floating in them, making them look coal black. A sharp pain ripped up his arms and Willis's head felt heavy and tunnel vision took over. The last thing he remembered was the black eyes staring at him as they ripped apart his flesh.

He woke up the next morning in the same field he was in but the man had left. Everything seemed normal. Willis checked his arm and all that lay as evidence was a strange symbol embedded in flesh. It resembled an old scar and was hardly noticeable. Willis had seen the symbol before. It translated to mean spirit, one of the five elements.

3

"Let me see," said Karen. Chase reluctantly surrendered his arm to be scrutinized. "That looks bad."

"I swear I don't even feel it," Chase lied, but his face cringed as he moved his arm too quickly, giving him away.

"You sure you don't want a painkiller?" Karen asked.

"I said I was fine," said Chase stubbornly. Karen sighed and dropped the subject. Once he dug in his heels it wasn't worth even trying to change Chase's mind.

"It still bugs me. Why the hell would Mathew just show up here like that in the first place," Karen muttered mostly to herself as she cleaned the kitchen up from their late night dinner. Shannon and Catherine left an hour before but they all agreed nothing could get done until the daylight. Mathew was still around and until then she didn't know if it was safe. She made sure to go around and lock the doors and windows but living out in the country finally had a downside. Two police officers didn't seem like enough anymore in a town where crime was nearly unheard of. A murder and an attempted murder in the same day was enough to uproot any feelings of safety. What would be next?

"Mathew said he was going to tell you that the woman you are replacing quit and the job is yours next year." Karen spun around to face Chase. The tension was high and it hadn't been so awkward between them since the day Melinda showed up and Chase accused her of being mentally unstable.

"Why the hell would you tell me that?" It came out harsher than she intended.

"I just thought you would want to know," said Chase, his eyes were cast down at the table purposefully avoiding her gaze.

"I-I'm sorry. I shouldn't have yelled. I'm just so stressed out and scared right now baby," said Karen and her eyes filled with water, threatening to spill over her cheek. She quickly wiped them.

"We both are, Karen. Everything will be okay. We are both okay," said Chase. Karen looked down at the bandage on his arm. The blood was already soaking through the gauze. She didn't say anything but Chase noticed her stare and hid his arm in his lap under the table. Karen pulled out one of the kitchen chairs to sit closer to him.

"I don't know what I'm supposed to do now," said Karen, and she rested her face in her arms. Now all she could do was wait.

4

Mathew locked himself in his apartment, lost in self-reflection. What happened to him today? How did he get into the woods and how did he lose track of so much time? He felt as if his body wasn't his own anymore and was merely a shell while someone else held the puppet strings. He wasn't himself and everything felt wrong, like he was living in a nightmare but not even in his darkest nightmare was the murderous being himself. Mathew knew the only logical answer to his situation was a mental disorder. Maybe he had multiple personalities, he saw that in a documentary once. He wasn't safe to be around and Mathew knew he needed to turn himself in before he hurt anyone else. He nearly hurt Catherine when she was being kind enough to drive him home. She was only worried about him and rightfully so. Hell, she was probably terrified of him too. It was no ones fault but his own.

Catherine was a nice girl, a little bit of a drama queen but she could have been nice company when he was lonely. She was as real as it could have been if he ever chased anything attainable. Mathew was always that kid in the sandbox who wanted the shovel only after one of the other kids started using it. The challenge was the real fun but now he knew he screwed up. Mathew knew he owed everyone in his life an apology. Maggie, Karen, Catherine. Most of all Karen. He shuddered at the image of Chase unconscious and bleeding in his own home. Mathew didn't stay around to check if he was breathing. There was a good chance he was a murderer now. Karen would have called the police, or Catherine, but the police would be involved.

Mathew walked into the bathroom and looked at himself in the mirror as he stripped out of his bloodstained jeans and put on a fresh pair and a presentable shirt. He checked his hair but movement caught his eye. In fact it was his eyes. A black mist was floating across the whites making them appear darker and almost evil. Mathew jumped back; maybe his mental illness progressed to hallucinations. He didn't have much time. Mathew ran down the steps of his apartment and into the frigid late spring air. His truck was still where he left it in the ally and he backed it out and drove past the bar which was hopping with an above average number of underage high school students out celebrating their impending graduation and start to freedom. Mathew stopped out front of the community center, which doubled as the police station. The cruisers were parked out front and a light was left on. The officers were working overtime tonight. Mathew took a deep breath and stepped out of the truck and took in his last bit of freedom before surrendering himself to what he deserved.

5

Karen didn't think she fell asleep but when the phone rang on the bedside table she was startled awake and pushed over the snoring Chase to get to it.

"Hello, this is Karen Williams?"

"This is Officer Grierson. Mathew Barry turned himself in last night for the assault on Chase Williams." Karen was stunned into silence. "He confessed to breaking into your home and stabbing Chase."

"He just turned himself in?" Karen was still in a daze, and the math just didn't seem to add up.

"He showed up at the station last night claiming we needed to lock him up for the safety of the community."

"Um, can I talk to him?" Karen asked. She didn't realize how much she needed to confront him.

"The F.B.I. have taken him to their office for questioning."

"Is Mathew a suspect in Mrs. Elsing's murder?" Karen assumed.

"I really can't say," said Grierson grudgingly.

"Thanks for calling, officer." Karen hung up the phone and wondered whether she should wake her husband. Chase mumbled something muffled into his pillow that sounded like, 'who is it?'

"The police called. Mathew willingly turned himself in last night." Chase pushed himself upright in bed but grimaced as he put too much weight onto his injured arm. Karen was about to ask how he was but Chase gave her a discouraging look, so she held her tongue.

"That's good," said Chase but Karen could tell he was just as confused as she was.

"Yeah, it is but something doesn't seem right."

"Maybe he felt guilty?"

"Mathews guilty of everything. It never seemed to bother him before," said Karen.

"So the devil has a soul." Chase suggested and they both laughed. It felt good to be almost back to normal, but then Karen remembered Mrs. Elsing was murdered. It didn't sound like Mathew confessed to the murder, only to his involvement with Chase's maiming. If he was going to put himself in jail over one crime why not the other?

"I'm jumping in the shower. Care to join me?" Karen dragged herself out of bed and headed towards the bathroom stripping her nightgown off as she went. Chase smiled and waited until the water was running to chase after her.

Everything around them was so wrong but neither of them acknowledged it as they went on as best they could manage. Besides from changing Chase's bandage the day seemed normal until Karen turned on the TV while they munched on a bowl of sugary children's cereal. The morning news was on and Karen was startled to notice herself in the background of the footage being shown from outside Mrs. Elsing's house.

"Is that you?" Chase questioned, raising one eyebrow. "What happened yesterday that I missed?" Karen realized in the middle of the drama she never told Chase about the murder. Flashbacks of the day before came back to her, and she saw the stretcher bringing out the body once more and Tammy's blood stained hair as she was wrapped in a blanket.

"There was a murder yesterday in town. My old boss is dead." There wasn't a need to say more because the network's anchor came back on with updates.

"Police have told us Maggie Elsing was found dead in her home yesterday. Her daughter Tammy Elsing discovered the body in the early afternoon and the police were called. F.B.I. agents are investigating and have ruled the crime a homicide. New information claims they may have a suspect in custody this morning but no word yet as to whether murder charges have been laid." The news cut to a commercial break after the story and Chase still hadn't said a word.

"Melinda called me after work and told me about the police and reporters out there so I thought I should see what was going on. I still can't believe it!"

"I wondered where you were. Do you think Mathew is who they were referring to?"

"Yeah, the officer on the phone said something along those lines."

"He didn't do it," said Chase, startling Karen.

"Why the hell not?"

"He was all the way out here when the murder was called in. If it happened at noon there's no way he could have gotten this far on foot so fast without being noticed. He had to have hiked in from the other direction to get onto our property."

"The murder was called in at noon but it could have happened sooner, there's no way to know for sure. Didn't you say he was already covered in blood before he got here? And wasn't he acting weird?"

"I guess you're right. I hope he did it, because if he didn't that means there are two people that are capable of murder in this small town and I really don't like those odds."

"I know." Karen was entertaining the possibility of Mathew's innocence but if he wasn't involved then who else would want Maggie dead and be malicious enough to go through with it. Mathew clearly was capable of murder and Karen was always able to sense something not quite right with him. Tammy found the body and didn't get along with her mother but Karen didn't think she was homicidal. Was she capable of blackmail? Possibly. But murder?

There was a banging on the front door. Karen wasn't expecting anyone, so it was most likely a noisy neighbor who noticed the police and ambulance in front of the house last night.

"I'll get it," said Karen, knowing whoever it was would probably make a spectacle out of Chase's arm. Karen looked out the peephole before opening. She saw an augmented stranger in a suit along with the officers from last night. "Here we go again," Karen mumbled to herself in frustration. She wanted nothing more than to be left alone by the police but like everything else she was always getting inadvertently involved in the towns problems. Karen slowly opened the door to the four people standing on her porch.

"Hi Mrs. Williams, I'm special agent Lisa Thornton, with the F.B.I. and this is my partner Agent, Ross Tomlin. We need to request access to your property in relation to a crime yesterday."

"My husband was stabbed but I thought you already had Mathew?" Karen's stomach dropped. Maybe he somehow played the system and got released.

"Mathew is in custody but we are looking for evidence in a murder case."

"What does this have to do with my property?"

"We'd really appreciate it if we could just look around. We can get a warrant." The agent sounded friendly but Karen could tell it was just a front. She wouldn't be wise to argue with this woman.

"Sure, anything you need. If it helps figure out what happened to my old boss, I'll be glad to help," A dog barked from one of the agent's cars. Karen looked past the police for the first time and she felt faint when she noticed Mathew sitting quietly in the back of one of the cruisers.

"Mrs. Williams, did you know the victim personally?" Karen didn't like that the question seemed more like an accusation.

"She was my boss at the elementary school before she quit. We never really talked on a personal level but I knew her daughter

Tammy." Special Agent Thornton's eyes narrowed a bit and Karen reminded herself she should probably be careful of what she said in order to avoid becoming a suspect.

"What is he doing here?" Karen finally cut in changing the subject. It was eating at her, even from behind bars and probably handcuffs Mathew's presence made her nervous and fidgety.

"We're sorry for the inconvenience Mrs. William's but he is necessary to our search," said agent Tomlin and he did look genuinely sorry.

"Didn't you request to speak to Mathew Barry this morning?" Officer Grierson stepped in.

"Yes, but I didn't want him anywhere near my house or my husband!" Karen said.

"Karen?" Chase called from the living room.

"The F.B.I. is here," Karen yelled back at him, although he probably figured it out by now. She heard Chase get up and he came to stand beside her in the now way to crowded entranceway.

"Nice to meet you Mr. Williams," Special agent Thornton greeted extending her hand. Karen didn't like the sudden change to over friendliness again. She already detested the woman's façade.

"They were about to search the property for something," said Karen sharply. Chase gave her a look sensing the tension she was feeling.

"Can I ask what you are looking for?" asked Chase, he looked confused.

"We are simply doing our jobs, sir." Agent Thornton stepped back and left the porch leaving the others to follow. Karen and Chase watched as they led two dogs out of the back of a black SUV. There was a German Sheppard and a chocolate lab both donned in black vests that read F.B.I. Whatever they were searching for it was serious.

"Let's go back inside," said Chase as Mathew was being let out of the cruiser. Karen took once final look and went inside the house and away from the chaos going on in her yard. She'd had enough share of drama for a while.

6

"Show us exactly where you were yesterday," said agent Thornton to Mathew the moment he was let out of the cruiser. The handcuffs were tight and bit into his flesh and he was convinced it was on purpose. He's spent the early hours of the morning going from county jail to the F.B.I. precinct and interrogated heavily. Maggie was murdered. Mathew had trouble getting past that reality. Maggie was murdered and they accused him of the crime. It stung but worst of all he had no idea if he was guilty or not, it did look suspicious. Agent Lisa Thornton was a hard ass, and Mathew knew her type well. She was over achieving and ambitious and desperately wanted to put the case to bed. There wasn't going to be no as an answer even if there really was nothing to be given. Agent Tomlin was easier, he played the good cop and he knew it would be wise to get in his good books, because despite Thornton's domineering ways,

Mathew was able to determine Tomlin was the higher respected of the two.

"Can you loosen my handcuff's at least," Mathew pleaded, and was met with harsh glares, but Agent Tomlin did undo his handcuffs and loosened them into a much more comfortable position. He could still feel the metal but at least he would have skin. "Thank you."

"Start walking," Agent Thornton spat and Mathew tried his best to back track his path from the day before, bypassing the detour inside the William's residence. Agent Tomlin released the two search dogs that immediately started sniffing at the ground and taking cues from the agents. The local police trailed behind for security reasons mostly but they were obviously out of their league. Mathew never saw Officer Grierson so complacent. The man was a weekend regular at Morgan's and could be seen flashing his badge at every opportunity.

Mathew walked around to the backyard and saw Karen and Chase watching from the window curiously. He tried not to make direct eye contact and picked up the pace on his way further into the property. The dogs ran on long leashes and were running back and forth smelling the ground in no logical order. The Labrador darted closely in front of Mathew, nearly causing him to face plant into the ground.

"Stupid dog," he muttered under his breath. They walked in silence for the most part, and there wasn't anything to be seen. Mathew knew there was a lot of ground still to cover before he could go back to his cell. He wasn't sure if it was a good thing or not, on one hand he wanted to go curl up in a ball and wait for everything to be over and done with but on the other he didn't want to be back in the cold boring room in F.B.I. headquarters or even worse in a jail cell in the city.

"Hey, I think Benny has found something," said agent Tomlin breaking the silence. Mathew looked and the Sheppard did seem to be picking up a scent. Tomlin gave the dog more lead and followed closely behind but the Sheppard was all work and didn't lift his head, pulling heavily on the leash.

"That's weird," said Thornton who looked at Mathew suspiciously after the dog suddenly stopped without warning, seemingly coming to a dead end with the trail.

"I swear he had something," said Tomlin and the pair looked at each other in confusion.

"Is there anything we should know about?" Thornton asked Mathew firmly. He just shrugged it off, fairly certain that even in his black out nothing would have happened here.

"Let's keep going," Officer Anderson suggested. There were plenty of trees and foliage on the property and the view of the pond was still blocked. After a few more moments it slowly came into view and Tomlin stopped dead confusing the group.

"What is it?" Thornton asked impatiently.

"I think we should check the pond over there." He said.

"For what? We don't even know what we are looking for?" Thornton said frustrated. She just wanted to get this over with, they already had the body and DNA evidence was in the works. The tests would be back shortly and Mathew would be either cleared or finding himself in a bad situation. The investigation seemed to be more or less a waste of time, in hopes of securing some form of a murder weapon.

"It was just a thought," said Tomlin not impressed with his partner.

"Mathew what did you do when you walked though here yesterday?" Officer Anderson asked, stepping out from the background.

"As I told you already, this was the first house I came to when I was lost. I promise I didn't ditch anything in the pond." Anderson felt Mathew was being genuine. The man looked him in the eye and there was no reason to lie. Mathew was already guaranteed jail time and appeared to be co-operating. He turned himself in for god's sakes and that had to account for something, didn't it?

"Let's move on." Thornton grumbled and followed Mathew beyond the line of trees boarding the William's property line, leading into a small forest of pine trees. Tomlin wasn't satisfied and made one final look at the pond before catching up with the group. The water was too cloudy to see anything but his gut was telling him the pond was the perfect place to ditch evidence and the dogs did seem to be picking up something which was unsettling. The cadaver dogs were trained to find human remains and he hadn't seen them act that way before without a reason. Tomlin wanted desperately to retrace their steps but Thornton was on a mission and on her own agenda.

7

"Do you think they're gone yet?" Chase asked, glancing at the clock.

"I don't know," Karen looked out the window from behind the curtains, "the cars are gone."

"It's about time. They were out there for at least six hours. Do you think they found anything?"

"I hope not," said Karen. She didn't want to think about the possibility Mathew was hiding a murder weapon or worse in her backyard.

8

Karen left Chase inside the small church while she quickly intercepted Catherine at the entrance. The two hadn't spoken since she gave a statement to the police when she helped Mathew flee her house.

"Can we talk?" Karen asked and Catherine wordlessly made her way down the chapel steps and into the not quite big enough parking lot.

"I'm sorry about the Mathew th—" Karen cut her off.

"Its alright, that's not what I wanted to talk to you about. I just wanted to ask you how Tammy was and if you talked to her yet?" Karen interjected.

"Oh. I haven't yet but I was on the phone with Suzie yesterday and she said Tammy is taking it really hard, especially since the F.B.I cleared Mathew as a suspect yesterday."

"WHAT!"

"Yeah, apparently they told Tammy his DNA didn't match what they found on the victim, I mean Mrs. Elsing. God, this is all so terrible to even think about." Catherine looked as if she was about ready to burst into tears from the stress of it all. Karen felt the pressure as well. The implications of the potential new murderer were too much to consider, since Karen had already condemned Mathew in her mind. She noticed the parking lot cleared and the depressing organ music started playing.

"We better go inside. I fucking hate funerals." Karen declared on her way up the steps. She quickly skirted down the aisle to her seat beside Chase. He gave her a disapproving look, before focusing on the minister who was clumsily making his way behind the podium. That casket was closed at the front of the room and Karen tried hard not to picture what horror lie inside. She saw Tammy in the front row sitting beside a man in his mid sixties that must be her father. She was sobbing silently into a balled up mound of Kleenex, but the older man just sat motionless staring past the minister in a daze.

"We have gathered here today to celebrate the life of Maggie Elsing that recently came to a tragic end earlier this week. Maggie was well respected and known to all at the public school. There wasn't one little face she didn't recognize…" The minister went on glorifying the life of Maggie Elsing in a biased but respectful way. Karen spent most her time watching Tammy and wondering if she were in her shoes how she would react. Karen wasn't particularly close with her mother but wasn't estranged like Tammy had been. She knew she would be devastated but to be the one to find her like that...Karen shuddered. Chase noticed and squeezed her hand bringing her back to the minister's eulogy. The speech went on for another ten minute or so before he invited family and friends to say a few words. Karen was thankful for the religious mumbo jumbo to end. Church made Karen uncomfortable and she was fidgety in her seat.

Everyone waited for someone to offer to speak but it was Mrs. Langley who stood up first and wobbled over to the podium.

"Maggie has been a great boss and colleague over the last twenty years. She took a chance on me and gave me the opportunity to work with children and do a job I loved and I'll be forever thankful to her for that. One of the saddest days was when Maggie left her job to go to Florida, but I'm sure she had her reasons. She'll be remembered in the hearts of all the children who had the chance to get to know her and she'll never be forgotten at the school as long as I still work there. A plague has been placed in the main entrance dedicated to Maggie because the school was important to her and its only fitting that she continue to be apart of it in death."

Mrs. Langley stepped away and swiped a tear threatening to spill down her cheek. The secretary clearly had a deeper friendship with the principal than Karen realized. There were a few awkward moments of silence while the entire crowd was waiting to see if the family would speak. The personal issues were common knowledge around town and Karen was starting to believe neither her husband or daughter were going to share but eventually Tammy rose from the pew. She appeared composed as she cleared her throat and stared out at the roomful of family and friends there to support her.

"It's no secret my relationship with my mother was a rocky one," she said. "But now my biggest regret is not getting to know her more for the strong woman she was. We butted heads a lot, especially in the last few years but I see now she didn't deserve how I treated her and I wish more than anything I could tell her I'm sorry now. She was human and as a human she made a few mistakes but so do I, and so does everyone else. I'm not going to lie and say my mom was easy to get along with because she wasn't. My mom was hardheaded and stubborn as a mule, but that is what made her great at what she did. A little closed off at times, but she was a damn fine principal."

"Here's the part where I should insert a story from my childhood but I'm going to stop here while I'm ahead. I want to remember my mother for what she succeeded at in life and I don't want to let her death define her. I'm choosing not to remember her as the cold mask of a woman I grew up with and instead see her as the children she taught see her. Please don't let her memory live on as the story of her fate, but even as I say this I know it's pointless because that's the only reason everyone came out today. It's the only reason I'm here, and it's the only reason nearly everyone in the room is here. I'm talking about you!" Tammy angrily pointed out the row of reporters standing at the back of the church who slowly inched towards the door awkwardly. Karen wasn't sure exactly when things went wrong but somewhere Tammy lost control and turned on her supporters. She wasn't wrong and the look of guilt wore heavy on the faces in the crowd. Suzie took her chance while everyone was noticing the reporters to quickly escort Tammy back down to her seat, although the ceremony was over. Karen thought it might be wise to avoid the wake and from the looks at the crowd others were having the same thoughts.

9

She was drowning. Karen clawed at her chest frantically fighting for air as her lungs burned and felt as they were about to burst. The dark water swirled around her in all directions, she looked up and saw a clear light shinning and she knew it had to be up. She tried to swim towards the light but she couldn't be fast enough. Some invisible forced was pulling her deeper into the dark depths towards the bottom away from the beckoning light. As her energy weakened she found a calm come over her as she just took in the beauty of the bubbles in the water rippling around her. No matter what she did nothing seemed to take her any closer to that sweet breath of air. She sunk deep into the clay bottom, as the air left her lung in one giant whoosh of bubbles making their way to the surface easily, it was unfair. Then Karen lungs could take no more and she involuntarily took in a giant breath.

***

Karen jumped awake gasping frantically for air before discovering she wasn't really breathless. She was sweating profusely, and already soaked the sheets on her side of the bed. The movement woke Chase who slowly was brought back to consciousness.

"I thought the nightmares were over," he said realizing the cause of his disturbance. He pushed himself upright into a seated position, leaning back on his pillow.

"They were." Karen said immersed deep in thought. "This was different. Jennifer needed to show me something."

"I thought we agreed to not mention that name." Chase said sadly, already knowing there wasn't going to be more sleep tonight. His eyes were pleading with her to go back to bed.

"No, I know where Jennifer is!" Karen flung the off the duvet and searched for her slippers in the dark without finding them.

"Karen. Now is not the time for this." She just ignored him and quickly dashed out of the room leaving him alone in the dark. He contemplated going back to sleep before dutifully following her down the stairs. Chase found her wearing rain boots and a sweater over her thin nightgown digging frantically through a drawer in the kitchen.

"I need a flashlight." She mumbled, not even bothering to look over at him on her mission. Chase found it at the top of the fridge, where he kept one in case the power ever went out during a storm.

"Where are we going?" He asked giving up and flicked on the flashlight. "You don't really expect to find Jennifer do you?"

"Not Jennifer, just her body." Karen said flatly as she slid open the sliding door with Chance dumbfounded a few steps behind.

"Um, excuse me? Karen?"

"I need the light. Are you coming or not?" Karen ripped the flashlight from his hands, Chase hadn't seen Karen so determined since she was drunkenly looking for that blackmail picture she found in her laptop bag. It was best to let her do her thing, but Chase was getting a bad feeling about this. Karen was nearly running nimbly in the dark with only the light of the flashlight to guide her, she was placing each foot as if she knew exactly where she was going. It was as if she'd done this many times before. Chase struggled to keep up and his foot kept catching on tree roots. Karen stopped so suddenly he nearly rammed right into her in the darkness.

"She was right here. I don't know how I didn't see it the first time." Karen said, looking off into the distance. Her mind was back to the vivid dream when she chased Jennifer out to this very spot, much like Chase was chasing her now. That night she watched Jennifer disappear into thin air over the pond and she knew it was her attempt at communicating.

"She's in there," said Karen and she shone the flashlight into the depth of the pond. The water was dark and there was nothing to see. Chase walked up to the waters edge and attempted to make out any shapes at the bottom. It was too dark to see anything but black but he knew instinctively Karen was right about this. He didn't know how or why, but he knew Jennifer St. Claire would be found at the bottom of his pond.

10

"Dad?" Tammy called out, she could have sworn she heard someone in the kitchen but the house seemed quiet. Tammy checked the living room and found him sleeping in a giant lump on the couch. The TV was turned on to white noise and she quickly powered it off and watched her father sleep long enough to convince herself she was just hearing things. Tammy did the rounds, making sure all the lights were turned off before calling it a night and retiring to her bedroom. Tammy sank into her mattress glad the day she was most dreading was over. Suzie managed to keep her mostly sane and she was thankful. Tammy didn't have to say much at the cemetery, and she silently watched her mother get returned to the earth. She was concerned for her father. He didn't show any emotion at all during the funeral and burial ceremony. The wall of silence would be normal if she believed it was truly his way at dealing with his loss but Tammy wondered if his demeanor wasn't more malicious. Her father made her jumpy and she wanted him gone before her mother died, but she couldn't find it in her to ask him to leave now.

BANG! The crashing sound in her kitchen startled her out of her reverie just as she was feeling like she could really sleep again. Tammy debated whether she should investigate, this was one of the circumstances she wished she had a baseball bat handy. Tammy slipped silently down the hallway listening for any little sound. She mentally prepared herself before ducking her head into the kitchen, half of her expected to see Mathew standing there with a knife in one hand and her mother's heart in another. She told herself it was a stupid fear and was relieved to find the room still vacant as she left it. Tammy hit the lights and checked in on her dad, but the couch was empty except for his pillow and blankets. Tammy backed up a few steps and ran into something solid.

"Looking for me?" He father's voice whispered in her ear. Tammy spun around and screamed as she looked into the eyes. They were black as coal, and not at all remorseful as he held up a large knife to her throat. Tammy screamed but it was cut short.

Sacrifice

1

"Karen, what's happening?" Chase asked, and his expression was all it took to know something else happened. The police weren't coming.

"Trust me you don't want to know."

"The police are too busy with another murder," said Chase, understanding the gravity of what that meant. They both knew this wasn't a random act by some deranged serial killer. This was happening for a purpose, a purpose that was around for generations.

"What are we supposed to do?" Karen was frustrated. She felt like she was getting somewhere for the first time, right on the edge of figuring out the real answer to what happened to the St. Claire family but instead she was met with yet another hurdle. Karen's cell vibrated on the counter signaling a text. It was from Catherine and read, *'OMG Tammy. Turn on the news now!'* Karen felt a sinking feeling and obediently turned on the TV, she didn't have to fiddle with the channel because the breaking news story was the first thing she saw. Yes, this was bad.

"And the second homicide victim was discovered just miles from where Maggie Elsing was found earlier this week. This time Tammy Elsing was found dead in her house just outside of the small town where her mother lived. Both bodies had their throat slit and were found with the heart removed. Police are looking for Michael Elsing who has gone missing and was living with his daughter at the time of the attack. If anyone has any information on his whereabouts please notify the police or call Crime Stoppers. This is Diane Riley for DC News."

Karen stared at the screen open mouthed as the news hit her and she stumbled in need of a seat.

"Karen, are you okay?" She just nodded. She needed a minute.

"Tammy's dead. I just saw her yesterday… Oh my god!"

"Its terrible. Whatever it is needs to be stopped!" Chase said and hammered his balled up fists on the counter.

"Their hearts were missing, Chase! Who does that?" Karen knew she was right on the boarder line of a mental breakdown and she took in deep breaths to center herself. There was nothing she could do now but hope they caught whoever did this before anyone else was killed. "I'm going to call Melinda."

Melinda answered on the first ring and already saw the news report on Tammy and claimed she was just about to call. Karen asked her if they could meet as soon as possible and Melinda must have picked up on the urgency because she agreed to drop everything to head over now, although not without first asking if Chase was going to be present. He certainly left an impression during the last visit. Despite some hesitation Melinda was sitting in her kitchen within fifteen minutes.

"I could tell you seemed anxious on the phone, I know you knew Tammy this must be extra hard on you," said Melinda warmly. "Its terrifying thinking about it. Its not safe in the streets anymore!"

"I knew Tammy but we were never close. I can't believe she's gone. It was really only a few days ago Mrs. Elsing was found. The worst part is I think it has something to do with that curse or whatever it was you told me about back in May. But I'm crazy right?" Karen said, Chase was listening in and made an appearance joining them in the kitchen.

"Oh my god, what happened to your arm? Are you alright?" Melinda shrieked and Karen felt guilty realizing how little Melinda was kept in the loop. She didn't even think to call her in the mist of all the drama over Mathew, the police search and the funeral. Everyone forgot about poor Melinda.

"I'm fine." Chase clarified and Melinda still seemed confused.

"Um, Chase and Mathew had a surprise meeting and it ended up with a knife incident,"

"Matthew did that?" Karen could tell her friend was thinking Chase got off lucky. She must not know Matthew was cleared from any murder. His DNA wasn't found on Mrs. Elsing and he was in jail during Tammy's attack.

"He showed up here when everyone was preoccupied when Mrs. Elsing was found. Chase was lucky to get by with a few stitches and Matthew turned himself in and must be enjoying a cell by now," said Karen. Melinda didn't seem upset about being left out, which bother Karen more. The poor woman was so used to always being on the outside of the circle.

"If Mathew's in jail…" Melinda came up with the same worrisome conclusion.

"I don't think Mathew is the only one whose been poisoned," said Karen, and Melinda met her eye contact understanding the real reason she was called over.

"The husband." Melinda mouthed and Karen nodded. If the original story held true then anyone in a bad place are susceptible to the darkness. It wouldn't be a stretch to say Michael was at a low point himself after his wife had an affair and left him. His soul would have been weak for the taking, as the dark force claimed him. He had a clear motive for Mrs. Elsing's murder but not an obvious one for Tammy. If there was any merit to Melinda's theory of an old campfire story then it meant he might be more dangerous than even Mathew. His next victim could be anyone, even a completely random target.

"I think we need to stop this," Karen declared.

"Yeah, but I don't think we can. We don't even know if it's true. How can we even know that we aren't the crazy ones?"

"Well then at least we aren't killing people. What harm can we possibly cause?"

"True but I wouldn't even know how to go about starting to make sense of this and I doubt you can. I think we need to leave this Karen, and maybe its time we both consider moving before it gets even more dangerous." Melinda looked concerned, thrust out of her comfort zone.

"I think I know where to go for help," said Karen and Melinda looked doubtful. "I know this is going to sound crazy–,"

"Crazier than this?" Melinda interrupted.

"There was a woman who lived here before me. I think she's trying to help me. I think she wants me to end this."

"You're right that does sound crazy." Melinda snorted. She looked back at Chase, probably waiting for him to kick her out again. Chase met her gaze with a serious expression and Melinda seemed to understand the depth of her reality. Yes, it was completely insane but at least thinking they were doing something was better than sitting around waiting for someone else to take action. "You're really not kidding?"

"Honestly I wish I were. Last night Jennifer showed me where her body was and if I can prove that it's there will you help me?" Karen pleaded.

"I probably shouldn't be saying this but you can count me in." Melinda finally agreed. There was a knock at the front door, which startled them both, "Whose that?" Chase went to answer the door while Karen waiting anxiously. They weren't expecting anyone else.

"Yes, its out back. I hope you can drain a pond," said Chase. Karen couldn't hear who was talking but knew it must be one of the officers checking up on their call. She heard the sound of the door closing and Chase came back into the kitchen. "Agent Tomlin and Officer Anderson are here with one of their cadaver dogs. Apparently they were more interested then I was led to believe. I was originally told not to expect anyone until at least tomorrow."

"That's weird, but I'm glad they came," said Karen. If she was forced to wait a few more hours the anticipation probably would have drew her to wade into the pond herself.

"Should I go?" said Melinda, looking unsure.

"Aren't you the least curious if your going to help me or not?" said Karen and Melinda gave her a half-smile.

"Um, how long ago did you say Jennifer went missing?" Karen hadn't even considered the possibility there might be more than bones to find.

"She's been gone over 14 years. I doubt there will be anything to see but bones, if she's even there at all but if it makes you uncomfortable I wont hold leaving against you."

"No I want to stay. This is kind of cool," both Chase and Karen gave her a disturbed look. "I just mean it's not something you see every day. Not that it's a good thing or anything!" Melinda defended herself.

"I know what you mean," said Chase. "We should get out there." They all walked back to the pond where the two agent had already ran a hose connected to a pump.

"Where would be a good place to drain the water?" Officer Anderson called when he noticed the group.

"Behind those trees would be okay." Chase answered, referring to where the backyard started to turn into denser bush. Anderson stretched the hose and started the pump. Once the humming sound started Karen felt the butterflies in her stomach, as she started doubting herself. How can she be so convinced about something just from a simple dream? Karen reached out for Chase's hand for reassurance while Melinda watched silently. The water was rushing out into the bushes quickly but the level didn't seem to be dropping in the pond. Every second felt like an eternity.

"I think I see something," said Melinda breaking the silence. Karen saw it too but it wasn't what she was expecting. The water still had a bit to drain but Karen could see the top of something that appeared to be rusted metal with some sort of broken cable tied to the top, an end of the cable floated on the water still left at the bottom. Soon with only inches left remaining Karen saw exactly what she expected to see. A toothy grin and hallow eyes look out at her from the muddy abyss. *Hello Jennifer.*

Agent Tomlin was on the phone in seconds summoning up the coroner and an agent to examine the bones. Karen already knew the cause of death, she'd seen it before and the presence of the bones told the same tale. Jennifer was thrown down a flight of stair breaking her right leg and her spine during the fall. Karen saw the woman's throat slit surgically with a hunting knife. That was as much as Karen could stand to watch but Jennifer's body showed clearly what happened next. Her ribs were broken badly as if ripped apart completely as if someone had forced their hands in and physically pulled them aside. The organs and flesh had long ago disintegrated completely but Karen knew if found earlier her heart would have still been missing.

The F.B.I. agent seemed to have arrived at the same conclusion because he was knee deep in the muddy pit assessing the shattered bones carefully. The correlation between murders seemed too big of a coincidence to not consider. Officer Anderson stood in the background with a worried expression on his face, deep in thought.

"We have a serious problem." Melinda whispered in Karen's ear fearfully. The three of them stood back and tried to move out of the way of the small investigation. Karen didn't like the way Anderson was gazing at the remains, like he knew something he shouldn't.

"Is the St. Claire case going to be reopened now?" Karen asked, walking up the young officer.

"Oh, sorry I was zoned out a bit." He looked embarrassed.

"So I guess we know what happened to the St. Claire's now." Karen repeated.

"I wonder which one of them that was." Karen fought back the urge to mention Jennifer's name but decided Anderson may perceive it wrong, and she knew explaining how she figured it out wasn't exactly an option.

"Do you think there's a connection between the murders happening today?" Anderson got the funny expression again and Karen knew he at least came up with a theory.

"I think there's some bigger issue in this town. It almost seems like history repeating itself," Karen tired another tactic and she waited for Anderson's reaction.

"You might just be right," said the officer and he abandoned the conversation to join Tomlin down in the hole where the pond used to be. Karen sensed he knew more than he was letting on and she wanted to figure out just how much. He may be able to prove helpful.

"Hey Karen!" Melinda was waving for her attention. "I think I've seen enough. I have an idea where I might be able to find more information on what ever it is that's going on."

"That's probably a good idea. Call me if you find anything." Melinda quickly made her way back towards the house and Karen was distracted when Agent Tomlin came trudging up to meet them with his German Sheppard dog.

"If you don't mind I'd like to search the property just in case there's any leftover evidence." Agent Tomlin didn't wait for an answer before he sent his dog free to do its job. Karen was about to try to get a closer look at Jennifer's remains while Tomlin was busy but the dog quickly caught her attention. It was intently smelling the ground and picking up speed in excitement and determination. It looked like it may actually be on to something. The dog ran to the back of the property where the bush grew denser and the trees were closer together and disappeared from view. Tomlin followed closely behind and Anderson sprinted to catch up.

"Do you think?" Karen said looking at Chase with a concerned expression. A dog's loud bark and some yelling answered her question.

2

Jennifer was fully awake and others joined her ranks. The Lost Souls were anxiously awaiting their fate and preparing for a fight. The darkness was growing and feeding off of the fear of the people and creating more susceptible victims with every move. It was different this time than the others, the debt was paid and it should be over but it wasn't prepared to leave. The power found the perfect vessel to use as a host forged of flesh and blood, walking the edge of both worlds. It was going to take the combined power of both worlds to banish the darkness for good…if it could even be done. The living were getting closer to the truth with every passing second, Jennifer was just the messenger, and she believed she'd finally found her prophet. It was beyond her now, but the closer the truth came to being discovered the stronger her world became. The stronger the Lost Souls became. It was time to end the reign of terror of their corrupt home.

3

Melinda was finding herself directly involved in something bigger than herself for possibly the first time in her life. It was both a liberating and terrifying feeling and she didn't know what to do with such power and responsibility. She drove herself over to the nursing home her grandfather lived in but she couldn't bring herself to go inside. She'd been pacing back and forth in the parking lot for over five minutes without being aware of the passage of time. Melinda was lost in thought, all the hidden warnings he's given her as a child and she'd ignored then. This place was dangerous, something dark was lingering here and anyone could be a victim or even the perpetrator. The best thing to do would be to calm down and avoid stress in order to ward away what her grandfather had once referred to as the black poison. Melinda leaned against her SUV and took two deep breaths to calm her nerves. *I can't believe I'm doing this,* she thought. Melinda entered the home and took the elevator to her grandfather's room. She hated being here, the chemical smell and sterile walls made her uncomfortable and immensely guilty every time she visited, which was only once in the last year.

She walked the long hallway passing wheel chair bound patrons who seemed to not notice her presence in drug induced mental states. She knocked on the door of her grandfathers room and heard his raspy voice echo through the walls, 'who I it?'

"It's me grandpa," Melinda declared awkwardly. There wasn't a reply but she entered his suite anyway and found him sitting up in his hospital style bed.

"Melinda?" He seemed surprised and pleased to see her, as a smile spread across his face making her heart go out to the man. She felt the guilt of her absence.

"Hi Grandpa." She said, and she pulled up a plastic chair to his bedside, noticing he was hooked up to new machines beeping rhythmically by his bed. "I know you weren't expecting me but I need you to remember something," said Melinda hopefully. His expression dropped instantly and she feared she may have offended him and made a mental note if she ever got though this she would visit at least once a month when she could swing it. He deserved better.

"It's happening again isn't it?" She saw his lower lip trembling.

"What's happening?"

"The black poison. Its back isn't it?" Melinda could sense his fear and it brought her back to reality.

"I think so, there's been two murders already. I've felt its influence grandpa, but I don't know what to do!" Melinda's eyes welled up and she paused to calm herself. She was feeding off of the fear and felt helpless and utterly useless.

"Melinda, be careful and it's important to stay strong. Find the sacred ground. I don't know if there's anything to be done but if you find the ground you may just have chance. This town is born of evil and it all started at that place."

"How do you know that?"

"It got to your grandmother, when your mother was still a girl in 1956. I loved her and it took her from me. I'd seen the evil first hand, and I tried to warn her but it was too late. It was in the eyes of her sister and she trusted her. Look at the eyes and you'll know."

"What about the eyes grandpa?" The machine beside the bed started to get louder and beeped at irregular intervals. In seconds the room was filled with at least four nurses who surrounded his bed doing their job and Melinda forcibly pushed out of the room in the crowd.

4

"What have we found?" said Grierson in awe standing at the edge of the newly dug up pit of doom. Just a few feet into the forest outside of the William's property line was a shallow mass grave with an undeterminable number of skeletons inside. It was going to take hours to sort through all the bones and come up with an exact number and figure out their owners. The crewmembers and agents stood motionless staring into the pit not wanting to believe the horrors they witnessed and not understanding how something so terrible was hidden for so many years. It was becoming clear the fantasy of a clean safe crime rate was nothing but a façade. This was the work of at least one talented serial killer, and it had been going on for years. The age of the bodies made it doubtful the new homicides were related but an investigation was inevitable. The town was going to be rioting once the media caught a whiff of the discovery. Mass hysteria was already beginning and the new murders would be enough to start a whole new level of panic.

Old troubled memories were getting dredged up and Grierson felt the pressure of letting the original St. Claire case run cold. He may have only been a small town officer back then but if only he investigated the disappearance that one-step further. If only he talked to more people, maybe he could have done something. The early analysis found the pond skeleton to be an adult female–Jennifer St. Claire. It wasn't official yet but the early speculation was that she was beaten before her death, and like the new victims it was quite possible the shattered ribcage could mean her heart was taken. That was the thought that haunted the team. It was apparent to everyone here that these murders, all the pit skeletons and Jennifer St. Claire might be connected. They seemed to be apart of some sort of terrible ritual that could even span decades.

5

Karen and Chase walked back in silence both not knowing how to react, both knowing what the other was thinking. The sun was setting beyond the trees and the darkness was beating the light for dominance in the sky and it was getting eerie outside. There were different F.B.I. agents and police all over the property, combing the areas for clues that probably wouldn't be found. The number of bones was staggering, and the body count was climbing which made her fear they were in for slaughter. Chase almost became a victim himself and there was no way of knowing who was affected. Now it was obvious Mathew wasn't the only once poisoned from town she was worrying just how many people were already gone or will be affected. Anyone could be a possible threat, even the police.

"What do we do now?" said Chase.

"Lock all the doors and windows," said Karen, absentmindedly. She was wondering the same thing. Karen did everything she knew how to do, but it somehow wasn't enough. Packing up and driving back to Manhattan seemed like a good idea but she felt like she was somehow meant to help, like it was her destiny to save this place. It was all crazy, and stupid and she didn't understand any of it but Karen decided to go with her instincts and trust herself. It was easier with Chase by her side and with the evidence of dreaming Jennifer's watery grave but it could just as easily been coincidence.

Karen slid the back door open and fumbled around for the kitchen light switch in the dark. Karen's fingers found it the same moment Chase jumped. It took her a moment longer to process the message, written in red letters across the wall, 'Find my daughter.' The meaning was unmistakable.

"That's not written in what I think it is?" said Chase shakily. The intrusion affected him, but Karen was getting all to use to the unexplainable. Ever since the night spent in the cold basement Karen tried to get the woman to show herself again, to no avail. She got a closer look.

"Its ketchup."

"How do you know?" said Chase unconvinced and unwilling to move from where he stood frozen in place in the doorway.

"There's a half empty ketchup bottle open on the floor." Karen declared bending to pick it up and close the lid. It pooled into a puddle on the floor and after the events of last week it could easily be construed as blood. 'Meow,' Timbit the cat entered the room causing both of them to tense.

"Timbit seriously?" Karen scolded, and the Persian gave her a dirty look before trotting out of the kitchen looking pleased. "I've had way to long a day. I think it's time for bed." Karen yawned as if on cue.

"We need to eat something first," said Chase reminding her stomach just how famished she was, there hadn't been a break all day.

"I feel weird cooking in here with that message staring at me," Chase declared. Karen agreed it was making her uncomfortable to. *Find my daughter,* it was a plea for help and a command. Karen turned it over in her mind. Molly could be anywhere, living or dead. She might even be one of the pit skeletons although she doubted Richard would have dumped Jennifer in the pond if he had known about the pit. It didn't make sense. If Molly St. Claire were dead, she'd be on the property.

"Karen!" She jumped out of her reverie. "I said, would you mind cleaning that off the walls while I make us both a sandwich?"

"Um, yes…sorry." Karen mumbled still processing the meaning of it all. She was just dampening the cloth when someone rang the doorbell.

"One of the police officers?" said Karen, looking up from her mindless task. The doorbell rang again, and Karen dropped what she was doing to answer the door. Melinda stood on the other side looking anxious and panicky. "Melinda?"

"I'm sorry, I wasn't sure if you were busy or not, I probably shouldn't have come." She looked as if she was about to turn and walk away.

"No, no, come in please!" said Karen and ushered her friend inside. Karen almost led her to the kitchen but remembering the writing still prevalent on the wall she steered her to a seat on the couch. "Did you find anything?"

"Yeah, I visited my grandfather today and he gave me a warning and a message," said Melinda. She seemed a little shell-shocked and Karen wondered just what all went down during the conversation but she didn't want to ask. "He said we might be able to stop it if we find the sacred place."

"That's good news," said Karen, although the expression on Melinda's face was worrying and made her question what it was she though she could do.

"I guess, but I'm not sure we will be able to make a difference. I've been thinking about leaving. It's all too much to comprehend and I don't think I'm strong enough." Melinda welled up and stared down at the floor looking ashamed. Karen moved to sit beside her and rubbed her back reassuringly.

"You don't have to do this if you don't want to, but you are strong Melinda. Remember when you confronted me in the bathroom when you thought I was having an affair with Mathew? You were brave that day and you stood by your values. I know when you need to you can handle anything!" said Karen.

"That was stupid of me though, I should have let it be." Melinda muttered, looking a little more comfortable.

"No, it wasn't stupid. You were wrong but what you said needed saying. It's why we're friends. Anyway, remember how you marched over here in the pouring rain in the early hours of the morning to warn me about Mathew even though it didn't make sense." Melinda giggled and Karen relaxed.

"I guess that was pretty crazy of me."

"You can be pretty badass when you want to be and when you're determined enough. I'm not going to ask you to help or do anything you don't want to, but you're far from weak Melinda." She smiled but the expression fell almost instantly but Karen knew she was getting somewhere.

"I think I got you in trouble though that day. I hope it wasn't too bad for you." Karen thought back to Chase's protective attitude and concern over her mental health. She was glad those days were behind them.

"You might have stirred up a little something but it's really not a big deal," said Karen.

"I want to help," said Melinda suddenly making up her mind. Karen could tell by the determination in her voice she meant it. "What happened after I left?" Karen realized Melinda was still in the dark about the pit skeletons and wasn't sure how to word it without causing Melinda to rethink her new determined stance.

"The police found something in the woods out back, there's a lot more bones buried. There's too many to just be from the St. Claire's." Melinda's eyes grew big and wary but she remained unfaltering.

"How many bodies?" another question Karen was hoping to avoid, it was enough to shake her to her core and Melinda seemed so weak and fragile.

"They haven't removed and sorted out all the bones yet but there were at least 5 skulls that I could see. I stopped counting after that." Chase entered the room with three cups of black coffee and offered one to Melinda and Karen. The night barely began but exhaustion and stress levels were high all around.

"Did you see any police cars on your way in?" Chase asked, wondering if the investigation ended for the day.

"Only one police cruiser. I didn't see any of the F.B.I.'s vehicles," said Melinda. It seemed weird the local police would be the last to hang around. They spent the majority of today in the shadows almost as much as Karen and Chase themselves.

"Should we go see what they're doing?" Karen asked turning to look at Chase, who seemed confused as well. He looked as if he wanted to go crawl up in a hole and tune out the world until everything went back to normal.

"I want to see the pit." Melinda chimed up surprising Karen.

"Sure," said Karen, unsure of what to make of the dramatic change. She looked suspiciously at Melinda.

"We have to find the sacred ground to end this, maybe the pit…" Karen caught on excitedly.

"Can this wait until tomorrow?" said Chase knowingly, met with two pairs of pleading eyes. "I'll grab my sweater." He sighed and went off back towards the kitchen, mumbling what sounded like, 'I'm never going to sleep again.' The women waited in silence for a few moments, listening to the sounds of Chase moving about the house. Karen was lulled into a lack of sleep-induced trance but a sound snapped her out of it and she shrieked as her eyes focused on a smiling figure looking in at them. It was only there for a moment and was cloaked with dark shadows leaving Karen shaken and unsure of whether it was real or not.

"Karen?" Melinda asked, and Chase's footsteps ran down the stairs before appearing in the doorway with his coat on and a half-eaten sandwich in hand.

"I thought I saw a face in the window over there?" Karen pointed but nothing but darkness could be seen beyond. Chase went to the window and looked around but no movement could be seen in the darkness. He drew the blinds.

"I probably am just seeing things. I haven't slept in nearly 24 hours."

"That and we are all stressed out. I'm sure its nothing," said Chase who wrapped his arm around her, comfortingly. She still had tears in her eyes but she felt better and was sure it was just the stress combined with exhaustion prompting her vision. Melinda still looked concerned but Karen waved it off and gave Chase a dirty look for sneaking food. Karen felt slightly lightheaded from the hunger but the thought of eating just made her feel sick from all the stress. Her body was operating on fumes.

"Um, Karen?" Melinda stopped dead eyeing their new kitchen mural nervously.

"Yeah, I was meaning to warn you about that."

"It-It's not blood is it?"

"Ketchup." Chase jumped in, easing Melinda's nerves but only slightly.

"What does it mean?" She asked, walking closer to inspect the writing.

"The St. Claire's had a daughter who went missing. I think Jennifer is using me to find her," Karen quickly explained.

"Isn't Jennifer a skeleton in your pond?"

"How do you think I knew where she was?" Melinda gulped nervously, and again Karen waited for her to snap again. She didn't and they slowly made their way outside, the air had cooled down and had a bite to it. Melinda drew the hood of her sweater around her face and Karen snuggled into Chase for comfort and warmth. They led the way with the flashlight and followed the little circle of light along the path they walked the night before.

"Do you think Molly survived?" asked Melinda.

"I think the best place to look might be at the bottom of that pit," said Karen and they all got quiet again. Chase's arm around her stiffened and Melinda jumped back as two shadowed figures emerged from the darkness ahead. They both held flashlights and as they got closer Karen saw it was Officer Grierson and Anderson heading back for the night. They both looked just as startled by the three of them and everyone stopped and stared at the others unsure whether to acknowledge the others as both parties were clearly doing something inappropriate.

"We were just heading out," said Grierson nervously.

"We were just checking up on you, Melinda saw your car still parked on the road." For a moment Chase thought they bought it.

"So the three of you decided to see us off?" Anderson asked suspiciously. "There's a killer on the lose in these parts, it would be best to stay in tonight and lock your doors."

"What were you guys really doing here so late?" Chase inquired accusingly, choosing to ignore Anderson.

"We could ask the same?" said Anderson curiously.

"You wouldn't believe us if we told you, we had a theory about those pit skeleton's. Its probably nothing." Anderson raised an eyebrow.

"It wouldn't happen to be a long string of ritual killings would it?"

"I don't know about that but we do think whatever killed those people is more powerful and dangerous than anyone could consider and has been doing it for a long time," said Karen, remembering how earlier it seemed Anderson might have insight into these deaths.

"You know what's responsible," Anderson said, clearly against Grierson's wishes, and who was giving his deputy a reproving glare. "I know there are reports of missing persons and a string of homicides every fourteen years. That's fourteen years exactly." Karen instantly caught on.

"I don't think its really a who that's responsible, we believe its more of a what."

"The Black Poison," said Melinda. None of them spoke for a while it was clear they might have similar interests much like Karen wondered. The police had valuable information and knowledge about the crimes in the town that could prove useful. The question was whether they had an open mind. Karen caught site of movement behind Grierson's shoulder and her attention was pulled away the group. She strained her eyes and thought she saw a figure standing in the darkness beneath the cover of an Elm tree.

"What are you looking at?" Chase asked, noticing her gazing off into the distance.

"There's something over there" whispered Karen. Grierson shinned the beam of his flashlight in the direction she indicated but there was nothing.

"I swore there was something there?" She felt the hair on the back of her neck stand up.

"I have goose bumps," Melinda declared, looking around nervously. Karen was increasingly becoming aware of how small she really was in the world.

"Are we doing this or not?" asked Chase, regaining the attention of the group.

"You were going to the pit?" Chase and Karen led the way followed by Melinda and then the officers. No one dared to speak and Karen was on the look out for her mysterious shadow figure. She was under the impression Jennifer was nearby. At least she hoped it was Jennifer. Her mind went back to the task at hand. She needed to find the daughter, Molly St. Claire.

They fought there way into the trees and down a short ravine that luckily wasn't to steep. Karen nearly stepped into the pit before Chase pulled the back of her shirt saving her from getting a close and personal view of the numerous victims. Melinda fought her way between them to see into the abyss for herself.

"There's so many of them!" She whispered surprised and horrified.

6

Mathew rolled over in the cot in his cell. He had a small window high in the cement wall and the moon cast eerie shadows across the room. There was a repetitive dripping noise coming from the pipes and it was slowly driving him mad. He had the unnerving suspicion he was being watched but the place was empty of any conscious entity. A drunken man in his mid forties was dragged in an hour earlier and passed out within minutes of arriving. Mathew could hear him snoring softly from a couple cells over. Muffled sounds of late night TV were coming from somewhere and Mathew closed his eyes and tried to make out something coherent. He nearly dozed off again but the sensation of falling ripped him out of it fully conscious. From the moment he opened his eyes it was clear the change was imminent. His breath came in labored gasps as he fought with the heaviness coming down around him. The sharp pressure in his skull was becoming too much to bear and his vision blacked out.

Footsteps echoed down the hallway and a door creaked open signaling the guard pulled himself away from his TV and crossword puzzles long enough to make his hourly rounds. There wasn't time for thought, Mathew quickly fumbled around and tore a spring from the bottom of his cot. It was already loose and pried away easily without much effort, it wasn't surprising for how aged it appeared. Mathew clutched it into his palm and concealed it under his sheet as he pretended to sleep. The footsteps slowed at Mathew's cell and continued on down the line to check on the sleeping drunk. As soon as he moved on Mathew through himself into a spasm and fell painfully hard onto the cement floor, thrashing around uncontrollably. The guard ran to see the commotion and threw open his cell upon finding Mathew in a seizure. The unsuspecting man ducked down to get a closer look but Mathew expertly placed the metal spring deep into his neck puncturing the jugular. Blood spurted out of his neck and sent him careening into the wall and sinking to the floor. Mathew felt around for the set of keys, and tore it from the still barely conscious man. He dashed out of the jailhouse unnoticed, even the drunk didn't stir in the commotion. He let himself out into the night air and ditched the keys at the door. He stripped off his orange shirt and followed the faint sounds of house music to the nightclubs in search of a taxi. He was free but there was something he still had to do.

7

Melinda piled yet another shovelful of dirt into the growing mound. The body total had to be higher than anyone expected. She counted at least ten skulls and hundreds of bones. Some of the skeletons were mostly intact with remnants of clothing but it was difficult to tell much of anything from the remains. Karen searched frantically in the dirt on her hands and knees looking for anything that could have been the possession of a 16 year-old girl. There were a couple metal bracelets but nothing definitive. There wasn't any clue that this was the so-called sacred ground her Grandfather spoke about. The bodies were dumped here lazily in the woods and some of them were only a few feet deep into the ground.

"This isn't helping," Melinda decided, wiping her forehead and dropping her shovel outside of the pit. Karen looked up and frowned. "This isn't it."

"Isn't what? I thought we were looking for a teenage girl," said Anderson. The officers were sorting through the remains and tried to make sense of them but weren't being much help. Chase held the light but seemed to be losing confidence in the operation.

"She has to be here!" Karen muttered. "Jennifer needs me to find her."

"What if she isn't dead? What if she is one of these skeletons, what makes you think we would know?"

"I think I just would." Karen muttered displeased but even she doubted herself.

"We need to find the sacred ground, not the burial ground. This isn't it, and there's nothing more we can do," said Melinda. Chase reached down and pulled her from the hole, and Karen followed grumpily.

"When we were here for the first time we were looking for a place Mathew described. We never found it and since it sounded strange enough we didn't believe it existed," said Grierson. "There is supposedly a place in the middle of these woods where strange symbols are carved into trees and a man-made looking rock slab was in the middle, like some sort of ritual grounds." Melinda looked wide-eyed.

"The sacrificial grounds! Mathew is poisoned, it must have led him right to it." Melinda was nervous but felt for the first time they were on the right trail. Even Karen seemed excited.

"Which way was it?" asked Karen, eager to get going. The rest seemed to be thinking the same thing. If the police and their dogs couldn't find the location in the daylight there was no way the cover of darkness was going to bring them any luck.

"Karen, I think we need to go back now, it's late and we are all tired," said Melinda speaking for the group. They all nodded in agreement but Karen was having none of it, she was staring off intently into the woods with big eyes fixed on something in the distance. Melinda followed her gaze and saw a woman standing and watching them intently. She had a menacing grimace on her face that sent shivers down her spine.

"Hey you!" Melinda yelled and the mysterious intruder ran deep into the woods and out of sight.

"You saw her too?" said Karen surprised.

"We all did." Anderson added, and the two women turned to see the flushed pale faces of the men behind them.

8

Karen finally got a better glimpse of their intruder and was relieved to find it wasn't Michael stalking the backyard. It was a young woman around the same age as herself. At first Karen believed it might be Jennifer working in the shadows but this wasn't a figment of her imagination. There was a real solid person in these woods, watching them. The woman didn't seem pleased about it either, and it frightened her. She was brunette with a slight figure and a piercing stare. Her eyes were dark, but it was hard to distinguish in the night. Karen hoped they wouldn't have to get close enough to see if they were black like Melinda warned was the mark of the curse.

Karen knew she shouldn't but the urge to follow the woman overcame her, even though she would often complain about the people who did that in horror movies. Still the figure was a small woman who appeared to be alone and both Anderson and Grierson carried loaded handguns.

"It was this way," said Anderson pointing to the far left of where Karen wanted to go. The group started walking deeper into the bush but Karen still fought the urge to double back and find the woman. *Who was she?*

"Are you okay?" asked Chase whispering in her ear. She nodded and grabbed his hand, attempting to refocus on the task at hand. "We'll only go for a little while okay?" Karen didn't say a word but never protested. Her exhaustion gave way to being over tired and she felt full of built up energy. This was the last night she was going to be afraid. They walked in silence with only the light from a few flashlights to guide them. Karen tripped a few times on fallen branches and roots, the brush was getting thicker and it seemed like they were bushwhacking more than following any particular trail. Just as Karen was giving up hope and thinking of turning back the evergreens gave way to an old deserted dirt road.

"Where are we?" said Melinda astonished. There was some old ruble and a rickety old farmhouse horribly sunken in, Karen feared it would collapse at the vibrations of their footsteps. The small stable off to the side had collapsed leaving a pile of rotten wood and stone.

"I don't think any of these places have been lived in for a while. We were on this road with Mathew and he said he followed a path but it couldn't be found again."

"This is cool!" said Chase wandering away from the group to better examine some of the dated homes. By design they looked to be built sometime in the mid-eighteen hundreds. Undoubtedly Chase was fantasizing about a new novel setting and Karen went to drag him back. With strange people possibly under the influence of the black poison wandering around it wasn't the time for lone exploring.

"Chase!" He disappeared behind a house and Karen was following too far behind and he was gone. Now she found herself alone and susceptible. She found it harder to breath and a cool breeze came out of nowhere. "Chase?" She felt small. She was about to go back to the group waiting for her but backed into an icy wall. "Ah!" Karen flung around and a hand covered her mouth. She stiffened but saw her captor wasn't the strange woman. She was older and more familiar. Karen realized she was only restricted in her mind, and Jennifer stared back at her from a few feet away. Jennifer silently extended her arm and pointed to a small overgrown path across the road. It was easily overlooked and blended in with the greenery but it was there and impossible not to see once her attention was drawn to it. Karen looked back towards Jennifer but there was nothing but air. She jogged back towards the group and was relieved to see Chase was among them.

"That way!" Karen pointed out the discreet pathway.

"How did you find that?" asked Grierson shocked, the others looked equally impressed. Chase gave her a confused look and Karen knew he was thinking she came from the other direction. She would have to thank her messenger later.

"We've come this far?" Melinda pointed out and shrugged, acknowledging their short exploration adventure wasn't going to be as short as planned. Sleep could be sacrificed for the greater good and finding the way back in the dark wasn't really a possibility. Karen already forgot just where they came in through the trees. Grierson led the way down the twisty path deeper into the abyss. They were forced to travel in single file because the trees were overgrowing much of the old pathway. Melinda trailed on the end, having the most trouble with the footing.

"Can someone shine their light over here?" Melinda asked after a while of more hiking. Chase was closest and obediently illuminated the ground by her feet. Melinda kneeled down for a closer look. "That's a new footprint. Someone's been here very recently." Karen got an uneasy feeling in her stomach.

"What is out here?" said Anderson. For the middle of nowhere in the early hours of the morning this place was quite heavily trafficked. Karen looked down and could pick out two separate trails, and one was barefoot. They weren't alone. The trail ended suddenly with huge evergreen trees creating a sort of wall in front of them.

"This doesn't make sense," said Chase, Karen agreed. It seemed certain they were in the right direction but then nothing.

"Guys!" said Melinda, her voice unsteady. They all looked in her direction and saw the brunette woman quickly approaching. Karen was the first to break through the evergreens and found she was in a clearing on the other side, a strange clearing. This was what they were looking for, the Sacred Grounds. The others were quick to follow and Grierson had his hand on his weapon. Karen felt trapped and vertigo set in looking at the perfect circle of trees that walled them in, she already lost track of which direction they came from. She was so disoriented she nearly tripped on the suspiciously man-made looking rock in the centre. They all braced for the encounter unable to flee further but she never appeared. After enough time had passed to be certain they weren't pigs headed for slaughter, Karen started to relax and take note of the clearing. They all stood in amazement, every one of them feeling the same thing. There was a power here, a dark nefarious power.

"There's something engraved on this tree," said Melinda. No one recognized the foreign symbol, and after walking the perimeter another three trees seemed to be marked with similar but different insignias. They were a perfect ninety degrees apart and Karen wondered if they were the directions, north, south, east, and west. It could be how the people who made this place stayed aware of their bearings.   The perfect treed in circle was proving incredibly disorienting.

"Something's been burned into the ground here." Melinda pointed out, yet again the observant one. Chase kneeled down and picked up some dirt in his fingers. "It's definitely ash." The sun started rising in the sky changing the darkness into grey and everyone made out the clear pentagram shape, each point from the star coincided with a marked tree and the stone alter, as it seemed was in the middle. They were standing on an ancient ritual ground, and judging by the scorch marks it's been used far more recently than the surrounding area led them to believe.

"I don't like this," said Grierson, full of paranoia. Karen felt it too. Everything was too still, too quiet. They found the place, but now what? She moved to stand beside the altar, inside the inner triangle of the black scorch marks in the ground. The wind eerily picked up and Karen heard someone approaching. The brunette woman gracefully crossed the wall of evergreens followed by two men, which flanked her on either side. Melinda gasped from behind Karen, as everyone recognized the one on the right as Mathew Barry. Holding her ground Karen stared the woman down, her eyes were black as coal and soulless. But the face was familiar.

"Molly," a voice whispered close to her ear. The presence of Jennifer appeared behind her, and Karen noticed they weren't alone. The translucent figures circled the Sacred Grounds in a protective wall; they watched the scene in solidarity. Karen stole a glimpse at the others. Each seemed to be witnessing the bizarre stand off between the spirits and their tormentor. Each one of them stood beside a spirit and Karen watched as all at once the bright mist lost its form and disappeared. Then seconds later she saw the same light appear in the eyes of her friends. There was a chill on her shoulder as another spirit man looked into her eyes, and she felt comforted. Then she felt some pressure then he was gone.

9

Karen was pushed out of her body, in one uncomfortable moment. She was swirling around in the air above her head and Jennifer reached out and took her hand. She pulled her towards the others, and Karen took her spot in between Chase and Jennifer. The circle was completed but the real action hadn't started yet. The line between the two realms was never closer, for in this sacred place the power existed long before it was used for evil. It was powerful enough to manifest the spirits and bring them together, and with power comes corruption. One dark spirit's will to live unleashed a curse and Karen understood what needed to be done. There was one final sacrifice that needed to be made on the altar. Each of them took their place by one of the elements.

Karen was spirit, the one who supplied the motivation behind them all. Chase was water, free flowing and able to go with the flow. Melinda was air. Her mind was everywhere at once not missing anything. She was warm but could unsuspectingly settle into a storm. Anderson was earth, grounded and the calmest of them all. Grierson was fire.

10

Karen woke and the sun shining in her eyes. It was already fully above the trees. She scrambled to find Chase curled up to her left and she shook him awake in a panic.

"Chase?" He grumbled and opened his eyes to Karen's relief. They both sat up and found the rest of their friends slowly stirring.

"Are you hurt?" Chase asked his eyes wide with concern. Karen looked down at herself, taking inventory. Her coat was soaked with dried blood, and her hands were plastered up to the elbow with dirt and gore.

"Ew!" She screamed and jumped up to her feet frantically scrapping her palms against her jeans, but she was fine

Karen found the source at the same time as Chase. The lifeless body of Molly St. Claire still lay on the altar. Her eyes were open and Karen saw the black had disappeared, and was replaced with a gorgeous shade of green. They were the same as Jennifer's. Hopefully they were together now, both no longer trapped in the dark world forever repeating its doomed cycle. Karen reached out and gently closed Molly's eyes. The girl's spirit had died long ago, hopefully now it saw peace.

"Did you?" said Chase.

"Not me," Karen answered. Her body may have killed Molly but not her soul. It would be a secret she'd take to her grave. The events of the day in the sacred grounds could never be repeated again. The rest joined them, and Mathew and Michael were the last to wake. The black gone from their eyes, both men were confused but uninjured. The others didn't know what to do. It didn't seem right to persecute them for actions beyond their control but yet there was something that had to be done. The town recognized them both as killers, and there wasn't going to be any way to avoid that chaos.

They walked back much faster in the daylight, no one spoke much and it was mutually agreed their activities of the night didn't happen. The grounds Mathew told of didn't exist. It was just a cover for his weird activities but he was really on a drunken stupor. Against Mathew the charges were dropped and in a bid for forgiveness he quit as principal. Kevin Hull was to replace him and the staff was secretly relieved. Mathew never held up to Maggie's high standards and rumor quickly circulated he was arrested for murder. He would have been fired if he hadn't willingly left, but no one wanted to piss him off. Despite the new discoveries it would be a long time before the town forgot. Michael disappeared soon after another body was found with the same MO. She was Mathew's old mentor but it was never questioned Michael was involved. Molly's body went unreported and a 'mysterious' fire broke out after Karen and the group left the clearing. There was nothing left to show for their night's activities. The old abandoned section of town was forgotten and disappeared with nothing left to show but ashes and bits of old blackened chunks of metal.

For once they were free.

Epilogue: The Girl in the Woods

1

Molly William's was sitting on the tire swing behind her house. She could hear the sound of her mother's piano playing in the distance. She was with a new student and every other note made a horrible bellowing sound that butchered the integrity of the classical piece he was trying to play. Her father was away on a book tour or else he would have been outside away from the sounds coming from the living room. It was a beautiful spring day, and the flowers from the garden were just reaching full bloom and Molly didn't mind being outside. Pretty soon the school year would be over and she would be outside everyday. Sixth grade was hard work and she looked forward to the holiday.

Molly planted her feet in the ground and spun in circles watching as the rope coiled up above her. She kept going until the swing was too high for her feet to touch and she let go suddenly and the swing came to life spinning her around faster and faster. As she watched her backyard spiral around in blur she noticed a dark figure standing behind the trees. Between rotations she thought she saw it wave at her but when the spinning stopped there was no one there. Clumsily Molly walked towards where the person was, and decided to go explore the woods. A branch snapped in the distance and she jumped and looked up in time to see a teenage girl standing thirty feet from her. She looked about sixteen, and had green colored eyes that stood out like emeralds.

"Hello?" Molly called but the girl just started running and she lost her in the trees for a while. Then she stumbled onto a clearing she'd never seen before. It looked like the scene of a forest fire long ago. Some trees were blackened, with many fallen logs and new greenery sprouting to take its place. Some new trees even looked big enough to climb but something was different about this place. A bad feeling crept over her and the sensation of being watched. The girl was nowhere to be found and Molly turned back and ran home. The clearing felt wrong, and almost evil. She would never speak of this place again.

2

The bond was broken and the Lost Souls were freed. Molly awakened and was met by her mother's smile. It a heart warming victorious smile that she would remember forever.

"Where am I?" The last thing she remembered was sprinting out of the house dodging her father. She'd fallen down the stairs during her escape and she should be in pain but instead she felt nothing.

"It doesn't matter we're going home now," said Jennifer calmly. Molly noticed the others unconscious on the ground. There wasn't any blood and they were breathing. They were alive.

"They saved us," said Jennifer.

"Are they coming with us?"

"No, they can't." Jennifer backed away and Molly was able to see one casualty lying in the grass. Molly recognized herself lying lifeless in the center of the bodies.

"We're both dead," she said knowingly still unable to look away from herself.

She had known it somehow and she accepted it. This was always to be her fate. Jennifer reached out and took Molly's hand, giving it a squeeze. Both had tears in their eyes as they followed the other Lost Souls into whatever happens next.

About the Author

Teanna Dorsey was born and raised in Southern Ontario, Canada. Spending a decade in the small village of St. George, ON which plays a large role on her writing. She earned an advanced diploma in journalism before going on to teach English in Vietnam. She's currently at work on her fourth novel.